DEVIL'S ENTROPY

JT CUNNINGHAM

Tea With Coffee Media

CONTENTS

PART I: NIGREDO   1

1. The Harrowing of St. Anthony West   2

2. Warning Shot   18

3. The Philosopher's Stone   42

4. Leg in a Bear Trap   61

5. Dead Gull   76

6. Napoleon Crossing the Alps   88

7. In the Labyrinth   103

PART II: ALBEDO   117

8. Norseland   118

9. Götterdämmerung   136

10. A Sisyphean Effort   151

11. The Cruel Chains That Bind   179

12. Am I My Brother's Keeper?   195

13. Rubicon   211

14. Katabasis   224

PART III: CINRINITAS   235

15. The Long Scouring of the Soul   236

PART IV: RUBEDO   267

16. Anastasis   268

17. Skål, Cambions   282

18. The Valley of Dry Bones   297

19. The Seventh Seal   308

20. Blood of the Lamb   327

21. Woman Clothes in Sun   342

22. Pentecost   355

PART I
NIGREDO

I

THE HARROWING OF ST. ANTHONY WEST

T HE BLOODIED STUMPS OF his horns itched. Though he was usually careful about it, he must've had too much to drink last night and carved a little too deep into his forehead. Corman rubbed the stitches hidden underneath his thick black hair and his fingers came back dotted with scabs. Although he more or less botched the impromptu surgery, he knew he didn't look out of place for the district's standards.

Snowflakes fell gently down from a slate gray sky as a frigid wind picked up from the northeast. A sharp breeze soaked itself into his bone marrow. Amongst the decrepit and foundationally unsound warehouses and abandoned apartment complexes, people walked close together, beads of sweat managing to pool on their foreheads despite the cold. He noticed them peeking over their shoulders periodically, eyes wide and pupils dilated. Walking in the opposite direction, Corman Ryan didn't bother with fear; he already knew that all of theirs were real, and waited for them around every darkened corner. After all, he was one of them.

Dim sunlight, as though acknowledging its failure to break through the clouds, began to fade. It'd be night soon, and as Corman knew perfectly well, all things dark and wretched would be coming out to play.

Dried and frosted over plants tried their best to claw out of the pavement to reach new heights of the buildings they grew next to, and all of them failed. All of the warehouses on this stretch of the St. Anthony district were adorned like this. Old brick exteriors destroyed by years of disuse, excessive graffiti, and various shootouts the eastside gangs brought to the steps of the west. Examining one of the archways that once led into a luxury highrise, Corman saw traces of where the bullets hit. *Violence begets violence, but peace doesn't solve anything either*, he thought.

A dull pain throbbed through his left arm that petered out into a prickle when the skin on his palm ripped open and stitched itself back together to reveal an eye, big and brown and singular.

"Are we there?" Edgar asked.

"Just about," Corman replied, holding his arm out so he could get a better look.

He walked across another empty intersection, all of the cars present either shackled with wheel clamps or missing their engines. Symptomatic of the district as a whole; the majority of St. Anthony now consisted of abandoned construction sites, burglarized residences, and squatters' camps. Nobody really lived there, so much as temporarily existed before moving on to the next rundown section of town.

Dilapidated warehouses falling apart at the seams lined up one after another a few blocks from the riverfront, pieces of them crumbling onto the streets where couples and dog walkers and joggers used to convene in the summer, back when the city took vibrant breaths; when all of the color of life hadn't been sucked out. *That time's just a myth now*, Corman thought, hopping over a chunk of upended concrete.

Down Hennepin Avenue, just before the road stretched across the Mississippi, Corman hooked a left onto Main Southeast. Once a rare instance of cobblestone streets, the entire neighborhood was now in possession of cracked and broken boulevards. Passing underneath the Central Avenue bridge, he saw some of his fellow cambions tucked underneath it, hanging around a few limp tents. They were the kind that lurked in shadows, too afraid of being seen in the daylight, lest a couple of passing Knights got the bright idea of beating them to death. Out of the corner of his eye, Corman saw them huddle close together and away from him.

A quiet hissing noise emanated from within the storefronts to his left. There was virtually no traffic in the area; no other sounds besides the pathetic whimpering of the cambions. One look at Corman, and all their eyes darted to the ground. All of them, except one.

"They're in there," one said, pointing with the lone finger that remained on their hand. "They're in there. Them's wiemca."

"Shh, you," another hissed. "He could be one of them."

"Look at him, he's not," the first cambion argued. "He's come to *kill* them."

"Well, he's not one of *us*," a third piped up. "So quit jabbering."

Good enough, Corman thought as he entered what used to be a small movie theater. How long since they showed films there, he couldn't say. It'd been busted up and left to rot for years, just like every other building on the block.

The lobby reeked of cigarettes and dried vomit. Rats scurried from one hole in the wall to the next, squeaking as Corman's feet intersected through their paths.

"Ew," Edgar murmured.

Voices poured in from the right, through a doorway that connected the theater to the other businesses operating out of the same building. Corman crouched behind it and listened to the low, rasping chanting. What was being spoken was a dead tongue used only by the wiemca. He'd heard it enough times to know the specific cadence and pronunciations that went with it. Poking his head out, he saw a darkened room illuminated only by portable lanterns. Slowly, as to not arouse suspicion, Corman crept toward the room.

Judging from the decor, namely the elongated rectangle attached to the western wall, it was used to be some kind of ballroom or bar.

Now, however, the wiemca occupied it. Tall, gaunt figures dressed in thick, black robes stood around in a circle, each attended by a lantern. At the far end of the circle, a figure even taller than the rest of then, adorned with a hood that tapered off into a point far above its head. Wooden antlers stuck out on either side. A golden Seal of Solomon glistened on its forehead, signifying it as the Witch, leader of this particular coven.

At the foot of the Witch was a bright red Seal, intersected by a pentagram and scribbled over with runes. Whatever the runes spelled out detailed the purpose of that particular ritual; they were too obscured from where Corman presently stood.

Accompanying the Seal was a young woman, bound at the limbs and gagged in the mouth.

"Another sacrifice?" Edgar asked quietly as the wiemca began to chant in their crooked, sandpaper voices.

"Looks like," Corman said.

The Witch shrieked in the dead tongue.

In unison, the wiemca raised their arms, the sleeves of their robes falling to their shoulders to reveal the skeletal pallor of their arms. Thus began their synchronized dance; the ritual could commence.

Flailing fanatically, their chanting grew louder. The circle grew tighter, all of their heads pressed together, until they abruptly split apart. The hostage was laid at the foot of the Witch and the other wiemca turned their backs on it. With withered, greenish hands, the

Witch removed its hood to reveal a decayed death's head for a face the color of putrid flesh. Its eyes were white and sunken, its cheeks almost one with its teeth. Wisps of black hair sprouted from its scalp. In a motion much quicker than its physique would suggest possible, the Witch lifted up the woman and laid her in the very center of the Seal. Its robes whipping around its legs, it returned to its original spot and stretched out its ghastly arms.

Corman grabbed the billy club attached to his belt. Time to knock a few heads together. Flicking his wrist, the club shot out into a five-foot staff. A curved blade clicked into place.

"We have the element of surprise here," Edgar whispered. "Don't go rushing in."

Corman rushed in.

One of them sniffed the air and screeched, snapping its head toward him. All the others followed suit; their guttural shrieks coalesced together in one long, ugly cacophony. From the shadows across the room, a chimaera appeared. A malformed griffin, its leg bones jutted through its back, flaps of skin barely sticking to the bone, and its head was crooked. Four of its six eyes looked in the wrong direction. It looked at Corman. It was pissed.

The chimaera burst forth to chomp down on him, squawking through its fanged beak. Corman leapt back on his heels and used the momentum to spring forward, slicing at the chimaera's throat. He missed. Next thing he knew he was hurling through the air. Next thing after that he smashed into the drywall and collapsed in a flurry of dust and plaster. Coughing, he got to his feet. The chimaera pounced, claws at the ready.

Gripping the scythe with both hands, Corman swept it up into a wide arc; the blade pierced the side of the chimaera's head. Blood seeped into its feathers as it flailed and squawked, twisting and turning its head. Just as Corman ripped the blade free, he saw the wiemca surround him with bone-hilt daggers. A few managed to stab him, ripping through his overcoat and all the way down past the skin. Blood seeped into his clothes as he frantically swatted at them with the scythe. There was no ground to be gained; more and more knives entered him. Then the chimaera burst through the mob and rammed its beak right through the side of his gut. It flailed its head around wildly, as if it had skewered him on accident. Through the force of its head waggling, it flung Corman through the front window of the building, right out into the street in a storm of broken glass.

"Fuck," Corman grunted, clasping his stomach. He could feel the blood draining out of him, the frigid wind cutting through the open wound.

"I told you not to fucking rush in!" Edgar snapped. "You'll be lucky to survive this."

"We have very different ideas of luck," Corman coughed up blood. Yet even with his entire body compromised, Corman stood back up, his legs shaking and knuckles about to buckle. He grabbed the scythe tight enough to whiten his knuckles; the wiemca poured out with the shards of glass into the street.

Swinging the scythe out, he sliced open their chests. Over the spilled entrails he stepped, whipping Samael around in a circle to decapitate the rest. Heads rolled, clunked together as fountains of blood sprayed out of severed necks; it was nothing less than a wiemca graveyard. *Good*, Corman thought through his lightheadedness. *That's good.*

Brick and mortar came crashing at his feet as the chimaera busted through. A massive paw came swinging, and before he knew it, Corman felt the ground rush up to meet his back. His chest about to cave in; his ribs rumbled and cracked; his wound lashed a fiery whip across his body.

"Ed…" he murmured, "you gotta heal me. Before he fucking…" The chimaera increased the pressure. "—fucking *kills* me."

"I don't have enough time," Edgar protested. "All I can do is flood you with adrenaline."

"Then fucking do it!" Corman barked.

"All right, all right, quit being pushy."

It was like an injection of pure, unadulterated anabolic steroids. His blood pumped faster, his muscles pulsated, and his anger grew. Roaring, he lifted the paw up off of him and over his head, then in one twist of his arms, broke the chimaera's ankle. It flopped to the ground, buckling over. Corman threw himself at it and grabbed it by both ends of the beak, frothing at the mouth as he ripped it in half, breaking its jaw. The creature released something like a yelp from down in its throat as it thrashed around. Corman grabbed the scythe off the ground and raised it over the chimaera's neck. Once the blade touched ground again, the chimaera's head slid off of its massive neck into a vermillion pool.

Still gripping the scythe, Corman walked back inside, stepping over the broken glass. In the ritual circle, the Witch held one of the bone-hilt daggers above its rotted head, the woman at its feet. Though she desperately squirmed and twisted around, there was no getting out of there. Corman aimed the scythe's blade at the Witch's neck and let loose. The blade went sailing through its throat. Its body crumpled into a heap, and the head went rolling away from the woman.

"Please tell me it's dead," Edgar said.

"Then I'd be lying, wouldn't I?" Corman murmured.

The Witch's body started to shake. Its limbs sprang back to life and twisted around to push itself off the ground. Two more limbs burst out from both of its sides. Its stomach expanded, steadily growing until it gave birth to the head of a spider, bright green fluid gushing forth onto the floor. As its head twitched, its chelicerae clacked together. All eight of its eyes were then immediately on Corman.

"Why'd it have to be a *spider*?" Edgar moaned.

Corman took off in a dead spring toward it. At the end of his run, he held the scythe behind his head and leapt into the air over it. Samael's blade got caught in between its jaws. Arms rattling and breath ragged, Corman roared once more and ripped the scythe right down the Witch's middle, splitting it right in half. Its legs skittered and toppled together and with a disgusting squish, fell dead into its green blood as Corman landed. A quick glance behind showed him the outcome of his work.

"Is the girl okay?" Edgar asked.

"What?" Corman looked over at the the woman, still bound and gagged. "Oh."

Slowly, every step a walk through mud, Corman approached her. She squirmed and tried to get away, but he gently placed a hand on her shoulder and held her firmly. Carefully, his fingers shaking, he cut through her restraints using one of the discarded daggers strewn about the floor. She gulped in a breath of air and was just about to speak when Corman collapsed. The scythe clattered next to him, coated in blood and bits of organs. A sharp, stinging pain erupted from his stomach wound.

"So doc... what are we... what are we dealing with?" he asked.

Edgar sighed. "Four cracked ribs, two broken. Liver, stomach, and large intestine damage. Internal bleeding, internal bruising. Close to stage two blood loss. Multiple stab wounds. That giant hole in your gut."

"Is it fatal?"

"For anybody else, it would be," Edgar murmured. "I'm going to have to raise your body temperature and double your white blood cell count. I'm also going to have to reroute some of your blood flow. You might go into shock."

"Believe me, I already... already am."

"I'm increasing your natural levels of phenethylamine," Edgar told him. "Hopefully this will help your central nervous system acclimate."

"Oh, joy," Corman whispered as a jolt of pain suckerpunched him, as if his entire body was clenched between a vise. The bright blue light of the healing process lit up his veins. He wanted to scream, but instead, everything just went black.

When he awoke, it was still dark and gray out, but the hole in his stomach was closed up, as were his stab wounds. Sitting up, he couldn't felt the same pain he did before. Edgar had once again saved his sorry ass. And for nothing in return. *Well, that's not exactly true.*

Stretching, Corman felt his body parts pop back into their rightful places.

"Good work, Ed," Corman said.

"You're out of just about everything," Edgar told him. "Your iron, sodium, and potassium levels are dangerously low, and your blood plasma is—"

"But I'm alive, and that's what matters," Corman cut him off.

"Yeah, *barely*," Edgar said. "You have no idea how close you were this time. I had to rework so many of your necessary functions I'm surprised you're even coherent."

"It comes with the job," Corman said with a shrug, standing up. "Speaking of, I need to take a look at the Seal."

Inside his coat pocket was his little leather notebook, chock full of notes whose interconnectedness he was still figuring out.

"Hold on," Edgar said, "where's the girl?"

"The who?" Corman murmured, squinting at the Seal. "Damn, it's too dark. I can't make anything out. Is that the rune for 'moon' or 'sun'?"

"The girl who almost got killed?" Edgar yapped. "The one you just saved?"

"What about her?"

"Maybe see if she's okay? If she's *alive*?"

Rolling his eyes, Corman tucked his notebook away.

"It's safe," he called out. "They're all dead, in case you were wondering."

From behind the bar, she poked her head out. Her auburn hair was a mess, plastered to her face by sweat, and her blue eyes were wide with leftover fear. She aimed them at him.

"Nothing's gonna kill you. It's fine," he told her.

The skin on his palm pinched up.

"Say something *comforting*," Edgar hissed. "She's terrified."

"Like what?" Corman hissed back. "I'm not a fucking therapist."

"Who are you talking to?" the woman asked in a small voice.

"Thinking out loud," Corman lied, walking over to the bar. "You all right?"

Tears stained her cheeks and eye makeup ran down to mingle with them, but she nodded. "Yeah... I think so. I don't know."

As her eyes studied him, he wondered if she'd be afraid of his face. Scarred, disjointed, broken. Not the face of someone you'd want rescuing you.

"Are you... are you a cop?"

"God no," Corman scoffed.

"Be *comforting*," Edgar whispered.

"I'm a Knight from D.C.," he answered, heading back over to the Witch's body. "I specialize in these kinds of things."

That funky transmogrification was a neat little trick; he'd never seen it before. The chimaera they conjured was rowdier than most, too. But the wiemca weren't the innovative type. Why were they suddenly trying to be?

"*Forget* about work for a *second*," Edgar spat. "It can wait."

"In case you missed all that," Corman hissed at him, "I don't think it *can*."

"Are you talking to me?" the woman asked.

Looking back over his shoulder, Corman frowned. "No."

Edgar pinched his palm again. "*Comforting*."

"You got a name?" Corman asked.

"Abi— Abigail," the woman said. "Abigail Steward."

"You ever seen a chimaera before? The big monster thing?"

She shook her head, grabbed her left elbow with her right arm.

"And the wiemca? You know anything about them?"

"I've heard the stories, but I— I wasn't sure if they were even real."

"That's how they get you, all right," Corman said. "So you have no idea what they could've possibly wanted with you?"

Abigail shook her head again. "No, none."

"What happened when they took you?" Corman inquired, scribbling in his notebook.

"I was on my way home from work, and... And... *how* did you do all that? How did you... *do* all that without any help?"

"I clean up other people's messes," Corman said. "You get good at it after a while."

"You killed that thing by yourself," Abigail pointed out. "How—? And the... scythe?"

From inside his coat pocket he produced a leather ID case. Inside was his fabricated employee badge. "Corman Ryan, federal investigator. Like I said, I'm a Knight. Now, you were saying?"

"I was walking home from work, when I..." Her eyes started to well up. She sniffled and wiped the tears away. "I don't know. I was— I don't know what they wanted. I'm no one special or anything."

"You know about all the women that've gone missing within the past six months?" Corman asked her.

She nodded. "They... they took them, too?"

Indeed they had and in, as Corman jotted down, eerily similar ways.

"You know any of the missing persons?"

"Kind of," Abigail said. "I knew some of them from... Um, it's, I'm an actress. We were in plays together. Used to be. Before, you know."

"How many did you know?"

"Four, I think. I don't know, I'm—"

"Deep breaths," Corman told her, wanting to shake her by the shoulders and slap some sense into her. What was the big fucking deal? She was alive. Wasn't that enough?

Abigail did as he suggested and closed her eyes. "I'm sorry. I guess I'm just... I'm just kind of rattled, I guess."

"You know their names?" Corman asked.

"Names?"

He fought the urge to heave out a sigh. "Yes. The names of the women."

"Oh, I... I'm not—"

This was getting him nowhere.

"The cops'll be here soon enough," Corman said, writing out his phone number on one of the notebook pages. He tore it out and handed it to Abigail. "I'm investigating the disappearances. Call me if you remember anything you think might be helpful."

Abigail's eyes went wide. "You're— you're leaving?"

"Yeah?"

"Please, don't— don't leave me alone with these things," she begged him.

"They're all dead," Corman told her. "They won't hurt you."

"I know... but, please. I don't want to be alone with them."

Edgar pinched his hand again.

A bit of plaster dust fell from the ceiling. The bar was an ugly sight; dead, mangled bodies were strewn about pools of blood and internal organs. The Witch's corpse oozed out its green blood. Despite its premature end, the specter of the ritual lingered on.

Corman settled on waiting with her until the cops showed up; she brightened up at that.

It was nearly an hour later when Corman decided to pack it in. He'd been sitting at the bar, studying the Seal over and over again, trying to figure out which runes were which. No use; without a decent light source, it was pointless. He'd have to come back later. *When the place is crawling with cops*, he thought sourly. Outside, the gray world was turning increasingly black, and nights in Minneapolis were best spent inside with the doors locked.

"I don't think they're coming," Abigail said from the other side of the bar.

"Looks that way," Corman agreed, putting his notebook away. "You all right getting home by yourself?"

Edgar sent a sharp stabbing pain through his hand this time.

"Or..." He grimaced. "I can walk you home, if you want."

"Yeah," she said quietly. "If it's not too much trouble. I don't know if there's more of them waiting for me there."

Well there goes my fucking evening.

"We'll go when you're ready."

II

WARNING SHOT

H E WALKED MUCH FASTER than she did. In fact, he could've sworn she was dragging her feet on purpose; hunched over, hugging herself, she seemed to be in absolutely no hurry to get off the street and to safety. What the hell was wrong with her?

A stabbing pain shot through his palm. Corman glared at Edgar, who returned the glare right back.

"*What*?" Corman demanded.

"What do you mean, what's wrong with her?" Edgar asked. "She was kidnapped. She almost got *killed*. Cut her some slack, will you?"

"Yeah, so did I," Corman muttered. "Don't see me sulking over it."

"She doesn't have a built-in ER," Edgar said. "And she's not *you*, for that matter."

"You'd think the bastards cut off her legs," Corman said, glancing over his shoulder. Abigail's eyes were red and her nose was runny; he heard a small sniffle.

"Are you even listening to me?"

Corman shoved his hand into his coat pocket.

"She's not in a good mental state right now," Edgar continued. "She's terrified. Can't you see that? Can't you be just a *little* sympathetic?"

"Oh, sure, I *could*," Corman said with a shrug. "But what would be the point? Not my fault she didn't see this coming. She's gotta learn somehow."

Edgar groaned. "Don't start."

"Hey, *you* brought it up," Corman said. "All I'm saying is that if you're too weak to protect yourself, maybe don't go walking home alone at night."

"And how else is she supposed to get home?"

"There's plenty of ways," Corman said. "Maybe she's too stupid to think of them."

"*Corman*," Edgar hissed. "That's *awful*."

Corman smiled maliciously. "Yeah, and so's the world. Don't blame *me* for understanding how it works. Either you learn, or you die. Simple as that."

"You're being an asshole."

"I'm the asshole who saved her life, aren't I?" he asked. "You could factor *that* into your criticism. If it's not too much trouble."

All things considered, what happened to her was nothing short of a miracle. She'd managed to escape the wiemca with all of her organs intact. How many people could say that? She still had all her limbs in working order, too. What else was she expecting? Not to be attacked in the first place? *Bad shit happens*, he thought. *Worse shit than this*.

"Slow down a little," Edgar said. "Let her catch up."

"I don't owe her that."

"Idiot, you don't know where you're going."

True enough, Corman thought, slowing to a stop. A few moments later, she finally reached them. She didn't look up from the ground.

"Ask her if she's okay," whispered Edgar, pinching his palm.

"*No.*"

The pinching got tighter; Edgar cut through his skin.

"How are you, uh, holding up?" Corman asked as he wiped his hand on his pants.

She replied quietly. "I'm okay."

"We going the right way?"

"Yeah, it's just... it's just up Fourth Avenue," Abigail murmured, still not looking away from her shoes. For the first time, Corman noticed the blood. It was splattered here and there, mostly on her arms. *They're not suddenly performing blood transfusions, are they?* he wondered. One of the nice things about the wiemca was their predictability, but recently they hadn't been acting like themselves.

The last thing he wanted to deal with was a wiemca that had their shit together.

"We'll cut through the park," Corman said as he crossed the street. It was next to an old elementary school, one which had no students and hadn't for nine years. Children were a rare sight in Minneapolis, most families having packed it in and moved back out to the suburbs. Eagan, Bloomington, St. Louis Park, some even as far as Savage or Lakeville. Some poor souls even got moved out to Apple Valley. They were safer, if only nominally. The shadows they fled still loomed overhead.

"Hold up," Corman told her, holding out his right arm. In the middle of the park were a few members of the Sun Kingdom, standing around with their swords like a bunch of assholes. "Goddamn it."

"Don't tell me they're on your shit list, too," Edgar murmured.

"What's wrong?" Abigail whispered. "Who are they?"

You really don't know shit about the fucking place you live, Corman thought, frowning. "They're Sun Kingdom. Bunch of idiots pretending to be samurai. See the armor?"

"I've never seen them around here before," Abigail said.

"They're treading dangerously close to Sons of Odin territory," Corman said. The

boundary line was Broadway Avenue to the north, but the Sons claimed the cleaving Central Avenue Northeast as their own. But since it ran from Broadway down to the Mississippi, the Kingdom naturally contested that claim. Unless they wanted to declare war, which happened every few months or so, both gangs stayed away from the area. Saint Anthony West was considered contested territory, and so it was difficult to gain any sort of real foothold. *And so the wiemca set up shop.*

"Let me handle this," he told her. "Stay behind me."

And then, with just enough acid in his voice, "And keep up the pace. You have to look like you're with me."

They made their way across Holmes Park, and to his surprise, Abigail stayed close to him. Maybe she wasn't a complete idiot.

"Halt," one of the Kingdomers barked. They were each about six feet apart, all four gripping the kashira of their katanas. "What business do you have crossing into the Sun Kingdom?"

Christ, here we go. Corman rolled his eyes.

"Just escorting my charge home," Corman said. "I'm duty-bound to lead her to safety."

"Is she a sister or cousin?" another Kingdomer asked.

"I saved her from a chimaera," Corman said. "She'd be dead without me."

The four Kingdomers exchanged a brief look, which even under their kabuto Corman could tell was a worried one.

"Oh yeah, they're operating just a few blocks south of here," he told them, pointing. "Might want to get on that before they annex your entire territory."

"The wiemca are of no concern to us," the first Kingdomer announced. "Emperor Wukong has not declared war on them."

"Yeah, he might want to get on that," Corman said. "I can't be the only one keeping their rotting asses in check."

"You?" a third Kingdomer scoffed. "You're the size of a mini fridge."

"Silence," the first Kingdomer snapped. "Speak out of turn again and I'll have the wiemca collect you."

"Oh, they're not interested in you," Corman said. He nodded to Abigail. "They have a taste for the feminine as of late."

"You're saying they'll be after our women?" the fourth one asked.

Corman shrugged. "If they haven't already. Might want to let the Emperor know."

"He's trying to instill fear, nothing more," the second Kingdomer declared. "To allow himself to pass freely."

"Uh, no," Corman said. "I got *her* for that. Just passing along information."

"The wiemca are of no concern to us," the first Kingdomer reiterated, though his cheeks looked a little more than flushed. "Speak no more of such things. You may pass."

"Great thanks," Corman told him, bumping into the second Kingdomer. "Sorry, I have the spatial awareness of a mini fridge, too."

The second Kingdomer bit his lower lip and glowered, his knuckles turning white against his kashira.

It was only when they a block away down Southeast Third that Abigail spoke again. "They... they don't seem too bad."

23

"All things considered? Yeah, they're not the worst. They all follow bushido. Part of initiation is memorizing the rules and all that shit. To really *embody* the code, I guess."

"Bushido?"

"Way of the warrior," Corman said. "The moral code of all samurai. The Zonbi have something similar. Daisy's Girls protect women. The rest live by survival of the fittest."

"How did you get to learn all of this?" Abigail asked meekly, her voice hardly louder than a whisper. "If you're from D.C.?"

"It's called doing your job," Corman told her. "They don't send you in blind."

"I didn't know we had so many."

"No," Corman said. "But this city's always on the verge of a five-way gang war. If you want to live very long around here, it's a good idea to know how they tick."

"How... how do they?"

"The Sun Kingdom lives by bushido. They always fight head-on. No stealth, no espionage. The Zonbi do what Shaka Zulu did. They fight with the bull horn formation. The Sons of Odin, Pilate's Disciples, and the Howler Monkeys run things like any other gang. No embedded moral code. They run on murder, extortion, and torture. The Golden Hermetic Order are the only ones who don't really fight. They mostly just do blackmail and racketeering."

"And the wiemca?"

"Freaks," Corman said. "The worst out of all of them. Even the Sons, and the Sons are all bastards. Nothing is too fucked up for the wiemca. So long as it serves their god. Who, by the way, is characterized primarily by them not knowing what the fuck it is."

"They don't know what they're worshipping?"

Corman barked a laugh. "That's the point. They worship the unknown. Mankind was meant to know jackshit. As in, people knowing anything besides the time of day is blasphemous. Bunch of goddamn luddites."

So this new trend of theirs is especially fucking worrying.

"It's, um, just around here," Abigail said as they turned right onto Southeast Seventh Street. Out in front of her apartment building, underneath the dull orange glow of the streetlamps, Corman took out his notebook and jotted down his phone number. Ripping out the page, he told her to call him if she could remember anything important.

"Anything at all," he said. "And I mean that. Any small amount of information might help. You never know with them."

With a shaking hand, she accepted the page.

"Th— thank you," Abigail said, her reddened eyes glistening with tears. "We don't even know each other..."

"Part of the job," Corman said. "All right, have a nice night."

Spinning around on his heels, he bolted down the street and rounded the corner back onto Third. *Jesus Christ*, he thought as he slowed to a walk. *Did she have to start bawling?*

"She was almost *killed*, Corman" Edgar piped up. "You could've at least seen her get inside okay."

"Hey, I just wasted a half fucking hour walking her here," Corman spat. "I get to complain about it."

"Well if it was such a pain in the ass, why did you save her in the first place?"

"Call it a marriage of convenience," Corman grunted. The aches and pains were starting to set; pretty soon he'd be nothing *but* aches and pains. It felt like his body was about ready to fall apart.

"It sounds impossible, but you *are* capable of doing good. You know that, right?"

"My coat's fucking shredded," Corman muttered, fingering a hole where a button had once been. "I don't think I have enough thread for a patch job like this."

"And you change the subject."

"I have a lot to worry about that's more important than some random woman," Corman said. "What was this last séance about? And what does a bunch of worshippers of the unknown want to *know*? What forbidden knowledge are they after? What's the revelation?"

"Save your energy," Edgar said. "You're dehydrated and dangerously low on blood. Common sense, too, but I don't think I can fix that."

"Ha ha," Corman muttered.

As he drove back to his own apartment near Loring Park, Corman watched the city pass by from his windshield. On the western bank of the Mississippi, there were still dim whispers of life. Some buildings kept the lights on past ten, but most were boarded up and tagged in bright letters with some variation of "fuck." The ones that managed to stay open had to write it in big bold letters on the wooden boards over the windows. Trash skidded across gutters, public trash cans either nonexistent or tipped over by rats.

He wondered how people like Abigail managed to exist, what kind of life they led. In *this* world? How the hell did she live? Constantly terrified? In blissful ignorance? For a moment, he almost felt sorry for her. But then he remembered she was an *actress*, one of the most pointless professions a person could have. What a complete and utter waste of time. Who the fuck could stomach *plays* anymore? People were dying, starving, running hysterical down the streets, and she was putting on *plays*. Minneapolis was not a place for actors, or musicians, or painters, or anyone with their heads up in the clouds. Minneapolis was a battleground and artists didn't belong in warzones.

Looking back on it, his time as a Knight was almost as pointless. It had all amounted to nothing. All the job entailed was the drudgery of paperwork, but with the added twist of writing reports about the scenes of gruesome murders, ritualistic suicides, and cult activity. How many fucking reports did he write on some religious zealot raping some innocent in order to impregnant them with the soul of their god? *Too many to count.* In truth, he hadn't done much of importance during his time with the bureau. Not that it mattered to the top brass, or really anyone else. So long as they got their promotions and titles and pay raises. All it amounted to was emptiness. Empty work, empty valor, empty promises.

Then Lilith showed up.

No, he told himself. *No, she's dead. The dead don't warrant thinking about.*

He needed to focus on more important matters. Matters that concerned the living. The living who hadn't stabbed him in the back. *Although that does narrow down the list.*

What exactly were the wiemca up to? There was, for the first time since he started dealing with them, a sort of common goal. Something all the individual covens wanted, and were seemingly willing to allow each other to pursue. No other gang would likely be involved; everybody hated them. But nobody hated the wiemca quite as much as the wiemca. Each coven believed in their own variation of the core dogma, and that every other coven was composed of a bunch of heathen Philistines determined to usurp them and install their own interpretation as law. Nobody knew how the ouroboros was born, but everybody was smart enough to stay as far away from it as possible.

Something was *very, very* wrong. They hadn't been fighting each other. They hadn't been leaving human remains on the other covens' doorsteps as a warning. There was, strangely enough, *peace* between the covens. Something, or someone, had united them. That was the only possible explanation for it. And whatever it was, it had to be *thoroughly* convincing. The wiemca were a paranoid, delusional, conspiratorial group. Only something that penetrated through the denominational differences and struck at the very core of their entity could be responsible.

And that freakshow, where did he learn how to do that? Though wiemca weren't exactly human, they were still limited by human physiology. That transmogrification... he'd never known a single wiemca, Witch or otherwise, to be able to do that. *Unless handing your soul over to the dark abyss suddenly comes with a starting bonus, that Witch was on some different kind of shit.*

Putting his car into park, he sighed. He might actually be in trouble with this one. A united wiemca... surely that was one of the signs of the apocalypse.

Breath visible before him, he set off for his apartment. A shadow moved out of the corner of his eye near another building's dumpsters. Corman stopped and took hold of the billy club, and the shadow moved again. Flicking out the scythe, he pivoted and swung the blade at the shadow. In the dim, flickering fluorescent light of the side door, he saw a hunchbacked cambion shivering under cardboard.

"Please," he begged. "Don't kill me, please."

"Jesus," Corman said, collapsing the scythe. "The hell are you doing scrounging in the fucking trash for?"

The cambion sized Corman up with his mismatched, bulbous eyes.

"Do you have a dollar?"

"Oh, go fuck yourself," Corman spat.

"Please!" the cambion pleaded after him. "Please! Just a dollar!"

"Do I *look* like a fucking charity?"

"It's a *dollar*, Corman," Edgar muttered. "Yeah, and what business is it of mine to hand them out?"

He shoved his hands into his pockets as the cambion's pleas went unheeded into the cold, solemn indifference of the night.

Waiting for him in his apartment was Yue Sunisa, sitting on the arm of his sofa and smoking a cigarette. She was in her Knight uniform, a gray polyfiberous outfit designed to resemble plate armor, including a flak jacket made of fiber-reinforced plastic reminiscent of surcoats marked with a coat of arms displaying their precinct. Hers, and formerly Corman's, was a gold phoenix flying across a maroon sky.

"This is a nonsmoking floor," Corman said, throwing his coat at her.

She caught it. "You really ought to have a curfew. I've been waiting for almost an hour."

"Not my fucking problem," Corman muttered. "And get off my fucking couch."

"Keep running your mouth like that, and you're grounded," Yue said, pointing her cigarette at him. "Honestly, I have no idea why King hasn't authorized a warrant already."

"Warrant," Corman repeated under his breath. "And what exactly have I done?"

Yue smiled. "You think you can be coy. Adorable."

"I'm not being coy," Corman told her. "I haven't done anything."

"Unless you count breaking out of a federal penitentiary, forging government documents, impersonating an officer, theft of government property, trespassing, breaking and entering, and general obstruction of justice," Yue said. "You *are* aware that we get calls about the lunatic with the giant scythe every day, right?"

"Who says that's me?"

"You're not gonna bother to at least *try* denying the allegations?" Yue got off the couch and went into the kitchenette, her cigarette hanging limply from between her fingers. "Trash?"

"Under the sink," Corman said. "And no, I'm not going to deny anything because I haven't done anything. You want me to implicate myself."

"So do me a favor then, and knock it the fuck off," Yue said. "If you had *any* idea how much reports I have to go through—"

"It's not like you're not assigned to my case," Corman said, moving to his dining table.

Yue narrowed her eyes at him. "Yeah? You think so?"

"Why would they—?"

"You think I got off easy after all that?" Yue sat back down on the couch arm, letting one leg dangle over the edge. "You think I didn't almost get canned?"

"I didn't ask you to testify," Corman grumbled.

"No, I guess you didn't," Yue said. "But nobody asked you to stick your nose in this wiemca business, either."

"So we both go beyond the call of duty," Corman said. "We should get commendations."

"All right, asshole," Yue spat. "I'm here to tell you to quit this shit *now* before you really do something to fuck things up. And you are *dangerously* close to that."

"Sure." Corman laughed harshly. "Even if you *do* force me in front of a judge, it'll be thrown out for lack of evidence. Hate to break it to you, but even *you* need to have *something* to convict someone. I know you guys aren't big fans of that, but—"

"You were one of us, too, shitsucker," Yue barked. "You don't get to take the high road on this shit. *You* were part of this once."

"*Was* being the operative word," Corman said, holding up a finger. "*Was.* You, on the other hand—"

"Fuck you and fuck your moral posturing, Ryan," Yue snapped. "Stop getting involved and stop making life harder for everyone else. There's more to this than just you. Not that I would expect *you* to understand that."

"Funny, because it seems to me that nobody else is doing jackshit about this," Corman said. "You know how many human sacrifices I've seen in the past six months?"

"We *are* doing something about it," Yue argued. "And we might have even solved the goddamn problem if we didn't have to constantly do damage control."

"How many Knights on the case?" Corman asked. "You got Sasha on it?"

Yue frowned. "No."

"It's not on Lancelot's caseload? Then how much of a priority is—"

"No, idiot, Sasha isn't Lancelot anymore."

Corman slumped into his chair a little, one arm hanging over the back. He blinked, chewed the inside of his cheek, scratched at his stitches.

"Big fucking surprise, right?" Yue murmured, arms crossed. "But we *had* to be made examples of, lest somebody else might get the brilliant idea to defend your dumb ass. But with all the stupid shit you've been pulling, I don't think anyone with a brain in their head would."

"So you got moved to just doing street rips and Sasha was—"

"Demoted to Percival," Yue answered. "She's lucky she didn't get kicked from the Round Table altogether.."

"Hey, I didn't—"

"Ask. Yeah, I know." Yue hopped off the armrest. "And look, it wouldn't just be you making my life easier. You get caught, you're in deep shit."

"Deeper than the shit I'm in already?"

"You're looking at extrajudicial extradition," Yue told him. "King is foaming at the mouth for a case like this to break. Imagine the press we'd get for locking up an escaped, dangerous, and *armed* international fugitive. You know, the one who almost caused the apocalypse. *And* in the interim, you stole property from a federal agency and are actively impersonating a federal officer. I don't know if D.C. knows yet, but if Arthur gets wind of this?"

"Guantanamo?"

"The last eight years have been... *good* for the intelligence community. Drones pick up nearly every piece of intel in any given warzone. So much so that D.C. is lobbying for another military prison just to hold everyone who's since been put on their shitlist. It's part of Arthur's plan to expand the Knights into the middle east. Afghanistan, Israel, Syria. A global, internationally sanctioned police force. And imagine the outpouring of support he'd get with you back in chains."

"So you guys do military contracts now?" Corman asked, letting the news sink in.

"Have been for a while," Yue said. "It's part of the reason why King hasn't put you in the yoke yet. Resources are being diverted into Central and South America. Seeing what 'peace' we can offer to places like Venezuela and Nicaragua. We also may or may not be fighting the Taliban."

"They gonna give you the football, too?"

"I wouldn't hold my breath," Yue said with a sigh. "But, Jesus... we're supposed to fight monsters, not install dictators."

"Finally coming to your senses?" Corman asked. "Quitting would be the next step."

"I'm not quitting, jackass," Yue said. "How would I do anything about this?"

Corman pointed both of his thumbs at himself.

"You're doing it on *our* dime with *our* shit."

"Oh?" Corman offered her a cold smile. "And who's to say I'm the one with the scythe?"

Yue rubbed her temples. "Who *else* would be this belligerently fucking stupid?"

"You've ruled out copycats?"

"Of course we have. Nobody in our records besides *you* has a history of eviscerating chimaeras like this." Yue lit another cigarette. "Nobody else has the training, the experience, or the motive. All signs point to you, acting without executive oversight. Which, as you might imagine, looks bad. On you *and* us."

"So why haven't I been arrested yet? Can't just be the budget."

Yue sighed, rubbed her forehead with a thumb. "You *are* right about the lack of evidence. We throw the book at you now, it'll just be declared a mistrial. There wouldn't an impartial jury. Not to mention the complete lack of willing attorneys to take your case. Everybody in this city knows you, and everybody who knows you hates your guts. All our public defenders are staying as far away from this as possible. Even the fucking D.A. wants nothing to do with you."

"Which means I'm getting out on a technicality."

"If you consider you being so thoroughly unlikable that having a fair trial is impossible, then yes. You're getting out on a technicality."

Corman allowed himself the victory. "That's the best news I've heard in a minute."

"Don't get me wrong, Ryan," Yue said. "King wants your head on a plate. The *second* she gets what she needs for a conviction, you're fucked."

"Whatever King's up to doesn't concern me."

"You know what'll happen when she catches you. You'll never know peace again."

I've never known peace to begin with.

"I imagine there's another reason you decided to pay me a visit this late?" Corman asked, feeling like she'd left something out.

Yue puffed out a large cloud of smoke. "You remember Kyle Woods?"

"He Lancelot now?" Corman asked.

"Yup," she said. "And imagine the commendations *he'll* get for bringing you in. He's chomping at the bit. Clock's ticking, Ryan. War's coming. This was just the warning shot."

"And yet I don't have a bullet wound." "No, but keep this shit up and you will," Yue said. "It's only a matter of time before they get you. As far as I'm concerned, you're already dead."

"So why bother telling me all this? Why help a dead man?"

"Being an insufferable prick isn't grounds for execution. Wasn't then, isn't now." Yue opened the door and stepped on through. "Night, Ryan."

Except for the sirens blaring outside, the apartment was blissfully quiet. Corman held up his palm, releasing Edgar. From there he turned into a ball of energy, floated to a windowsill, and transformed into a black cat.

"Feels good to get out and stretch my legs," Edgar said.

"God, life was so much simpler in prison," Corman muttered, opening a bottle of whiskey. He took large gulp and let it burn his throat. *Still feels better than getting chewed out*, he thought.

"Simpler but worse, wouldn't you say?"

"Fuck if I know," Corman said, sighing. He slumped down onto the couch. "Why am I the only sane person in this fucking city?"

"Are you not including me because I'm a cat, or..."

"You know what I mean." Maybe not the only sane person, but certainly the only person with their priorities straight. He had exactly what Yue said he did. The training, the experience, the motive. So why shouldn't he take action Why *shouldn't* he solve the problem? Whatever she might believe, Yue was wrong about the Knights getting involved. They weren't, and would never. People went missing all the time, didn't they? So why bother it at all? *Fucking unbelievable.*

Corman stared up at the ceiling as he took another swig of whiskey. The wiemca needed to be dealt with, and nobody else had stepped up to the task. Fine. *I draw the line at the fucking Knights lecturing me on accountability.* The murderous, treacherous bastards. And now they were looking into military conquest. But then again, what else were knights for, if not expanding the kingdom's borders? *Bloodshed and war, that's all we're good for,* Corman thought. How had he not seen it before? That he was nothing more than a weapon to them? *I'm not the scythe anymore. I'm the motherfucker holding the scythe now.*

Picking up his overcoat, he examined the damage. Ripped in a hundred different places, missing a button, and coated in dried blood. *Might have to get this thing dry cleaned for once.*

A sewing kit was in the basket he kept on the endtable. Taking thread and needle, he started on the laborious process of mending. Though his hands were shaking, he'd done this enough times to be able to ignore it. He felt Edgar's eyes on him.

"What?" he asked.

"Maybe you *should* bow out, let the Knights handle this," Edgar suggested.

"Ed, are you fucking crazy?" Corman spat, not taking his eyes off the coat. "You really think *they* are gonna do anything? No. I don't care what threats they level at me."

"You're really okay with the possibility of life in a military prison?"

"Suicide's always an option."

"*Corman.*"

Corman set down his sewing and gave Edgar an incredulous look. "I'm not going to let those idiots muck this up. Thirty-eight women have already paid the price for their incompetence. I'm not letting a thirty-ninth pay, too."

"Maybe you could go to one of the gang leaders, or—"

"Since when do the gangs give a shit about anyone besides themselves?" Corman asked. "Zonbi, Kingdomers, Sons, Knights. They're all the same. You want something done, you do it yourself."

"But *one* man can't. Not this."

"Maybe, maybe not," Corman said, taking his notebook out of his coat pocket. "Take a look at the Seals I've drawn from the séance sites."

Edgar pawed through the pages. "Okay, so we have the... forty-eighth, the thirty-eighth, and the... twenty-first."

"Forbidden knowledge. Ancient knowledge. Esoteric knowledge." Corman took up his sewing again. "What in the fuck do a bunch of people who worship the unknown suddenly want to *know*? A better skincare routine?"

"Something those women knew."

"No, those women didn't know a goddamn thing. It was something *in* them. Something they carried inside themselves." He lifted the coat up to examine his work; his arms ached. "Their genetic makeup. Their blood type. I don't know. But it was something only blood magic would allow them to know. What *I* need to know, then, is what the common denominator is. Why these thirty-eight women? What specifically are they looking for?"

"You don't think it's random?" Edgar asked.

"No, this is too targeted. There's no room for coincidence here."

Edgar closed the notebook. "Okay, so what next?"

"I get what I can on the victims," Corman replied, setting his coat aside. He'd finish it in the morning; his entire body was screaming for sleep. "Medical records, coroner's reports, passport information. See where that takes me."

The shadows of his dreams were always warped, splaying across walls with too-sharp of angles and whose dimensions didn't fit together. Faceless phantoms floated together, their bodies nothing more than black stick figures with their limbs blurred. Time didn't work as it should here, Corman moving forward and backward in the continuum and existing at two different points simultaneously.

She would always be there, too. Upon her brow, over her raven black hair, was a bleeding crown. It cascaded over her sharp nose, her chromium blue eyes, her painted lips. In her thin, withered hand was a bone-hilt dagger. A forked tongue lapped the blood off from the blade.

Suddenly he was wrapped up by the body of a giant snake. Squeezing tighter and tighter, Corman could no longer breathe. The snake bowed its head toward him and opened its mouth back so far that he couldn't see it anymore.

Lilith's head grew from the snake's throat and smiled at him, her tongue wagging back and forth in anticipation.

"Pathetic," she hissed. She squeezed once more, and as every bone in his body shattered, he heard her cackling from somewhere off in the distance. Then he saw it. Her standing before him, Corman on his knees, knife in hand. He couldn't see their faces, but he knew. Lilith grabbed the knife from him. Corman, falling out from the snake's vise grip, tried to scream. Screamed until his throat cracked and bled. But he allowed Lilith to stab him through the chest.

As he continued to fall, everything melted away until he was alone in the void again. He tasted blood on his lips. Beneath him, the eyes of the snake, forked tongue approaching fast. Everything slowed as he dropped into the snake's mouth, and as its jaw closed, everything went black, too.

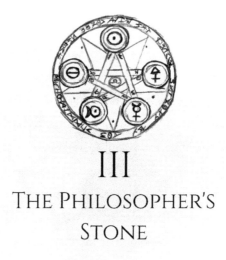

III
THE PHILOSOPHER'S STONE

L AST NIGHT TURNED OUT rougher than he thought; sweat drenched his chest and back, his stumps burned, and blood seeped past where the skin broke. Anxiety and stress, as he'd learned since he first started sanding them down, induced premature bone growth in his horns. Try as he might, they wanted to grow out. Thus, they were locked into a battle for dominancy that Corman was determined never to let them win. *It'd be easier to just let them*, he thought as he threw off his comforter. Feeling his sheets, his fingers came back damp. The outside matched his mood: gray, dull, and rainy.

As he put on a pot of coffee, his chest ached and his back felt pinched off. There weren't any painkillers left since his last bender a month ago, back when he started his investigation in earnest. One unseasonably warm night he chugged half a bottle of vodka and oxycodone and slipped into a blissful reverie that got interrupted by Edgar desperately trying to restart his heart. *Last time I had any goddamn peace*, he thought.

In the bathroom, he checked his hairline. Sure enough, his horns had pierced through his skin and grown about two inches during the night. They were hardly more than nubs, but even nubs invited hostility. Corman brought out the power sander from under the sink and got to work. First thing was biting into a tongue depressor, just in case he nicked a nerve the closer he got to his forehead.

As the sander whirred and shaved his horns temporarily out of existence, he could hear Edgar shouting from the kitchen. More than likely, it was a lecture on the futility of denying one's true nature or some such bullshit, and Corman was not in the mood to deal with that. Eventually, Edgar leapt onto the sink counter and glowered at him. By then, his skull was free of protrusions and blood was dribbling down his cheeks.

"Good God, I can smell the cortisol from here," Edgar said.

"That's probably just the coffee," Corman told him, putting the sander away. "Cheap shit always smells terrible."

"You had another nightmare," Edgar said. "What about?"

"That I used up all my painkillers," Corman said. "And just imagine what I woke up to."

"You didn't sleep very well, either," Edgar noted.

Corman poured himself some coffee and sat down at his desk, where Edgar joined him. "I never sleep well, Ed."

"Your blood pressure is up, and your heartbeat is irregular," Edgar said. "Whatever it was, it's still bothering you."

Corman took a sip of his coffee, looked into the mug. *Dirt.*

"Take a wild guess as to what that is," he said. "List is pretty narrow."

"I have an idea, but something tells you don't want me saying it."

"I'm glad we finally understand each other," said Corman as he rifled through his notebook. Time to search for those elusive similarities. Thirty-eight women, a potential thirty-ninth, all women. All with knowledge the wiemca wanted but didn't have, and should never have. *Chimaera necessary or just precaution? Witch learned new trick,* he reread. What forbidden knowledge do actors have access to, the intricacies of the Stanislavski Method?

Blood dripped from his forehead onto the page.

"Ed? You got this?"

As he closed up the wounds, Edgar asked, "Are you actually gonna eat anything today?"

"Depends," Corman murmured, scratching his chin with a thumb. "I think I need to pay a visit to the site. See what kind of sigils they used. I need to narrow down the common ones."

"What do you have so far?"

"Mercury, salt, sulfur. The typical symbols used to denote curing disease," Corman said. "So naturally they show up on the Thirty-Eighth Seal every time. Air and fire are used a lot too, but not always together, and not always with the same Seal. Then there's the Sun, which is used as the epicenter of almost every Seal the wiemca use.

"What's really interesting is this one here. Mercury, Copper, Silver, and Magnesium. So we have the 'cosmic womb,' the representation of the female, the brain, and eternity. And no Sun. So far the combination's only been used once, but it was the first one we found. It stands to reason that it was the blueprint for the rest of the Seals, but..."

"What?"

Corman frowned. "Copper is never used again, and neither is that exact combination of symbols. It's also weird that it's the only Seal where Silver is used, but not Sun. All the others have both. There's definitely a pattern, but I have no fucking clue what it's leading toward."

"You think a thirty-ninth is going to help?"

"It could be what solves everything," Corman said with a shrug. "Or it'll be a colossal waste of time. Only one way to find out."

"I think we can assume it'll be the second," Edgar told him. "We don't need to go diving headfirst into the mouth of the beast."

"We're further than that," Corman said as he left the desk. "We're already in the belly."

A shower helped the pain, in both his head and stomach. Not much, but enough so that Corman felt like he could actually leave the apartment without breaking down. Throwing on his overcoat, he examined the holes and rips he'd neglected last night. *Good enough*, he thought. *I'll fix it later.*

"It's going to be cold today," Edgar, sitting on the windowsill, announced. "Put on something under your coat."

"I'll be fine."

"At least wear a scarf or something."

Corman stood by the door, hand held up and eyebrows raised. Sighing, Edgar slipped into a ball of pure energy and returned to his palm.

"If you get cold, don't blame me," Edgar said as they headed down the hallway. "Don't say I didn't warn you."

"Oh, yeah, because you'd hate to be the guy who told me so," Corman said. "Here. Let me button up. That better?"

"When we get to the car, put on the gloves I had you leave in there. Your fingers don't get good blood circulation."

"Ah, so this is all for *your* benefit," Corman said.

"My benefit is *your* benefit," Edgar told him. "Or did you never wrap your head around symbiosis?"

"I thought it was parasitical," Corman said, getting a sharp jab to the hand.

The Knights weren't supposed to be there. By all means, they *shouldn't* have been there. Nothing about it struck Corman as something they wouldn't give two shits about, especially considering the other thirty-eight instances where they never bothered showing up. But this one for whatever reason garnered a significant police presence: barricades were erected, uniformed cops idled around, and armored, jet black Corvette Stingrays were parked up and down the street.

"I wondered where all the education budget went," Edgar murmured.

"Probably have anti-mine sensors if Yue was right," Corman said.

"But who can afford mines anymore?"

Corman pulled out his falsified ID badge from his breast pocket. It had earned him more than a few debts to the Golden Hermetics, but when it came to fraud and deception, nobody did it better. That being said, they were insufferable pricks. They looked down their noses at anybody not apart of their "club," as they liked to call it, and even to someone they actively assisted like Corman, took every opportunity to be condescending assholes about it. All of the Minneapolis gangs were emotionally draining in their own way; the Hermetics got so high off the fumes of their own shit they believed it was actually gold.

Approaching a uniformed cop standing guard, Corman flashed his ID badge.

"Sir Mador," Corman told him. "I'm on special assignment from D.C. Thanks."

"Oh, I, um— Go on ahead," the cop stammered.

Without a flicker of recognition, Corman made his way through the massive hole in the exterior left by the chimaera. Its body, as well as the bodies of the wiemca, had been removed from the scene. Their bodily fluids, however, had not. Glancing for familiar faces, his stomach sank. Between a thick cloud of smoke were Sirs Kay and Bors, the sons of Knights who failed upwards. Despite their titles, they were low ranked; they didn't even have the security clearance to know what went on most of the time.

Meaning King wants to keep this quiet, Corman thought.

"Holy shit, if it isn't the devil himself," said Kay in his grating, nasally voice. Both Knights were looking at him now. Kay had the face of a ferret and the complexion of a rotting pumpkin. Bors was a fleshy man, with a weak jawline and an even weaker chin.

Goddamn it, Corman thought, bracing himself. He offered a terse smile.

"Word around Camelot is some lunatic with a gardening tool is making trouble," Bors said. "We had a pool going. Either it was you or some idiot who looked like you. And it looks like half the department owes me."

"Figured you'd go and stick your snout into our business," Kay said, sneering. "There aren't any truffles around, sorry to say."

"What were you hoping to do, billy goat? Eat the dead bodies before we could bag them?"

"Actually I was gonna piss on them first," Corman said.

"Doesn't surprise me," Bors said.

"Why would you piss on something you're gonna eat?" Kay asked, cocking his head to the side, his beady little eyes narrowed.

"Piss is sterile," Bors told him.

"No, it's not. It's fucking *piss*."

"I didn't say it was *clean*, dipshit. I said *sterile*."

"What's the fucking difference?" Kay demanded, throwing his cigarette onto the ground.

"Way to dirty the crime scene," Corman said. Both Knights turned to glower at him. "Unless you think cigarette ash is sterile."

Kay stomped the cigarette out. "Well, whatever. What are you even doing here, mooncalf? I don't know who you brainwashed or hypnotized or *whatever* to get in here, but you should probably get the fuck out."

Corman showed him his badge. "Got transferred to D.C., actually. I'm here on business. What, you think I just up and left?"

"I was hoping you got executed, myself," Bors told him.

"No doubt about that," Corman said with a shrug. "But unfortunately for you, I'm very much alive. And unfortunately for me, that means I need to get to work."

"Hold it." Bors held out a hand. "What the fuck is D.C. doing, sending *you* here? There's nothing here they care about. Not to mention we just got your stench out of the office."

"All right, cool it dickhead," Corman muttered, shoving his hand out of the way. "This isn't major. Just doing a routine inspection."

"*You're* the dickhead," Kay snarled.

"I'll give you that," Corman said. "Now get out of my way so I can work."

"Fuck you, mooncalf," Kay spat as Bors led him away. "This ain't over."

"Turns out having a department full of fucking idiots might be a good thing," Corman snickered, taking out his notebook.

As soon as they were out of earshot, Edgar scolded him. "They won't buy that forever. They might not even buy it at all."

"Yeah, and?" Corman crouched in front of the Seal, sketched out the sigils.

"They might get you extradited," Edgar told him. "Did you not listen to a word Yue said?"

"Several, actually," Corman murmured, cross-referencing his sketches. "Relax, Ed. If the Hermetics did their jobs right, there's no paper trail to follow."

"This was a completely unnecessary risk to take, Corman," Edgar said.

"Seal forty-eight," Corman noted. In the spaces in between the pentacle's points were the symbols for sulfur, mercury, and salt. In the middle was the staff of Asclepius. "Forbidden medical knowledge. Now what could they want with that?"

"All right, you got it. We should go now."

"Think there's some infection going around? Some sort of virus endemic to the wiemca? But they're all half-dead, so..." Corman jotted some of his thoughts down. "So what could they—?"

"Bors and Kay are coming back," Edgar whispered.

They strode up to Corman and stared down at him, Kay with more than enough menace for the both of them.

"This what a routine inspection is?" Kay barked. "Looks like you're fucking up our crime scene."

"You're gonna have to pack it in, man," Bors said. "Fuck off."

"Sure," Corman said, standing up. "I was just putting my dick away."

"Why the fuck was your *dick* out?" Kay demanded.

Bors started to explain, but just sighed instead. "All right, you had your fun. Now *fuck. Off.*"

Shrugging, Corman tucked his notebook away and started off. "Mind the piss, boys. It's slippery."

It was only once he'd gotten far enough down Southeast Main, close to the intersection with Sixth Avenue, that he felt like the eyes were off of him. He sat on a bench near the old hydroelectric plant that had ceased to produce anything other than rust and algae and reviewed his notes.

"It's definitely medical related," Corman said. "They're trying to find healthy candidates for... something. Maybe get their antibodies? But—"

"Corman, you could've gotten arrested in there," Edgar interjected. "What the hell were you thinking?"

Corman closed the notebook and stared directly at Edgar's eye. "I have falsified papers. I have an alibi. I didn't do anything outside of my authority as a field agent. So what exactly about all that is so goddamn upsetting to you?"

"You were antagonizing them! You waltz into an active crime scene, already committing a felony, and then you go ahead and poke the bear. At this point, I'm starting to think you *want* to get the death penalty."

"You done?"

"If someone smarter than those two gets suspicious, they'll probably kill you without a second thought," Edgar continued. "It doesn't matter how well prepared you are if what you're preparing for is suicide."

Corman rolled his eyes. "That's an exaggeration."

"You're gonna get yourself killed."

"No offense, Ed, but I really don't give a shit," Corman told him. "If I have to weather this bullshit to stop the wiemca, then fine. I will. Everything else is tertiary."

"Are you *listening* to me?" Edgar yelped, raising the hand into the air. For a moment, Corman was taken aback; Edgar could do that? Then he felt his left hand strike him across the face, leaving behind a wicked sting. "Goddamn it, Corman. I'm trying to keep you alive."

"Nobody asked you to," he muttered, rubbing his cheek.

"*Fine.* I'm trying to keep *myself* alive. That work for you?"

"After a fashion."

"Like it or not, Corman," Edgar said, "what happens to one of us happens to the other. As above, so below. You can't escape that. You can't escape yourself."

"So what would you have me do?" Corman demanded. "Nothing?"

"I'd have you consider the consequences of your fucking actions," Edgar spat. "Before you end up getting us both shipped off to Guantanamo or God forbid, back to HADES. All I'm trying to get across here is to *be careful*. That's it."

"That possibility went out the window eight years ago," Corman said, opening up his notebook again. "They want to get at the very heart of their victims. To their personal aether. That's why mercury is written into every Seal. All other metals can be created by harnessing the right amount of sulfur in mercury. So they want to get to the origin of the victim to transmute something else. Something, or someone. This has to play into each of the covens abandoning their traditional dogma. Whatever this goal of theirs, it's worth it to them to forsake everything that came before it."

"And do you have any idea what that might be?" Edgar asked flatly.

"That's the thing. All of this is contradictory," Corman muttered, rubbing his forehead. "Nothing about this makes sense. Unless they're trying to manifest the Void itself into something comprehensible. Which is impossible. Cosmological chaos can't be rendered into *something* if all it represents is *nothing*."

"So it's not the Void, then."

"What else could it possibly be? The philosopher's stone?" Corman flipped through his notebook again. "They could be distilling the victims' aether in order to putrify and purify it, but..."

"Why would they bother with that?" Edgar asked. "It's not like they care."

"Immortality is seductive, no matter your affiliation," Corman murmured. "The wiemca are already undead. Maybe they want to prolong the process of decay."

"So all of these women have something that can contribute to the creation of the philosopher's stone, right? We just have to find out what that common factor is."

"I'd still need their autopsy reports. Medical histories if I can get them. No way I can figure it out otherwise."

"Okay, but how do we do that?"

The answer was a simple one, but it was one Corman was loathe to consider. But the path was narrowing, his options decreasing.

Nobody else could help him out with this. Nobody else he could trust not to turn him in, anyway.

"It's time to pay the old hag a visit."

"That's an awfully rude thing to call her."

"Yeah, no shit, Ed."

Stepping over cracked ice shelves that supplanted themselves atop the sidewalks, Corman felt his left hand twitch. Stopping, he turned his head and saw the mosque. Well, the old mosque; damaged so badly by the explosion, only the foundation bricks remained. Flowers and wreaths once laid down in the ashes long ago turned into dust themselves; they, like the congregation gathered that day, returned to the earth. Standing there, Corman couldn't formulate any one thought or another. What was there to grieve? It happened, there was nothing that could be done to reverse it. The dead stayed dead. Thus far, not even the wiemca managed to get out of that one. *Maybe that's the point behind all of this. They've divined the future and they didn't see anything good.*

But that was the nature of things. People were born, and people died. Usually prematurely. Not that it mattered. Nothing would change, the ouroboros would eat itself alive again and again. The mosque was just one of many to meet that fate. Synagogues, church-es, temples, all of them went down in flames. Nothing sacred re-mained in Minneapolis. The profane had eaten it alive and spat it back out. Prayers didn't stand a chance against bullets. When the enemy is dressed in full plate armor and carries .38 special revolvers, cardboard signs do little to deter them. Pleas for mercy did even less. The anger would rise and the protests would start; they would invariably end in bloodshed. *Rinse and repeat ad nauseum*, Corman thought. *Ad infinitum*.

What good these people probably thought they were doing wasn't the issue. They meant well, sure, but they were idiots. They were trying to kill chimaeras by throwing their shoes at them. Then they get angry when the chimaera rips their throats out, as if they didn't know what they were going up against. *Morons. Complete fucking morons, the lot of them.*

Much of the Warehouse District met a similar fate; it had been razed to the ground and left to rot in the time he'd been away. Those lost souls with nothing left in their hollow shells gathered there, having been emptied out and thrown away once they could no longer be utilized, whether by the gangs or by their families.

Old, tired men stood on street corners with broken teeth and worn out shoes. Young, malnourished girls hooked on opioids skulked in and out of alleyways looking for their next fix. Single mothers with wailing babes at their breast rocked back and forth in an futile attempt to quiet them. Cambions of all kinds walked listlessly down the roads of abandoned storefronts, their heads down and eyes wary. Their horns were at full length, their tails whisked behind them, their claws poked out of their dirty coats.

As Corman walked by, they looked to him with hungry, sunken, and desperate eyes. Surely, he must be well-off. He was clean, wearing clothes that fit him, and his face wasn't marred by pockmarks, scabs, or disfiguring scars. *If only they knew what I really was*, he thought. *Too clean for the gutter and too dirty for the rest of the world.* Even here he couldn't fit in. There was no place for him, even amongst the destitute and lost. Shadows of death lingered over their raw, windburned faces and blackened fingertips that never stopped shaking. *Maybe I'm still Death, after all this time.* He felt for the billy club under his coat and gripped it tightly. *I still have this. I'm still the master of my life and my death.*

From time to time, Knights liked to prowl in the area, usually drunk, looking for easy prey. Their nightsticks at the ready, they'd pick some poor sonofabitch and bash their skull in for kicks. Judging from the dried bloodstains and swollen eyes on the cambions he passed, they must've paid the district a visit fairly recently. These "incidents," as they were called, usually resulted in little more than a slap on the wrist. "Unprovoked assault" put the officer on two weeks of paid leave, only for them to come back ready to beat the shit out of another cambion on their way home from the precinct office.

"We got another dead hooker off of Third," Corman had once overheard as Gawain and Bedivere walked past his desk. "King's got on us detail."

"Wouldn't be so bad if we didn't have to write every single one up," Bedivere had murmured. "I mean, why bother? I can't think of anyone who would give a shit."

Gawain nodded. "It's too much goddamn paperwork for a ten-cent whore. A *mooncalf* whore, at that."

The building was a twenty-story highrise on the northern end of the district, a plain gray pillar of broken windows, graffiti, and graying, dying ivy. Corman entered through the lobby's revolving vestibule, whose glass was either smudged or shattered. Grime covered the lobby's walls, a mix of mildew and moss. The smell was pungent. The paint on the walls was cracked and peeling. On the areas still large enough for it were the prerequisite blotches of person tags. Fluorescent lights fizzled in the ceiling, their guts exposed by the lack of tiles. In the summer, moths danced around them as their shadows played on the derelict walls.

Fortunately, the elevator still worked. An old contraption in desperate need of basic maintenance, it had no door save for the iron wrought gate that was the only thing between Corman and a twenty-foot drop to the basement. He hit the penthouse button on the control panel, and the elevator began the arduous journey upward, a journey accompanied by the gnashing of broken metal.

Between the slits in the gate Corman observed the other occupants of the building, junkies, cambions, and the disabled, amble on about pointlessly, leaning up against the wall or lying on the dirty floor in ragged, moth-eaten blankets. They were very much like the ones in every other abandoned building in the city; after a pummeling by the cops, or a poorly-timed car crash, they got the usual treatment for those without health insurance: a few shots of morphine and an itemized bill. Cut to a few weeks later, and they were screening calls from the debt collector and from their drug dealer. Morphine was easy to come by; Corman had scene plenty of toxicology reports over the years that attested to that. Ten milligrams of morphine cost a hundred dollars. A week's stay at the hospital cost a hundred thousand dollars. Yet somehow it confused the outsider that they paid for the morphine instead of settling up their debt. Even a slow, painful death was more cost effective than paying to stay alive.

Vivaldi's *Four Seasons* grew louder as the elevator clanked and wheezed its way on up. Though it was being played on a phonograph, it still managed to blow out the speakers thanks to her ingenious audio set-up. Classical, death metal, jazz, it didn't matter what she played; she played it loud. *Music is a salve for the soul*, she'd told him. *Listening to it quietly is a sin.*

The electricity needed for this she got off the record courtesy of an old friend at city hall; it was channeled through a few backup generators and a rerouting of some of the city's power grid. Otherwise the building had no power; the owner had abandoned it during the Pagan Riots. He was far from the only one, but she was one of the few to make a home out of the decay left in the riots' wake. The far less adaptable got as far away as possible.

Corman shoved the gate to the side and stepped out into the penthouse's anteroom, a hallway that led directly to the apartment.

Entering without knocking, Corman looked around to see if things had changed in his absence. It had not, save for the painting taking up the entirety of the eastern wall. A floor-to-ceiling canvas portrayed a half-finished scene of apocalyptic visions: a sea of blood, monsters eating children, and a dragon looming overhead. On the opposite side of the penthouse, up a set of wooden stairs, was her room, a plaster mezzanine broken up by large panes of glass. Though he couldn't see her, she cast an amorphous shadow against the rest of the penthouse. The music faded out before stopping altogether.

"Rowan?" she called out, her voice an unearthly rumble that had no discernable source. "Is that you?"

"Corman."

One of her wings poked out from the mezzanine's door and unfolded to its full size. All seven of them were brilliantly white and feathery. Four pointed to the sky, three pointed down. All seven coalesced at her center, a collection of seven rings intertwined with each other, all constantly spinning. A ball of translucent fire enveloped the rings. Each wing and each ring had seven eyes each, and the fire occasionally popped to reveal another set of eyes hidden within the flames.

She floated down the stairs gracefully, her entire being taking up almost as much vertical space as the canvas did. All ninety-eight of her eyes outside of the fire looked down at him.

"Hey, Mom," Corman said.

IV

LEG IN A BEAR TRAP

"S O YOU FINALLY DECIDE to visit," Mom said, her voice so deep and distant that it sounded more like an echo. He'd forgotten how unsettling she could be when she wanted. "When were you going to tell me you were back?"

"Do we have to do this? Now?" Corman grumbled, rubbing his temples. "I just walked into the fucking room."

"Considering everything, I believe doing 'this' is in order," Mom said, floating toward him. Her wings shivered and twitched, and her core shone brightly to mask the transformation within the spinning rings. A blindingly bright light consumed the penthouse, a cyclone of hot air filled the room. A blonde woman in her mid-fifties stood before him once the light dissipated, completely naked. Corman shielded his eyes.

"Mom, come on, please," he muttered. "I get that you're pissed, but—"

"Oh!" Mom said. "If you'd given me some prior warning, I would've made sure to make myself presentable. Rowan always gives me notice before she comes over."

"Oh for fuck's sake," Corman grumbled, massaging his temples with his thumbs. To take his mind off of it, he turned to the canvas and got a better look at the details. Rotting corpses and skeletons danced in the throes of their madness, some grabbing their skulls in either ecstasy or pain. In the background, reds, browns, and blacks mixed together to form a scabbed-over river of blood. Drowning in it were the damned, screaming their exposed lungs out. *Hasn't changed her oeuvre, I see.*

"So how are my boys?" Mom called down from her mezzanine.

"Just fine, ma'am," Edgar chirped, flowing out of Corman's hand. He transformed into his cat form and kneaded the couch cushions. "You kept the Seal open."

"Of course I did," Mom replied. "I knew you'd be back eventually."

"From life in prison?" Corman asked.

Mom reappeared on the stairs dressed in a beige turtleneck, gray chinos, and black boat shoes. Walking back down to them, she said, "Call it mother's intuition. And pulling some strings."

"You still have strings to pull?" Corman asked, throwing his coat onto the couch facing the canvas.

"Believe it or not, other people like me," Mom said. "Convincing the head of the records department to lose yours was easy enough."

Oh for fuck's—

"That would've been nice to know beforehand," Corman said. "I spent the last six months busting my ass for the Hermetics to get fake papers."

Mom went over to the couch and scratched Edgar behind the ears. "Maybe you should've visited me sooner, saved yourself some trouble."

"Jesus," Corman muttered.

"Oh, is it so bad for a mother to want to see her son?" Mom asked. "Her son she thought she'd never see again?"

"You ever think *why* I didn't ever bother showing up? Why I didn't *want* to?" Corman spat. "*That* ever cross your mind? Or was it not enough about you?"

"You'll have to be more specific. What didn't you want to implicate me in? Your theft of government property? Your impersonation of a federal officer? Your general obstruction of justice charges?"

She knew. Of course she did. Why wouldn't she?

"You'll have to figure out an exit strategy," she told him as she went over into the kitchen. "You've essentially attached yourself to a time bomb."

"Funny, here I thought *I* was the bomb."

"And this chimaera business... what in the world convinced you going after the wiemca alone was a good idea?" Mom asked, filling up a kettle. "They're not be trifled with, even by you. And now that you don't have the Knights to back you up..."

"I'm aware," Corman replied, rolling his eyes. "Should I even bother asking how you know all of this? Or are we at war with Eastasia instead of Eurasia this week?"

"You jest, but your... *activities* have been well documented," Mom said, putting the kettle on the stovetop. "The mayor's office has been having a rough six months from what I hear. Even the governor has gotten wind of it. The mayor is facing mounting pressure from the city council to book you. You've become a bipartisan issue, dear."

"Can't say I'm surprised," Corman said. "Anyway, look, I'm here to—"

"Ask me for something, I'm sure," Mom interrupted him. "Why else would you just suddenly turn up out of the blue? Just because you, God forbid, *miss* me?"

"Christ. What, Rowan didn't ever see you?"

"I don't suppose you do, do you?" Mom rummaged through a cabinet for a box of tea. "And yes, as much as I've loved having Rowan around so much, I still have two children. I would like to see both of them more than every eight years."

"That part isn't *my* fault," Corman pointed out.

"Yes, but you not seeing me since you've been back *is*," Mom went on. "Is just calling me every so often too much to ask?"

Corman pinched the bridge of his nose. "*Mom*. Please."

"It's not so difficult, even for someone as *busy* as you, Corman."

"It wouldn't surprise me if my apartment was bugged. If King really thinks it's only a matter of time before I get caught, then—"

"Or is it that you just don't want to see me? I understand if you don't want to talk to me. I just wish you'd just be honest with yourself for once," Mom said. "Would you like earl grey or green tea?"

"Believe me, I'm nothing *but* honest."

"A little trust and respect go a long way, Corman," Mom told him. "Earl grey's probably a safe bet, I think. Edgar, would you like some tea?"

Edgar lifted his head up from his lap. "Yes, ma'am. Green, please."

"Don't encourage her," Corman hissed.

"At least *someone's* happy to see me," Mom said.

"Jesus." Corman rubbed his forehead.

"You act like seeing your mother is like getting a lobotomy."

Might as well be, Corman thought.

"I'm *not*," he said instead. "Look, I didn't come here just for you to admonish me."

"No, we've already established why you're here," Mom said. "But what does it matter? You're preoccupied with saving the city from devouring itself. As if *I'm* the one who's responsible for it. As if *I'm* the one who's getting in your way."

"Wow, and you wonder why I haven't seen you," Corman muttered, gritting his teeth. "The *second* I walk in here, you chew me out. Don't you think I get that enough from everybody else? You think I want to get it from my *mother*?"

"No, but I expect you to at least *listen* to me," Mom told him. "And what you're doing right now is a good way to get sent back to HADES."

"Did you happen to forget *you're* the one who sent me there?" Corman asked.

"To keep you from getting the needle," Mom snapped. "Did *you* happen to forget *that*?"

No, he hadn't. Of course he hadn't. The kettle whistled in the ensuing silence. So that was her game, then. Lording *that* over his head, as if it hadn't kept him from sleep for the last eight years. She saved him from the electric chair, so why didn't he just take an hour out of his day to visit her? It was, after all, the *decent* thing to do. Such a *simple* repayment.

And what a life she saved, he thought.

"No, I haven't," he said.

"You talk as if you had," Mom said. "I was beginning to worry."

As he was about to retaliate, Edgar shot him a look with his big, dilated cat eyes; he shook his head. Corman raised his eyebrows, but Edgar didn't let up.

Mom turned the stove off. "Cream and sugar?"

"Yes, please," Edgar said.

Glasses clinked together as Mom prepared her tea tray. Corman sat on the couch next to Edgar and rested his chin on the back of his hand. He could've screamed. Arguing with her was arguing with a brick wall that had also somehow fell on top of him. Time to concede.

Corman sighed. "I need a favor."

"Yes, yes, so we've established," Mom said, carrying the tea over. She set it all down on the coffee table and poured out the water into separate cups, one for each of them. In Edgar's she added the cream and plunked in a few sugar cubes.

Taking a seat in the plush armchair next to the couch, she crossed one leg over the other and folded her hands together. She looked to Corman expectantly.

"Thirty-eight women have gone missing over the last six months," Corman said, ignoring the tea. "Twelve of them are confirmed dead."

"And you're looking into it yourself."

"The wiemca are behind it, that I'm sure of, but I have no idea what they're after. I've broken up nine séances since this started, but eight of them had already conducted the ritual by the time I got there. The victim is always a young woman, and her body is mutilated and missing some vital organs. The other night, though, I managed to intervene before the victim died. Only thing is, she had no idea what they wanted with her. I'm at a loss. I tried figuring out what these women have in common, but I've come up short in regards to an answer. The bizarre thing about all of this is that the wiemca are acting against their dogma. Each ritual was performed by a different coven, and each one is acting blasphemously by their own standards. They're using the Seals of knowledge in the rituals, which is completely antithetical to their whole way of life. But whatever their end goal is, it's important enough to do that *and* bring chimaeras out to pull guard duty. They *really* don't want anyone getting involved."

Mom stared into her tea and frowned.

"And these séances, were they conducted around the same Seals of Solomon?"

"Yeah," Corman said, pulling out his notebook. "Forty-eight, thirty-eighth, twenty-first. But even the covens using the same Seal use different sigils in the pentacle. They're trying to find out something, and they each have different ideas on how to obtain it."

"So where do I come in?"

"I need to get the coroner's reports for the victims to see what they have in common. See what exactly the wiemca are trying to find inside these women," Corman said. "They want *hidden* knowledge. Hidden inside the human body."

"And you know this for certain?" Mom asked.

"Well, no, but—"

"So you're going out and almost getting killed every night on a *hunch*," Mom murmured. "The sheer amount of recklessness—"

"The wiemca are *unified*, Mom," Corman interrupted. "Some thirty-odd covens, each one loathing the other thirty, and they're working *together*. They don't do that. Something's united them. I need to find out what and put a stop to it.

"You need to?" Mom gave him a significant look. "You can't leave this for the Knights?"

"The Knights haven't done shit about this in the six months it's been going on," Corman barked, standing up. "Half a year in, and only *now* are they even recognizing what's happening. Nobody's done a goddamn thing except *me*. Not the gangs, not the cops, not the Knights. *Me*. Me and me alone."

Mom sighed. "This is about Lilith, isn't it?"

"I tried telling him that," Edgar added.

"No, it's not about her," Corman said. "This is about the wiemca. Whatever's going on, it's not fucking normal. And this is about thirty-eight innocent women who nobody's fighting for. Who nobody's lifted a finger for. There's been no resolution for any but the dead ones. This has nothing to do with anyone else."

"Corman—" Mom began.

"You hear about the 'groundskeeping' they're doing at Loring Park?" he went on. "They're digging up the grounds there, and only at night. They're up to something."

"They're doing electrical work," Mom said. "Rewiring the underground cables. It was in the local section of the paper a week ago. Please, Corman. Just calm down. You're working yourself up."

"I'm not working myself up," Corman snapped. "The bullshit this city feeds on is working me up. Why am I the *only* one who sees that there's a problem here?"

"You're not—"

"Then why am I the only one doing anything about it? I'm close to something. *Close*. But everywhere I go, everyone's trying to stop me. Why? Why am I the only fucking person in this goddamn piece of shit city that gives a damn?"

Mom glanced over at her canvas. "This is the piece I'm going to showcase at the Blue Ribbon art festival next month. I'd like you to come." Blinking, first at her and then at the canvas, Corman could've ripped the thing to shreds. "*What*?"

"It'll be me and some other local artists. You should bring someone."

"Who am I gonna bring? *Ed*?"

"Well, that's a given, isn't it?"

"Wouldn't miss it for the world," Edgar said.

"*Ed*," Corman spat. "We're not going to some stupid art show. The *idea* is ridiculous. People are out there dying. Starving, Homeless. Crippled. Living under the thumb of a bunch of murderous cowards. They're fucked beyond measure and you want me to waste my fucking time at a monument to bullshit?"

"You could use a break," Mom said. "Do something relaxing for once."

Corman eyed the painting. "Oh, yeah. *That* shit's real relaxing."

"Subject matter aside, it's been therapeutic for me," Mom said. "You ought to take up some form of art. You're all wound up."

"I have better things to do," Corman grumbled, throwing on his coat. "You gonna help me or not?"

Mom sighed. "I'll see what I can do. But such an unusual request might not go unnoticed. I can't promise you anything."

"Great, thanks," Corman muttered as he headed for the hallway. "Ed, come on."

Edgar looked up from his tea cup. "But I haven't finished my tea."

Corman scowled at him until he flowed back into his palm. Without another word, he walked out to the elevator and punched the down button. *What the hell was I thinking?* Having those records would help, but was having them worth putting up with this bullshit? He shoved open the gate and stepped inside the elevator car.

"She just misses you, you know," Edgar said as they descended. "It wasn't fair of you to not tell her you were back."

"Really. Couldn't tell from how she was acting," Corman muttered. "Every time I see that woman, all that ends up happening is her putting me on another goddamn guilt trip."

"I'll admit she wasn't entirely in the right, either, but you should—"

"I don't want to talk about it, Ed."

"I'm just saying—"

"*Drop it.*"

They didn't share another word until they were outside again, where a cold wind cutting through Corman's coat. It would start to snow soon.

"For fuck's sake," Corman muttered.

"Maybe they're friendly," Edgar suggested.

"Don't hold your breath."

Across the street was his sedan, and a jet black Corvette Stingray idling with its lights on. Leaning against the driver's side door was a black woman dressed in a Knight's uniform, save for the helmet. Her hair was tied up behind her head and tucked underneath a steel gray headband, loose strands falling down over her face; she must've just gotten off her shift.

Fuck, Corman thought.

"You're a pain in the ass to find," Sasha greeted him. "Surprising, all things considered."

"That's more or less the point."

She pushed herself off the car and started toward him. "You know why I'm here, so I'll make this as quick as I can. I need you to hand it over."

Why bother denying it? "Yeah, and *you* know I'm not going to."

"That's what I thought."

In one fluid motion Sasha had her rapier out and brought it to his throat, the tip of the sword dangerously close to breaking skin.

"I figured you'd show up here eventually," she said. "Even *you* can't do everything yourself."

"Leave my mother out of this," Corman murmured.

"Sure, when *you* do."

Corman leapt backward and ducked just as Sasha swiped at him. Unfolding the billy club, he thrust the scythe up to meet her blade. He held Samael steady, Sasha doing her best to make his elbow buckle under the weight of the rapier. With a twist of the scythe's blade, Corman shoved the rapier away and got in a clean horizontal slice; he missed. Sasha thrust at him, but caught the scythe instead. That's when she sent a boot into Corman's chest, splaying him onto the asphalt. She poked his chest with the rapier.

Then she offered him her hand.

"Yue told me you guys were gonna cut my head off," he said as Sasha helped him to his feet. "So why is it still on?"

"She told you Lancelot was going to, not me," Sasha said, sheathing her rapier. "I have no interest in beheading you. But I *am* going to need the scythe back."

"You will, when I'm done with it."

"The longer you have it, the worse it's going to be for you down the line," Sasha told him. "This puts King's competence into question. And when people find out the crazy guy fighting chimaeras by himself is also the guy who opened a portal to Hell, *and* the guy who stole a Knight weapon, well... it doesn't look good."

"Third time in two days I've had my rap sheet read out to me," Corman murmured, folding the scythe back up.

"Maybe that should tell you something," Sasha said. "You're only digging yourself into deeper shit by doing this, Ryan. Eventually you're going to drown."

"Fine," Corman said, shrugging. "But I have some things I need to get done before I do."

"Look," Sasha said, looking like she was dealing with a particularly petulant child, that is to say wearily exasperated, "so far the only people who know for *certain* you stole the scythe are me and Yue.

You give it back now, we can pretend it was a clerical error. It got misplaced into a different lot at the uptown warehouse."

Corman weighed the billy club in his hand. "And if I decide to keep it?"

"Worse than me's gonna be after you," Sasha said. "With intent to kill."

"I cost you Lancelot," Corman mumbled. "Can't imagine anyone would have more reason to want me dead."

"Believe me, there's plenty of people with plenty of better reasons to want that," Sasha told him. "I'm here to give you fair warning. That's all. So what's it gonna be?"

"The wiemca are up to something. They're behind this rash of missing persons cases. They're looking for some hidden answer to some hidden question inside them."

"Inside...?" Sasha pointed to her chest.

Corman nodded.

"You have any idea what this 'answer' might be?"

Corman sighed. "No."

"You bring anyone from the department in on this?"

"I'm not an idiot."

"Your impersonation of a federal officer begs to differ."

"Christ."

"Walk with me," Sasha instructed as she started for her car. "You must have *some* hypothesis about all this."

"The fact that they're doing this so organized is weird off the bat," Corman said. "Trying to learn something about the unknown is even weirder. It's out of character. Goes against everything they believe in. Whatever they're after, it's *important* to them."

"And if they have chimaeras," Sasha murmured, "then they must not want anyone finding out what that is."

"More than usual."

Sasha opened the driver side door and lingered with her arm on the door frame, her face screwed up in thought. "They're going to keep at this until they get what they want. And *you* aren't going to stop until *you* get what you want, either."

There wasn't any need to confirm it; they both knew it was the truth of things. She got into the car and started up the ignition. "The department wants its property back. One way or another, they're going to get it."

"Buy me some time," Corman said, gripping the pommel of the club. "I'm close to something here."

"I can't promise you anything," Sasha told him. "But I'll see what I can do. Just... be careful, Ryan. You have your leg in a bear trap and you're trying to fight the bear. You need to get out of it before you get mauled."

"No promises," Corman said.

The windows of the Stingray rolled up as Sasha rolled her eyes. Corman watched as her taillights faded off into the dark of night.

"See, it's not so bad to have friends," Edgar said.

"We're not friends," Corman said. "She doesn't even know me."

"Yeah? And how do you figure that?"

"If she did, she would've tried to kill me."

V

DEAD GULL

TRASH SWEPT UP BY the wind went tumbling into the gutters outside the Trismeg Theater. Small, delicate snowflakes fell lazily from the darkening gray sky. Corman swallowed a slug of whiskey and let it warm up his throat. As he walked underneath the marquee, which told passersby that *The Seagull* would be showing until mid-December, he screwed the flask cap back on.

Posters from old productions adorned the empty lobby's walls. 'Arsenic and Old Lace,' 'Noises Off,' 'A Streetcar Named Desire,' 'Antigone,' 'A Long Day's Journey into Night.' An empty concessions stand stood off to the right, the bathrooms were off to the left. Stairs leading to balcony seating bookended the doors to the main auditorium. It was one of Minneapolis's few old school theaters still standing; it had somehow managed to survive all the riots, bombings, and shootouts that most of its peers didn't. Some, because of those things, had shut down anyway due to lack of public interest. A night of theatre in the middle of a warzone simply didn't hold any appeal. It seemed superfluous. *Which it always was,* Corman thought as he pushed open the auditorium doors. On stage, down the sloped center aisle, were Arkadina and Trigorin dancing around each other in front of a painted backdrop. It bore the scars and scratches and fading of a stage prop used one too many times.

"I think this is Chekhov's best play," Edgar said. "Much better than 'A Doll's House.'"

"That's Ibsen," Corman said as he walked toward the stage. In the front row, a diminutive woman wearing large glasses jotted down notes on a clipboard. An equally short but thicker woman sat beside her, also taking notes.

"Okay, why don't we back it up to the beginning of the scene," the bespectacled woman said, "and Levi, I want you to *really* put on the schmooze. Let's try it from that angle."

"So you want me to be, like, scummier?" Levi asked.

"Yes, I think I do. Now, let's— Emily? Is something the matter?"

Emily pointed at Corman. "We have a guest."

The director turned around and scowled. "And who the hell are you?"

Brushing it off, Corman walked up to the edge of the stage. "Abigail in?"

"That doesn't answer the question," the director said, standing up. "Who are you, and why are you interrupting my rehearsal?"

Corman showed her his ID badge. "I'm from the D.C. Camelot. Miss Steward called me regarding her recent run-in with the wiemca."

"Can't you people leave her alone?" the director demanded.

"Someone else has been around?" Corman asked, raising an eyebrow.

"Couple of your locals. Harassed us for almost a half hour. I kept telling them Abigail had nothing to say to them, but they just kept asking questions like the fucking morons they were."

"Sounds like one of ours," Corman said. "You get a name by any chance?"

"Kay and Bors," the thicker woman said.

"Figures," Corman murmured. "Anyway, I'm Corman Ryan. I imagine that name rings a bell?"

"*You're* him?" Emily blurted.

"Damn, you're short," Levi said.

"She never mentioned his height," Emily told him.

"Yeah, but like, he sounded *tall*. Hey, how tall are you, man?"

I don't have to be tall to beat you within an inch of your life, Corman thought. "Is Abigail backstage?"

"In the women's dressing room," the director said, pointing in its general direction. "Word of caution, Mister Ryan. You make her uncomfortable, or stressed, or *anything* other than safe, your ass is mine. Got that?"

"It's just a follow-up interview," Corman said, climbing onto the stage. "I'll be out of her hair in ten minutes."

"Better make it five, knight boy," the director spat.

All of the actors holed up behind the curtain stared at him as he passed. For the first time in a while, a group of people leering at him didn't have murderous intent.

"Where's the women's dressing room?"

"Are you Corman Ryan?" one of them asked.

"Yes," he muttered.

"I thought you were tall."

I'll be taller than you once I break your fucking legs. "Dressing room. Where is it?"

One of them pointed to a door near the back. "Take the first left down the hall."

As Corman left backstage, he overheard them discussing him. "Are we sure that's him? I swear to God she said he was like, six-five."

Actors. Christ. "You're not short," Edgar said once they were out of earshot. "Five-nine *is* the national

average for men."

"Average for men in general," Corman grumbled. He knocked on the dressing room door. "Course every guy in this fucking city is over six feet. Doesn't matter. I should be seven inches taller anyway."

"That'd still be short for nephilim."

"Better than being short for a human." He knocked again. And again.

"I'm just getting ready," a weary voice asked from the other side. "Be out in a minute."

"It's Corman Ryan," he answered. "You called me?"

"Oh, um, yes. Come in."

Edgar lifted himself up to be at eye level. "Be *comforting*. Her being okay is your first priority."

"My *only* priority is getting answers," Corman said. "I don't give a shit how she feels."

"The lady doth protest too much, methinks," Edgar said.

Sitting before a wall of square mirrors, Abigail's auburn hair was hidden underneath a blonde wig. Off to the side was a makeup palette, overturned and dumped out onto the counter. She raised her head at the sound of the door opening; her mascara trickled down her cheeks onto her chin. Quickly gathering herself, she sat up straight and tucked a few loose strands of hair back into the wig. She glanced over at him, her eyes red and puffy.

Jesus. This how normal people react to this shit?

"I'm sorry," she sniffed. "I look like a goddamn mess."

"I look worse than that every day of my life."

"Ha," she said, unconvincingly. She wiped the ruined makeup off with a wipe. "Sorry. I really should've been... God, I'm wasting everyone's time with this."

Corman took out his notebook and pen. "You have more information for me?"

"Yeah, and some other stuff I remembered, too." She examined the palette and sighed. "I've made a real mess of this."

"I know the feeling," Corman told her. "So. What did you need to tell me?"

"I knew... I knew some of the other girls that went missing," she said quietly.

Looking at her eyes in the mirror, he could tell the tears were gonna start falling again. *Keep it together until I get the hell out of here.*

But the longer he looked into them, the softer her eyes seemed. He cleared his throat.

"Did you know them well?" he asked.

"Sort of," she said. "I used to... we were in the same theatre program in college. We did some shows together, but I haven't spoken to any of them in years."

"You remember their names?"

Abigail produced a piece of paper of her own. "Miranda Anderson, Juno Schmidt, Florence Johnson, Julie DeVine, and Penelope Vargas. We all did Shakespeare together. Do you... do you really think they're all, um—"

"I don't know," Corman said, jotting the last name down. "But I'm going to find that out. Find out what happened to the other women, too."

"Any of you have any contact with the wiemca before, that you know of?"

She shook her head. "No. I know it sounds stupid, but... I didn't really think they were real. Just ghost stories. You know, to scare people into... well, looking back on it, I guess I wasn't really thinking about what."

"You don't have any idea why they might've taken you? Or the others?"

"None," she said, applying a fresh layer of lipstick. "I don't understand any of this. I don't know... I don't know why this happened at all." The tears were starting to well up. "God, I'm such a fucking idiot. I shouldn't have walked by myself. What was I thinking? I can't sleep, I can't eat. I just see those... *things*. Always about to *eat* me. Do they do that? Eat people?"

"No, they don't—" Corman said sharply. Then, softer, "No. They don't eat people."

"Oh, good." She started to cry, and her makeup ran again. "I'm sorry, really. I am. You're not here to see me cry."

"Here," Corman said, going over to her. "Can I touch your face?"

"What?"

"I know a trick that calms people down."

She sniffled. "Sure. Why not? I can't feel any worse, right?"

Placing his fingers gently on her temples, Corman let Edgar take the reins. He discreetly opened his eye and worked through her lacrimal apparatus, redirecting a flow of his endorphins into her limbic system. This in turn manipulated her lacrimal gland so the tears stopped secreting through the interlobular ducts. In an instant, her eyes dried. She looked up at him and blinked a few times.

"How did—"

"Magic," he said, pulling his fingers away.

Turning from him, she curled her fingers into fists. "I don't have anything else to tell you. I'm sorry. That's all I had. I don't know why they took me. Or them. Or anyone. I don't understand anything about this."

"Most people don't," Corman said. "Thanks for telling what you did know. It'll help." At the door, just before his hand reached the handle, he looked back at her. He wasn't sure if it was Edgar, or himself, but he felt the need to do it all the same. "You gonna be all right?"

"Yeah," she murmured. "I'll be all right. I need to get ready. Deb needs me on stage."

Back in the auditorium, Corman got his fair share of confused and concerned stares from the other actors in addition to Deb's look of scorn.

"Well? You make my lead cry?"

"No, she did that on her own," Corman muttered, hopping off the stage. "You might to want to check on her yourself if you're so fucking concerned."

"Hey, pal, you don't get to waltz in here and insult me," Deb spat. "This is *my* production. You're messing around with *my* actors. I didn't want you people nosing around in the first place."

"Oh, something's messing with your actors, but it sure as hell ain't *me*," Corman told her. "Maybe call off the show until she's not fucking bawling her eyes out."

"You do *not* get to tell me how to run my show," Deb barked. "I better not catch your ass around here again, or so help me God—"

As he walked down the aisle, Corman went ahead and flipped her the bird.

Researching the women online, a clear pattern started to show itself. They were all in their early-to-mid twenties, amateur performers, and were part of some actor's guild. They'd all gone missing within the past six months, and so far only one of them showed up dead, in a obituary dated November 15th. *Juno Schmidt*, Corman wrote down. It wasn't much, but it was something.

A voice over the loudspeaker announced that the library would be closing in ten minutes. Corman gathered his things and went back out into the cold. Snow drifts were beginning to pile up; driving back to the apartment was going to be a pain.

In the car, as he waited for the heat to start up, he noticed a dull pain in his palm.

He sighed. "What, Ed?"

"I take it you haven't noticed how much you've been flushed with hormones today."

"Ed, please. I'm very tired, and—"

"And for once, it wasn't just norepinephrine," Edgar went on. "I actually got a hint of *dopamine* in there."

"So I have a body capable of reacting to neurotransmitters," Corman said. "Great. Really wasn't sure about that."

He unscrewed the cap of his flask and chugged what was left of the whiskey. The burn mixed in the ache already in his chest. It was a strange ache, one he hadn't felt in a long time. He wasn't quite sure what to call it.

"So you calming her down was just a professional courtesy?"

"If it gets you off of my back, then yes, that's what it was," Corman said. "I can't stand crying. Just swallow it and be done with it. Not my fault she needs to grow the fuck up."

"So crying is a sign of immaturity?"

"It's what fucking children do," Corman spat. "If you're a grown-ass adult, then figure out another way to work your shit out."

"Some might argue excessive cursing is childish," Edgar said.

"Oh, this is the *perfect* fucking amount of cursing considering the circumstances," Corman told him. "Shit's fucked. I don't need to be clean about it."

Driving out of the library parking lot and onto the snow-driven streets, he absently watched the grim orange of the streetlamps flicker in the night sky. They pulled up at a stoplight. An electric outlet box on the sidewalk to their right bore cryptic, illegible graffiti. "Fuck gangstalking" was written on the side of an abandoned building nearby. Nobody else was out, driving or otherwise; it felt like a ghost had written it. Like a ghost had made all of this. Had put the city together in between the realms of the living and the dead, just to see how much misery it could conceivably concentrated into just one empty, decrepit landscape of squalor.

A few blocks to the west was a residential neighborhood, closed off in its quaint atmosphere of mid-century Americana, houses built in an era deemed worthy of nostalgia, houses with attics full of useless paraphernalia passed down through the generations of people far too attached to material goods out of a misdirected sense of respect toward the past, houses with four televisions and five computers, houses with people already dead but unaware of it.

To the east, a slum the size of the western neighborhood; it was all apartment buildings that fell apart at the seams in the eighties, rats that went dumpster-diving, long forgotten baseball diamonds used as the foundation for tent cities, cambions with venereal diseases and injection scars, prostitutes with missing teeth and missing genitalia, torn up roads without street markings, parasite-infested trees, closed storefronts, and dead bodies stinking up laundromats that had their machines stolen.

I don't fit in on either side, Corman thought. But did that matter? Did any of that matter? Nobody belonged anywhere. It was nothing more than living deterioration and decay, a rumbling storm of destruction. But it was slow, painfully slow. It chipped away at their vitality, seeping into their bone marrow when they were little more than children, so that when they were grown, their eyes were sunken and yellowed, their wispy hair coming off of their exposed skulls, their hands and feet cursed by gout and arthritis. And then, given enough time, somebody in a suit and tie, likewise decaying, took their guts away from them piecemeal. Intestines, kidneys, liver, gall-bladder. Stomach, spleen, heart. The rot would get to their brains one day. But by then, nobody would be truly alive to feel it. They'd just be more dead seagulls, killed fo no good reason.

The light turned green and Corman drove off.

VI

NAPOLEON
CROSSING THE ALPS

T HROUGH SMOKE AND CRACKLING flames, she appeared. Her fingers, long and serpentine, curled around his face. Try as he might, there was no getting away from her; she was everywhere. She was the smoke itself, wrapping herself around his throat. Strangling him. Oily black tendrils crushed his larynx, collapsed his esophagus. Tighter, tighter, and tighter still. Though all he could see was darkness, somehow it all got even darker until all that remained were her eyes. Shimmering, cerulean blues gazed upon him with an emptiness. He felt blood fill his mouth as her eyes burned their glare into him. He fell to his knees and vomited out the blood, though more and more kept coming up from his crushed throat. His ribs pierced through his lungs as she reached inside his chest. In her hand was his heart, sadly pumping away what little blood it still had. Smoke filled his nose. His eyes watered. She sunk her fangs into his heart. Skin peeled away from his bones, dissolved to become one with the darkness. Now nothing more than a skeleton, he reached out for her, the last of his muscles slipping away. But she tossed away his heart half-eaten and disappeared after it. *Don't leave me. Please. Don't leave. Don't leave me. Please. I hate you. I hate you. I—*

Corman woke up drenched in sweat. His phone was ringing. He checked his hands. Not a skeleton yet. He slipped out of bed with a nice little burning sensation in his neck. Though he barely registered it; his back had been killing him for months. *Feels like I'm dead, anyway*, he thought, picking up the phone.

"It's three in the goddamn morning," Corman grumbled into the receiver.

"Why do you still have a landline?" his mother asked. "Everyone I know has a smart phone now."

"Maybe this is just the human in me," Corman said, "but I need sleep. This is usually the time we do it."

"Do you not have one to be a contrarian? Or are you just— what's that word Rowan taught me? Someone who hates technology?"

Corman squeezed his eyes shut. "What do you want, Mom?"

Following an aggravated sigh on the other end, Mom said, "I pulled some strings with the county clerk's office. Mordred's agreed to help."

"You have that much pull?" Corman asked. "What does the county have on that weasel? His firstborn son or something?"

"So cynical," Mom said, clicking her tongue. "Anyway, you might want to head over to the morgue. He'll be waiting for you there."

"You couldn't have told me this earlier?"

"I just got word of it myself," Mom said. "You know these people. Work on their own time."

"Fine. And the word you were looking for is 'luddite,'" Corman said. He hung up.

As he threw on a button-up and jeans, Edgar said, "See? Going to Mom was a good idea."

"We got lucky," Corman muttered, buckling his belt. "Someone's clearly blackmailed Nathan into doing this. Can't imagine he'd stick his neck out for someone unless that was the case."

"Remember to wear a coat," Edgar said, going into his palm. "It's below freezing out."

Corman rolled his eyes as he shouldered into his overcoat. "When did you turn into my mother?"

"I'm more like your father, wouldn't you say?"

As usual, Edgar was right; it was fucking *cold* outside. Snowflakes fell in wet clumps; dawn would likely bring a fresh blanket of snow. On his way down the block to his car, Corman saw cambions in alleyways gathered around fires made inside steel barrels and inside of dumpsters, rummaging around for cardboard and maybe some half-ruined gloves somebody ditched. Creative problem solving could mean the difference between life and death out here; when Corman walked a beat all those lifetimes ago, he saw them using a dead dog as a pyre. Nothing had changed since. Cambions still huddled in their masses against the cold, still begged anyone who passed by for a crumb of mercy. Maybe a few of them had died, maybe some scrounged up enough cash to get on a bus to anywhere but there. But it was all still the same play, just without different actors. No dead dogs that night, though. Just the frostbitten and mentally ill, the usual players.

A block down the street from the Minneapolis Camelot was the city morgue: a squat, elongated rectangle made of gray brick. Other than the black plaque out in front that held the building's name and purpose, it was nondescript, unfriendly. The acrid, sickly sweet smell of burning bodies often wafted from the poorly maintained ventilation system inside; neither the ventilation or the furnaces had been properly repaired since their installation some thirty years prior. The city's money went into what killed people, not into what dealt with the dead.

In the grim orange light of early morning, it looked even more derelict than usual. Really, all of Minneapolis did. Its ugliness was hardly masked by the black of night. If anything, it exacerbated it.

The front door gave way easily. Corman walked inside, where red emergency lights flickered eerily from the white brick walls on either side of the reception desk.

"How does anyone working in this place not kill themselves?" Corman asked.

"Oh, we want to, trust me," came Mordred's raspy, thin voice. All limbs, he slunk out of the darkness beyond the desk. Nathan Alderman always reminded Corman of a snake, though without the intelligence usually associated with them. That didn't put him above Corman's suspicions, however. Betrayal didn't require smarts, just myopic self-interest, and Nathan had plenty of that.

As the Knights' official liaison to the coroner's office, he knew plenty of departmental dirt. Not that he told his associates; they were the dead, and they had their way of keeping secrets.

"And yet you don't," Corman said. "You just skulk around in the dark like a fucking weirdo."

"Wit is wasted on the likes of you," Nathan muttered.

"Tell me Nathan," Corman said, "who's got you by your balls? Unless you finally stole a heart from one of your bodies?"

"Some of us don't have problems of willpower," Nathan said. "Some us don't go weak in the knees when some woman smiles at us."

"Maybe you would if one ever did," Corman told him.

"Uncouth as always, aren't we?" Nathan murmured, starting to walk down the hall on the left of the desk. "Never had anything to say that wasn't sarcastic."

"How else could I be so belligerent with my coworkers? Goes right over their heads."

"Not mine."

Corman gave him an incredulous look. "Oh, no. Nothing gets past you, Nathan."

"You always *did* think you were better than everyone," Nathan said. "Seems like eight years as a federal prisoner hasn't changed that."

"According to who?"

"Have you ever talked to anyone who worked with you?" Nathan asked. "Everyone in the department hated you even before you almost caused the apocalypse."

"Opened a portal to Hell, Nathan. They're very different things."

"Maybe to you, you lout," Nathan grumbled as they reached the end of the hall. Behind a thick metal door to the left was a dank, grimy stairwell that led down to the mortician's laboratory. The entire basement on that side of the building was dedicated to a single room, one where autopsies were performed. It was divided in two by a wall of bulletproof glass. On the opposite side of the glass was the autopsy room itself, its walls made of mortuary lockers. Four autopsy tables sat equidistance apart in the middle, floor drains in between each table. Each table had an occupant covered by a sterile medical sheet. Nathan unlocked the magnetic door with his employee card; once inside the room, Corman was glad he kept his coat on.

"Rumor is that you haven't been minding your own business," Nathan said, switching on the ceiling lights. Corman was about to reply, but was promptly cut off. "Not that I care what you do. I don't. It's because I don't find you interesting, Ryan. I find you prosaic. It might be hard to believe for a textbook narcissist like you, but you are the least interesting person I've ever met. You're just another arrogant brute with a violent temper. You're nothing more than an attention whore."

"Been building up the nerve to tell me that for eight years, I take it?" Corman asked.

Nathan glared at him. "*But* I've decided to put my enmity aside, because, against all odds, you actually might be onto something. My work is piling up, and I have reason to believe what you're chasing is related to my sudden workload. Take a look."

Pulling back the cloth over one of the bodies, Nathan unveiled a young woman with a mutilated throat and eviscerated torso. Her chest cavity had been rearranged, her organs pulled apart and left to rot. Only a few of them were actually missing.

"The diener already cleaned her up some, but this is pretty much what she looked like when we got her," Nathan said casually.

"And—" Corman averted his eyes, stared at the still-covered legs. "The lower half?"

"Bruised. Internal bleeding, but nothing like what you're trying very hard not to see."

"And the, uh—"

"Yeah. The others are much of the same. One doesn't have her face, another is missing a leg and both of her kidneys. The fourth one at the end there is nothing but a torso with a half-missing skull. The only way we knew it *was* a 'she' was by dental records. And even that proved difficult, given that half of her teeth were ripped out of her head." Nathan motioned to the lockers on the walls. "Take a guess how many of the others met the same fate."

"You think the wiemca did this?" Corman asked, thankful for having something else to focus his eyes on.

"We have twenty-five corpses in here that are barely recognizable as people," Nathan explained. "More like slabs of ground beef. Some are in worse shape than these woman, if you can believe that. All of them, and I mean *all* of them, were DBs on-site of a wiemca séance or up river of one. There's chimaera saliva in them, too. Ran it through the CODIS. Every one of them had been torn up by the wiemca for one reason or another."

"That doesn't tell me anything I don't already know," Corman snapped. "Why you felt like showing me some poor woman's—"

"Hold your horses, Henry Fonda," Nathan said, as he held up a hand. "As I said, we had to go through dental records to identify most of them. By number ten, I was already starting to wonder just what was going on. So I complied all twenty-five records together, including what I could gather from their medical histories. They might be incomplete, but I did what I could considering the circumstances."

Over at a sterile, metal desk, Nathan produced a manila folder. "Now, I can't figure out much of anything from them. But you're obsessive enough. You'll find something. Try and lighten my load a little, huh? Do something for someone else for once."

"I *am*, asshole," Corman grunted, grabbing the folder out of his hands. Sure enough, there were twenty-five case reports on the bodies. A cursory glance told him something awfully particular. "They're all women."

"Not the first pattern you'll find, I'm sure."

"Why are you helping me, really?" Corman asked. "Everyone besides my mother and my left hand hates me now. If King finds out about this, she'll have your head."

"You think death scares me?" Nathan cocked a wiry eyebrow. "Please. I spend twelve hours a day amongst the dead. Look around you, Ryan. This is it. All that we are, everything we've ever done or will do, it all amounts to the same thing. You're just a body that knows it's a body, that's all. A few sparks from our neurotransmitters, and we think we're gods. It's pathetic to believe we're more than this."

Dawn hadn't yet broken when they left the morgue, but as Corman predicted, the snow was starting to get heavy around them, now enough to step in. Tucking the folder under his arm, Corman watched as Nathan skulked back into the dark hallways of the building, his thin chicken neck bobbing as he went.

"You didn't answer my question," Corman called after him.

"No, I did not," Nathan replied without turning around.

"Asshole," Corman muttered, stuffing his hands into his coat pockets. Then, to Edgar, "What was with all that stuff earlier? About me being a brute? What the fuck is his problem?"

"I think he spelled it out pretty clearly," Edgar said.

"Yes, Ed, I'm aware," Corman sighed. "But he was so... erudite. It means he's *thought* about all of that. Really put me under a goddamn microscope. *I'm* uninteresting? This asshole's the uninteresting one. Jackass."

"You're overthinking it," Edgar told him.

"Don't I have a right to? After all this?" Though he couldn't see it, Corman knew Edgar rolled his eye. "It got us a lead, didn't it?"

"That, or your paranoia finally resulted in something useful. It's probable enough."

"Paranoia? What the hell are you talking about?" Corman spat. "Last thing I am is fucking paranoid."

"You think the world's out to get you."

"Isn't it? Considering how many people hate me, I think that's a fair assessment."

"I meant in a more cosmic sense," Edgar said. "That the entire universe is conspiring against you. As of God himself is plotting your downfall."

"It wouldn't surprise me. If God exists, then he's a fucking cunt."

"Somehow I think your perception of God might be a little biased."

"Whose isn't? Either he's enjoying this or he doesn't care. Either way, fucking cunt."

"Or he has a larger plan we can't totally comprehend without the benefit of hindsight," Edgar offered. "Or because of the limited capacity of the human mind."

"If the plan's to let innocent people die to prove a point or whatever, then he can fuck off," Corman spat "I don't care if this is beyond my understanding. The bastard doesn't deserve to be let off the hook. Mine or otherwise."

"Oh, of course, what's God compared to *you*?"

Out in front of the apartment was the Stingray; Sasha, in a pink bathrobe and matching slippers, opened up the driver's side door. A scarf was wrapped loosely around her neck.

"I finally get Isaiah to sleep, and wouldn't you know it, but I get a call from dispatch about someone breaking into the fucking *morgue* at three in the morning," Sasha said. "Now, I understand what motherhood entails. A lot of nights where I don't get any sleep. You get irritated. I know I'm hardly the first woman to want to throw my kid off the fucking roof. But what I *didn't* know was that I'd get stuck with *another* baby who turned out to be a grown ass man. So tell me Ryan, why am I suddenly your nanny?"

"Not my fault they call you to change my diaper," Corman said. "You could've said no and gotten someone else out here."

"At nearly four in the morning? With the roads this bad?" Sasha shook her head. "Only someone as crazy as *us* would do it. So are the dead coming back to life, or should I be worried about what you're into?"

"The dead have answers," he said. "Well, their medical records do, at least."

"Sure. What were you actually doing over there?"

"I just *told* you," Corman spat, stomping over to her. He waved the folder in her face. "Twenty-five women are in lockers down there and they're all *mutilated*. Twenty-five out of thirty-eight. God knows what happened to the rest. Their bodies are probably still out there, rotting."

"So what else does your intel tell you?"

"Funny thing about that," Corman said, "it corroborates everything I've been saying. Organs, specifically organs, are being harvested. The corpses are missing an arm, a leg, a kneecap. They're being cherry-picked."

"You thinking there's some sort of wiemca black market?"

"It's possible. Not that you assholes would bother looking into it," Corman muttered.

"We've got other things to worry about, Ryan," Sasha said, sounding more weary than usual. "The Sons' beef with the Kingdom is getting worse by the day. Since Uthor died, their truce has gotten steadily more pointless. That whole fucking war of theirs, too. New blood's spent the last year pissing all over it. There's this kid named Wukong who's coming up in the Kingdom, and he's done nothing but invoke the Son's ire. He's running everything from Northrop to Powderhorn, and his managerial style leaves little room for the Sons."

"Who's got the U? Stadium Village?"

"Stadium Village is under Leftclaw, but Dinkytown is a warzone. Border skirmishes are going on nearly everyday now. Intel says that Wukong is gonna make a move onto Leftclaw's territory soon."

"Let them eat each other alive," Corman said, the cold unbearable now. Why did everyone insist on talking to him in minus twenty degree weather? "Then you can help me deal with the wiemca."

"The Sons and the Kingdom have military grade hardware, Ryan," Sasha told him. "There was a raid on our North Loop and Lowry Hill warehouses a few weeks back. Seems like you've engendered their confidence in stealing from us."

"So they got your guns, huh?"

"More than just firearms, but yeah," Sasha said with a sigh. "But give them a few more weeks. I'm sure they'll have enough firepower to overthrow King. You understand that you'll wind up being the scapegoat for that, right?"

"Unless of course this gang war spills over into your jurisdiction," Corman said. "Then you might have get your thumbs out of your asses and actually do something about it."

"King will find a way to blame you, believe me," Sasha said. "You're smacking the hornet's nest now, Ryan. What are you going to do when Mordred rats you out? You need to keep your head down before Kyle knocks it off."

"I don't care if he does," Corman told her. "I can finally establish a motive for all this. I just need a few more weeks to put it all together."

"You better figure it out faster than that," Sasha said. "I'm out."

Corman frowned. "What?"

"King's cracking down on *everyone*," Sasha explained. "On everyone and on everything. Outgoing phone calls, mail, our car's mileage. Anything that can lead her back to you. And if she finds out I was *helping* you? You might as well hand me a shovel, because I'm going to be as deep into the shit as you are."

"You *aren't* helping me," Corman argued.

"Unless she counts keeping her thugs from caving your skull in helping," Sasha said. "Which she most definitely does."

"You're barely doing *that*."

"But I *am*, and that's all that counts." Sasha sighed. "You know once she figures it all out, she'll go after our families. I can't protect you and my kids at the same time. I have to choose, and I'm choosing them."

"Yeah, no shit you are," Corman muttered.

"You have to choose too. It's the wiemca or your mother and sister."

"Nothing's going to happen to your family or mine," he told her. "I'll make sure nothing happens."

"Ryan, come on," Sasha said, not unkindly. "Contrary to what most people might think, you're not an idiot. You already know the consequences of sticking your nose in places it doesn't belong. Despite everything, you *were* a good Knight. And I mean that in the sense of what we're *supposed* to be. Not thugs, not bullies, not murderers. You believed in the mission. I know you did. I could see it. Everyone could. But that won't save you now. It didn't save you then. You're in over your head. Bow out. Right now, you're Napoleon crossing the Alps. You're not gonna make it to the spring thaw. And that's not just because you're short." Corman furrowed his brow. "Of course it's not. And I know the consequences of not following through on this. I don't give a shit what happens to me. I'm the only one doing anything, and I'll be damned before I give up on this."

The engine revved as she shut the door. Snow flew up from under the tires as the car pulled off into the street, a good bit of it landing hard on Corman's pants he could feel the cold seep down to his legs.

"She's right, you know," Edgar said.

Corman made for the front door. "Doesn't mean I'm gonna listen.

VII
IN THE LABYRINTH

DAWN WAS COMING. As its rosy pink cheeks appeared just on the horizon, Corman finished his fifth cup of coffee. Whatever he was supposed to figure out, he hadn't figured out. There *were* patterns, distinct similarities that applied to all of them, but if there was a reason behind all of it, he was at a loss as to what it might be. The how, when, and where was all comprehensive; the *why* remained elusive.

He scratched his stubbled cheek. "I'm missing something."

"Yeah, sleep," Edgar said, looking up from his seat on the windowsill. "It's five-thirty and you have almost six hundred miligrams of caffeine in your system."

"It *has* to be medicinal," Corman murmured. "They're harvesting bodies, trying to find a cure, I'm sure of it."

"A cure for what?"

"I don't know," Corman said, sighing. "The women have the same blood types, the same height, and they're around the same weight. They don't have any serious underlying health conditions. But then why mutilate the bodies if they're only stealing organs?"

"Anything else unusual?"

"None of them are cambions. There weren't any additional amounts of keratin in their osteocytes, or any of the proteins found in cambion ribosomes. They're all full-blooded humans. No trace of demon ancestry was found in the autopsies."

"Any genetic disorders?"

"Just your standards." Corman tossed the folder aside. "Minor autoimmune disease, family history of arthritis. The wiemca are looking for healthy subjects. But to what fucking *end*?"

"Are we running in circles? It feels like we're running in circles," Edgar said.

That was true. Six months in, and Corman knew just about as much now as he did then. They had reached a substantial roadblock, one he couldn't break through with brute force. *This isn't what you trained for*, he told himself. *They made you into a killer, not an detective.* His investigative skills were limited to tracking chimaeras and semiotics; the latter of which he received no formal education on. *But what use do the dead have for a cure?* They had nothing to lose; it was fundamental to their dogma. Slavishly devoted to the Void, loss was no perceived as such, but rather as victory over life itself. To the wiemca, and Corman himself to a lesser degree, existence was in essence a curse. A return to that primordial state of nonbeing, that was the ultimate gift one could bestow upon others. *They aren't wrong, it's just everyone else thinks of death a little differently.* The brutality of the ritual was, like so many primeval religious faiths, deemed necessary to satiate the deity being worshipped. The victim could not join the Void in any meaningful capacity unless their physical body was properly disposed.

That being said, the wiemca, until recently, performed perfunctory funeral rites for their victims in that bizarre, esoteric way of theirs. Now, though, every coven had seemingly decided to forgo the practice.

"Someone else is calling the shots," Corman said. "Someone the wiemca have decided is worthy of retaining the Void's authority."

"We might have to outsource this," Edgar told him. "To someone who's had their ear to the ground for the last eight years."

"There's not a ton of people who match that criteria," Corman said. "Adding to that the amount of people who want me dead—"

"You already know who I'm talking about."

"*He* wants me dead, too," Corman said.

"I know there's bad blood there, but—"

"No, Ed," Corman said. "I'm telling you this now because I know for a *fact* that dickhead is going to say the same thing."

"We haven't any headway in six months," Edgar protested, trotting over. He leapt up onto the mess of documents strewn about the desktop. "Look at all this. Lukkan will be able to make *some* sense of it."

"I said *no*, Ed."

"He's a professional," Edgar reminded him. "A *licensed* professional. He might actually be able to solve this. And then we can live an *actual* life."

"An actual life," Corman repeated flatly. "What the fuck kind of life could I even have?"

"If that's the reason why we're stalled—"

Corman held up a hand. "It's not. I'm just being realistic about my prospects post-this. Doesn't matter. This needs solving first. And I'm not fucking going to Lukkan."

"Just try talking to him. It couldn't hurt." Edgar put a paw on the back of Corman's hand. "Come on. What else can we even do at this point?"

Corman gently removed the paw. "Find one of the wiemca and beat the information out of him. That's always an option."

"We did that already," Edgar said.

"Yeah, but we can try it again."

Edgar gave him a look of disapproval. "What do we have to lose, Corman?"

"My dignity," Corman said. "We go to Lukkan, I might as well bash its brains in."

Collecting all the documents together, Corman started to feel a particularly ugly realization. That he was hopelessly out of his depth, and once more, Edgar was right. What he had in front of him was a jumbled mess of incomprehensible ciphers. Only a mind versed in deduction, forensic analysis, criminal psychology, and the goings-ons of the city would be able to break the code. That was to say, definitely not his.

"Goddamn it," he muttered. He looked out the window at the dawn. Icicles hung from the gutters of rooftops and snow lightly dusted those rooftops. A cruel, cold wind rattled the fire escapes and satellite antennae. In the streets below, he saw the visages of the wanderers, wandering alone and afraid. The addicts, the homeless, the damned. Some cambion and some human, some white and some black, some with their visible vestigial traits and some without. But all were forgotten. To suffer in silence and to die outside of memory. Everyone was born with a target on their back, but the ones belonging to the desolate wanderers were particularly large.

All of them were just murders in the making, cambions especially. Humans were barely treated humanely, so why should cambions be? At some point, he had been tempted to consider them his people. *Homo cambionsis* were closer to him than any *homo sapiens* ever could be. But even so, he belonged to neither. His species didn't belong to any genus or phylum. *Am I subspecies to the subspecies?* he wondered. But in order to answer that, he had to first answer which *homo* was the subspecies. Humans, or cambions? Who came first, and who dominated the other before now? Nobody knew. Cambion skeletal remains were remarkably similar to those of early modern humans, despite the claws and fangs and tails. The distinction between them had blurred thousands of years ago. Cambions didn't evolve from *homo erectus*, *antecessor*, or *neanderthalensis*. Yet, they somehow matched up with *sapiens*; their evolutionary lines were nearly identical. In short, as Corman understood it, they were both the exact same shade of human. The distinction came from certain humans who didn't see it like that.

His betrayal, he always felt, was to the cambions. Not to "humans." It had been easy for him; just sheer the horns, and he passed as one of them. Most cambions did too, but they couldn't get rid of everything that pointed them out. Claws were part of the fingers, they couldn't be clipped down. Tails and rudimentary wings could be disposed of but their removal simultaneously took out important bones, namely spinal vertebrae and the coccyx. The procedure to do so was likewise dangerous and often times fatal; half of the country prohibited it by law. Modern medicine had not advanced to incorporate a cambion's comfort. It simply didn't care.

So that left horns, which were made of hard tissue and unfortunately directly connected to the central nervous system. Corman was part of the one in sixty thousand whose horns were made primarily of keratin; this was seen in the wider medical community, to which it existed, as a rare mutation. Worse yet, he wasn't even a cambion. His horns, much like the rest of him, was merely a vessel for his angelic DNA. Genetically speaking, he was closer in composition to a star than to other human beings; his mass and weight did not correlate with typical human standards. It was thanks to his father's genomes that he had a fixed human appearance.

Which meant he could, if he wanted, pretend to be human. His fellow freaks weren't so lucky. Their fangs, yellow eyes, and serpentine noses weren't the product of a celestial body copulating with a terrestrial one. They were just humans who looked like that. No cosmic origin, no strange, seemingly paradoxical biology. Nothing exciting or fantastical. Maybe they descended from demons. Nobody knew.

Not that it mattered. In practicality, he was just another billygoat. Another mooncalf. One more goatfucker yet to be added to the pile of corpses. An auf ruining polite society. An inheritor of the violence. An unwanted reminder of the uncontrollable nature of the universe. A remnant of a world long past that belonged to neither the old or the new.

A grim reflection of how small and insignificant every living being was, regardless of what they thought of themselves. Cambions were the result of thousands of years of evolution that did not end the way ruling humans thought it should; the freaks, the bizarre, the people of color, the cambions, they ought to be nothing but bones at the foot of their shrine to modernity. But since they weren't, they best be made into it, and as soon as possible. To some of the ruling humans, it was unequivocally unacceptable that Corman and his ilk were allowed to roam free, ignorant, or worse yet disobedient, to the natural order of things. And if the freaks didn't willingly fertilize the soil with their flesh, then their betters would make damn well sure it would.

Some hundred and ten years ago, before the Second World War gutted it, Mom had taken him and Rowan to the Frauenkirche. At the entrance, underneath its famous towers, was its equally famous footprint. She had each of them place their own foot on top of it.

"There," she had said, "now you can say you've stepped on the devil."

"Why would we say that?" Rowan had asked. "Aren't we devils?"

"No, sweet one, we aren't," Mom told her. "No matter what people tell you."

"But I hear it all the idea at school," Rowan protested. "Cambions are from the devil."

"We're not cambions," Mom said. "But even so, cambions aren't the devil, either."

"Then why does everyone keep saying that they are?" Rowan stepped on the footprint again. "Why keep saying something if it's stupid?"

"Try to imagine things from their perspective," Mom told her. "Do you remember the labyrinth we walked yesterday?"

"Yeah, it was *boring*," Rowan said.

"Remember how you felt when you finally got to the middle, and I said that's all there was to it, besides walking back out?"

"Yeah," Rowan said. "I felt *stupid*."

"All humans are stuck in the middle of their labyrinths," Mom explained. "Just like all humans think they have to step on the devil. Even they don't understand why. Because they don't ever try to walk out. They stay stuck in the middle because that's where they got thrown, and they think that's all there is, and that, until they die, that's where they'll stay. So they don't see the whole thing. All they see a very, very small part of the whole thing, and because it's all they see, they think the small part *is* the whole thing."

Rowan pouted. "But that's *stupid*."

"You have the benefit of being an angel, dear," Mom told her. "You can see the whole thing, so you think it's silly that they don't."

"What about Cormie?" Rowan asked, tugging on Corman's jacket.

"Hey," he said meekly. "Cut it out."

"That's for another time, sweetling," she said as she tussled Corman's hair. "Corman will figure that out on his own time."

Staring out the window at the morning snows, Corman wondered if he ever would. *Well, Mom, was I supposed to have figured it out by now?* Mom had made a promise to him without having seen the whole thing, it felt like. He had a foot in both worlds, and belonged to neither. Perhaps she thought he would've chosen one or the other. Felt more at home with one of his species. But rather than that, he wound up feeling alien in both. Was there really a way out of the labyrinth? Was there even really a labyrinth? Plato had similar ideas that his mother did, though he wasn't sure if that made him feel better about any of it.

"Corman?" Edgar asked.

He blinked a few times, the reverie fading, then looked back at the cat. "What?"

"We should go see Lukkan."

"I don't see the point," Corman said, yawning. "He's gonna say 'no.'"

"Sleep on it," Edgar told him. "Decide when you're not delirious."

"Yeah, sure. Sure." Stretching his arms out, he yawned again. Despite all the caffeine in his system, he knew sleep would come relatively easily. Though as to whether it would be a restful sleep, he had doubts.

A hot wind rose from the Seal; the sheer amount of energy needed to break the Seal was tantamount to recreating the Sun.

In a white sundress and flats, she looked a dream. There was a hint of mischief in her blue eyes. Though was it truly mischief, or had it been malice aforethought? Twirling and dancing on her bare, pale shoulders was her raven black hair. A smile creeped across her blood-red lips. He couldn't tell if it was just the lipstick, or if she'd actually taken a bite out of some bastard's flesh. Maybe it'd been his. Who could say.

While he stared at her lips, she pushed a bone-hilt dagger into his hands.

"Carve the sigil," she whispered into his ear. "Be my missing piece. Be the missing part of my soul."

Dressed in a black robe, he had become a skeleton. His horns, which had become antlers, had grown to a size that his skull couldn't sustain. On his fingers bones lay the dagger, its ivory hilt shimmering in the light of the flames.

"I don't have anything left to carve into," he said hoarsely.

"Into your *soul*," she whispered.

"I can't," he told her.

"You *must*," she insisted, taking his hands into hers. The blade started inching toward his ribcage. "Your soul is the only way to open it."

"Where will I go?"

"Nowhere," she said. "Your soul will be transposed into the door itself."

"I can't, not if I'll never see you again," he protested. "I can't lose you like that."

"You'll lose nothing, my sweet," she said. "You'll have won me my kingdom. Your name will be celebrated throughout my halls for eternity. As the man who gave me everything."

"But I'll have lost you," he told her weakly. "You'll have lost *me*."

Her grip over his knuckles grew tighter. "But you *must*. The future I mean to build depends on it."

"I don't care about the future if you're not there with me."

"But *I* care about the future," she said. "Isn't that enough?"

"My... my family. My mother and my sister. What will happen to them?"

"They will bend, or they will be broken." He no longer had any control over the dagger; she pressed it to his ribcage.

"Promise me, Lilith," he said, "promise me you'll look after t hem.""You know I can't," Lilith told him, her voice growing with impatience. "They belong

to the forsaken. I cannot treat them with any kindness. They betrayed our people. They must be held accountable."

"I betrayed my people then, too," he said. "Both of my people."

"Offering yourself absolves you of your sins," Lilith assured him. "Your memory will light up my halls for eternity. For your place in creating this brave new world."

"Without you. And without them."

"They don't love you like I do," Lilith said, her hands shaking. The dagger would not pierce him. There was a small vibration rumbling in his left hand. "Nobody has ever understood you like I do. So you must understand that you must do this for me."

"I can't trade my mother's life for yours" he told her, wrapping his fingers around the hilt again. "I can't give up my sister's life for yours."

"You *won't* be," she hissed. "The only life I'm asking for is *yours*. I deserve that much."

"*Why*?" he asked, starting to cry. "Don't they mean anything to you?"

"*You* don't mean anything to *them*, Corman," Lilith growled. "But you mean everything to *me*. Your death is the only way I can earn my kingdom. Please. For *me*, Corman."

"If my family doesn't mean anything to you, then neither do I."

"We're ridding the world of all those who would steal from us our birthright. We're taking back what is rightfully ours. Humans, angels, they all have to pay for what they've done to us."

"I don't *want* to rid the world of *anyone*," Corman argued, finding it easier to push the dagger away. "I'm a human. I'm an angel. I can't choose between both if I *am* both."

"You *aren't* choosing. *I* am."

For the first time, Corman looked into her eyes. Really, well and truly, *looked*. And inside those cerulean oceans, he saw a dark, midnight blue abyss. Nothing but scorn and hate and fury lay behind them. She didn't look back into his. She didn't even *see* him. She had *never* seen him.

And she never would.

"Who has loved you, despite everything? Who saved you from a life of loneliness and fear? Who still loves you, though you no longer deserve it?"

"My mother," he said, flipping the blade around. "My sister."

He shoved the dagger into her heart.

"My left fucking hand."

Lilith grabbed his wrists and broke them; Corman fell to his knees in agony as a sharp pain ran up his spine. She ripped the dagger free from her breast and tossed it away.

"It was the blind leading the blind, Lilith," he told her. "I can finally see again."

"Then I will gouge out your eyes," Lilith said as the flames consumed them both. A thick, black cloud of smoke took its place. Cold cut through the heat and Corman opened his eyes, laying on his bed fully clothed.

Clutching the comforter with his hands, he recalled the frozen rain that pelted him as the portal closed, the sirens that blared in the distance, the feeling of Edgar snapping his wrists back into place. That sensation that he had won, but had lost. That he was still stuck in the labyrinth.

PART II
ALBEDO

VIII
NORSELAND

T HEY WERE VIKINGS COME again. At least that's what the Sons of Odin wanted people to think. In reality, they were little more than thugs on motorcycles wearing horned helmets, whose braids were so long they got stuck in the gears. Even when they were less of a gang and more of a loose collection of rowdy assholes who set cars on fire after a football game, Corman hated them. In the eight years since he'd last encountered them, they'd gotten increasingly territorial in accordance with their newfound respect for hierarchy, courtesy of Uthor the Fearless. According to police reports, he used to be some bank teller named David Crowne before he shaved his head and started crusading for a movement against the genocide of his kind.

Under his leadership, the drunken frat boys became full-fledged soldiers, annexing the industrial district before eventually taking over the entirety of northeast Minneapolis, from Columbia Heights to Saint Anthony West. Border clashes with the Sun Kingdom often got settled on Nicollet Island, which vacillated between a DMZ and no-man's land. The Kingdomers were doing what they could to stem the tide, but the Sons had their sights sent on Marcy Holmes, and only one of them had access to military grade weapons.

Civilians died in the crossfire no matter what, but only the Kingdom wasn't dedicated to eradicating half of them. Really the only thing the Kingdom had over the Sons was discipline and community support. The Sons, meanwhile, controlled the city's supply of steel, granite, and limestone, as well as any and all rail lines. There were rumors that the Sons ran guns for the D.C. Knights around El Paso, but of course the official word on the matter was a vehement denial by Arthur himself. And the King of all Camelots was not to be refuted. That was enough for Corman to know the Sons were *definitely* doing it. No doubt they got a nice kickback here and there as a sign of gratitude.

The remaining Minneapolis gangs —Pilate's Disciples, the Golden Hermetics, the Good Earth Tribe, the Zonbi, Daisy's Girls— all scrambled for either gang's approval. Even the Knights, who were doctrinally neutral, curried favor with both of them, depending on what they wanted that week. More often than not, though, they sided with the Sons. Which made perfect sense, given how well their unspoken mission statements aligned,

It was a dangerous thing for anyone not a white human to enter what the Sons had christened Norseland. After all, Uthor the Fearless was a descendent of Thor himself. Not that any factual evidence proved that; he descended from an English salesman and a Polish housewife and had never been out of the state. He did, however, have a rap sheet that almost rivaled Corman's. He had the privilege of reading that when Uthor was still Mister David Crowne of Bloomington, and was only just getting started on his particular brand of bullshit.

Parking on Marshall, in front of an old club, complete with derelict ferris wheel that had ceased operations back when the Sons set fire to the accompanying business, Corman caught sight of a couple of Sons zooming by on their choppers. Proudly displayed on their helmets and on their saddlebags were their usual insignias— eagles, Armanen runes, black suns, and seemingly arbitrary numbers. It was not the place to look different, and fortunately for Corman, without his horns he looked just like any average white guy. *Like any short white guy*, he thought sourly.

Across the street sat a dive bar that used to proudly display a local basketball hero's name and signature before it too got firebombed by the Sons for serving cambions. It now served as Lukkan's office, as well as the man's personal liquor cabinet.

"Go easy on him," Edgar said as they crossed the street.

"*Me*?" Corman barked. "The fucker's fifty feet tall. *I'm* the one at a disadvantage here."

"I'm saying not to antagonize him," Edgar said. "Both of you are powder kegs.

There's no need to light the fuse."

"Yeah? And why do you assume *I'm* gonna do it?" Corman asked as he walked inside. He was immediately met with a sawed-off shotgun from behind the bar. "Hey Klaus."

"We don't serve billygoats, Ryan," Klaus growled. He was a large, pale man with a beard so white it was nearly translucent; he tied it into braids at the chin.

"You're missing out on a gold mine," Corman said. "Half of us are trying to drink ourselves to death. Imagine the business you're sleeping on."

"Take another step and I blow those horns off your ugly fucking head," Klaus snapped, trailing him with the shotgun.

Corman made a show of putting his hands on his hips. "And here I thought I'd done that myself."

Klaus's finger went for the trigger and Corman dropped to the floor; the shotgun shells blasted the front door. Loud, heavy footfalls came from the back of the bar. Lukkan, the big, ugly lug, appeared at the foot of the stairs that led up to his office. Unlike Klaus, Lukkan's hair was cropped short and his beard was trimmed. No Sons paraphernalia adorned his clothing. He surveyed the scene before him and pinched his forehead.

"Goddamn it, Klaus," he grumbled, "you know the fucking rules."

"He's a goddamn *mooncalf*, Luke," Klaus spat, pointing at Corman. "And he has the fucking *gall* to walk in *here*?"

"He's also an idiot," Lukkan said. "Too dumb to live, really."

"Thanks for the vote of confidence," Corman muttered from the floor.

Instead of offering a hand to help him up, Lukkan crossed his arms and leaned against the wall. "You really *are* too dumb to live if you think you *won't* get shot at here. You know the rules, too. You know cambions aren't welcome."

"I have a job for you," Corman said, getting up. Tucked inside his notebook were the medical documents. He unfolded and handed them over to Lukkan. "Missing persons case, side of homicide."

"They cambions, too?" Lukkan asked.

"What, you won't take it if they are?"

"What do *you* think?"

Corman sighed. "They're all fully human. And, fortunately for *you*, almost all white."

"Almost?" Lukkan raised an eyebrow as he took the folder. "Well, guess it doesn't matter if they're dead."

"Is that how we end racism?" Corman asked. "Kill all of 'em?"

"You don't get to talk, Ryan," Lukkan said. "One of us almost ended the world, and it wasn't me."

"No, you just want to murder my people," Corman said. "That's *much* better."

"*I* don't," Lukkan told him, flipping through the documents.

"Just the people you associate with, right?"

Lukkan glowered at him, then tucked the folder under his arm. "You're lucky I'm even *considering* helping you. You might want to keep that trap of yours shut in the meantime."

"How generous."

"So what am I looking for?" Lukkan asked, sitting down at the bar. Corman, despite Klaus's scowl, joined him. "Anything in particular?"

"Hopefully what I couldn't figure out," Corman said "What you're looking for is the purpose behind the murders. Some M.O. Picking up patterns, figuring out what these women have in common and what the point of all this is."

"That's it?"

"That's it," Corman said, eyeing the bottle of whiskey Klaus poured out into a glass for Lukkan. "Consider it an easy paycheck."

"Watch where you look, billy," Klaus growled.

"Always watching, aren't you? Tell me, am I damned? You know how many times I jerked it this week?"

"*Lukkan*," Klaus hissed.

"Cool it, Ryan," Lukkan murmured, not looking up from the folder. Spreading out the documents on the bar, his eyes scanned the autopsy photos attached to each report. "You're only still breathing because of my say-so."

I could kill both of you in ten seconds, Corman thought, gripping the billy club. "Sure. And I thank you for your unparalleled hospitality."

"What angle are you coming at this from? You think it's some sort of serial killer's targeting these women?"

"The wiemca," Corman said.

Lukkan's eyes stopped scanning. "You're not fucking serious."

"They're unified," Corman told him. "The covens haven't been butchering each other for the last six months, and in the interim, they've been butchering young women. Something, or someone, has somehow convinced them to do this. To forsake their own dogma and know the unknown. That's heresy in any coven, and yet they're all doing it. They haven't shown up in any police report in that time, either. No property damage. No arson. No gathering without a permit."

"I haven't had a single wiemca case in almost a year, now that you mention it," Lukkan said. "I figured they all just killed each other off."

"They're too busy with *this* now. And every single woman, all of them twenty-five or twenty-six years old, were found on or near a séance site. Eviscerated and missing vital organs."

Lukkan gave him an incredulous look. "So what you're saying is someone had the wiemca get their shit together, and then pushed them to commit murder?"

"Not murder. Sacrifice," Corman said.

"Same difference in court," Lukkan said. "Not that any wiemca is sane enough to stand trial. Do you have any hard evidence it's for some bigger purpose?"

"No, but like I said, this goes against everything the wiemca profess to believe in. I've been a good number of the sites in the last six months, and the Seals of Solomon I've recorded are all about discovering some kind of knowledge. Medical knowledge, specifically. I think they're trying to find a cure to something. Death, specifically."

"Meaning?" Lukkan asked.

"I think they're trying to make a philosopher's stone," Corman replied. "And they're

using these women to do it."

"What do they want to turn lead into gold for?"

"That's not the stone's actual purpose. It's a statement, more than anything. A symbolic gesture. It's the external manifestation of the soul. See, you can't make it without first undergoing the four stages of the magnum opus, the end result of which is putrefaction and then purification, or turning a leaden soul into a golden one. It's a show of mastery of not only the prima materia, but of one's own understanding of it."

Lukkan frowned at the documents. "And the wiemca want to do that because...?"

"I don't think the *wiemca* are after that, but whoever's leading them," Corman told him. "You need all of the elements present in the human body as a foundation for the stone. But the thing is, you don't need multiple people's organs. Or multiple people at all. Just someone say, without diabetes or an iron deficiency. So why cherry pick these women's bodies? Why are the victims so similar to each other?"

"This is a *lot* of conjecture, Ryan," Lukkan told him. "Unless you have better proof about some grand conspiracy—"

"I'm not asking you to investigate that," Corman cut him off. "I'm asking you to look into these women. Find out why *they* were the ones used."

"*You're* the wiemca expert. Why the hell should I waste my time on this?"

"Because you this is your *job*, you fucking ape," Corman spat. "Or do you only take on cases you *like*?"

"I don't take work from mooncalves, for one," Lukkan said, collecting the documents together. "Much less mooncalves who fucked Satan's hellspawn."

Corman went red in the face; his horn stumps burned. Through his throat clenching up and his anger boiling up from his stomach, he felt Edgar give him a pinch on the palm. But it didn't matter, he was already on his feet with the billy club out.

"*Corman*," Edgar pleaded. "*Not here. Not with him.*"

Lukkan looked at the club and laughed. "You gonna hit me with that? Go ahead. Just know it ends with all of your teeth down your throat."

Then the door opened, letting in a draft of cold air. Three Sons walked in, all of them with long, blond braids and leather biker cuts.

"Finnbar, Morris, Drake," Lukkan welcomed them. "Have a seat. Klaus, this round's on me."

The fattest one, Morris, stopped dead in his tracks as soon as he saw Corman. "Luke, what the *fuck* is *that* thing doing in here?"

Finnbar and Drake both looked in his direction.

"You got a goddamn *mooncalf* in here?" Finnbar, the skinniest one, spat. "The fuck?"

"Yeah, the fuck?" Drake, an amalgamation of the other two, repeated. "What the *fuck*, Luke?"

"All right, calm down, all of you," Lukkan said. "He was just leaving."

"It don't matter if his head was up on your wall," Finnbar snapped. "Klaus, why didn't you shoot this piece of shit?"

"Lukkan told me not to," Klaus said.

Finnbar turned to Lukkan. "So why didn't *you* shoot this piece of shit?"

"I said *calm down*," Lukkan snarled. "I don't need another goddamn hole in my wall."

"The hole's in the door, though," Drake said, looking at the shotgun spread.

"Not the point," Lukkan said, getting off his stool. "He came here with a case. It's business, that's all."

"Business with a devilfucker?" Morris screeched. "Are you out of your mind?"

"No, but I *am* out of the Sons," Lukkan said, his blue eyes narrowed. "I can conduct business with whomever I want. Billy goat or otherwise."

"We don't fuck the devil, by the way," Corman said. "Most of us don't even see him that much. We get like one witches' sabbath card a year and that's it."

"You listening to this shit, Luke?" Finnbar barked. "He thinks he's smarter than us!"

"That's because I am," Corman said.

"Cut that shit out," Lukkan hissed at him. "You need to go. *Now*."

"Oh, no, Luke," Morris said. "He's already tainted this place. We gotta purify it now."

"No thanks, I already took my drug test this month," Corman told him. "Though you might want to go ahead and gut this place anyway. There's just *no* feng shui."

"Do you *want* to get killed?" Lukkan snapped at him.

"*Me*? Oh, no. If it comes to that, *I'm* not the one who's gonna get killed." Corman noticed Klaus picking his sawed-off back up. This seemed to be the signal; Morris slipped on a pair of bras knuckles, Finnbar slid out a hunting knife from his boot, and Drake slipped a grenade out of his pocket.

"You gonna do some demolition work there, pal?" Corman asked.

"Drake, what the fuck?" Morris snarled.

"It's all I had in my saddlebags, okay? I didn't know I was gonna be fighting today. I thought all we were gonna do is get shitfaced."

"Then do me a favor and do this outside," Lukkan growled. "*Nobody's* destroying my fucking bar."

"He has to die, Luke," Morris said. "For trespassing. For contamination."

"Seems a little excessive," Corman said. "I usually only get a slap on the wrist."

"That's your fucking problem, billygoat," Finnbar snarled. "You get away with *everything*. Nothing is *ever* your fault. It's always *us*. Just honest folks who are trying to make a better world."

"And what, pray tell, does that entail?" asked Corman.

"Cambions are *never* at fault, are they?" Morris shouted. "It's *always* the fault of people just trying to preserve their culture, isn't it? What's our crime? Ensuring a future?"

"For exclusively white children?" Corman said, hand on his elbow and finger tapping his chin. "Gee, I don't know mister. If only the *sturmbannführer* would enlighten me on the subject."

"Kill the bastard," Morris screamed, bursting into a run.

"Goddamn it, no! Take this shit outside!" Lukkan demanded, to no avail; Klaus sent another round of shells at Corman. Ducking out of the way again, Corman flicked the club out into the scythe. As Morris rampaged toward him, Corman sliced his legs open at the shins; Morris tumbled forward and slammed his head into a booth with a sickening crack. Klaus fired again and Corman cut across his torso, paring him down to the ribs. The shotgun shells were fired into the ceiling; the force of the blast sent Klaus into the liquor shelves. Shards of glass crashed all over the floor and onto Klaus's back.

Spinning the scythe around, Corman swiped at Finnbar and knocked the knife out of his hand, simultaneously slicing off the first digits of each one of his fingers. Finnbar shrieked. As he turned to Drake, Corman's eyes went wide. The dumb bastard had pulled the fucking pin.

Oh fuck.

"Drake, you throw that outside *now*," Lukkan said, hands held up. Finnbar and Klaus were still howling as their blood spilled onto the floor. "You're gonna kill *all* of us."

"*He* already did!" Drake screamed. "Fuck you!"

Corman took off into a dead sprint, launching into him. This launched both of them out into the street; he made sure his hand wrapped tightly around the grenade. Once outside, Corman held the scythe's blade under Drake's hand and severed it in one quick pull. Then he grabbed the hand and chucked it as far as he could. Immediately after it touched ground, the grenade went off. Bits of metal, asphalt chips, and gravel exploded forth in a cloud of dust. Corman looked down at Drake, who was wailing as he gripped his bloodied stump.

Standing in the bullet-ridden threshold of the bar was Lukkan, arms crossed and leaning against the doorway.

"At least you had to courtesy to destroy public property," Lukkan said. "I'll give you that. Thanks to these idiots, I'm gonna have to spend at least two grand getting all this fixed."

Corman rolled his eyes. "Yeah, *that's* what I was worried about."

"As repayment, I'll offer you this. There's a chop shop off of Broadway you might want to take a look at," Lukkan told him. "Heard they do more than just strip cars there."

"And you know this how?"

"You head over there, do me quick favor, and I'll consider giving you a discount on my retainer," Lukkan said.

Corman frowned. "What's the favor?"

"Disrupt their activities," Lukkan said. "Put them seriously behind their monthly sales quota."

"*You* can't do it?"

Lukkan shrugged. "Sure, I *could*. But it'd hurt my standing with the Sons. And as seeing as that's where most of my client list comes from…"

"I do this, and you look into these women for me?"

"That *is* what I'm offering, yes. You've bought yourself a bit of goodwill just now. It won't last, so you gotta take advantage before I realize how stupid I'm being."

Corman collapsed the scythe, then looked at the one-handed bastard writhing on the ground. "And I'm doing this just for a *discount*?"

"You get the tip-off at a discount, too."

Corman chewed the inside of his cheek, his horns itching like crazy. Edgar wasn't

pinching him, however. *Goddamn it.* "What's the nearest cross street?"

Lukkan's directions turned out to be redundant; a cacophony of metal scraping, power tools, and shitty alt rock blared out from the chop shop, and probably for six miles in every direction.

"Couldn't they play anything better?" Edgar asked as they walked through the parking lot. "This stuff's *awful*."

"You expect these dipshits to have good taste in music?"

Inside, sparks launched off of steel and plastic. The Sons wore welder's masks and leather aprons as they stripped a wide menagerie of vehicles for parts. Apart from the whole business being illegal, nothing seemed amiss. *Not that legality means much of anything.* Nobody paid him any mind as he walked through the shop. Even if they weren't focused on not sawing their fingers off, their masks made it difficult to see five feet in front of them. No security cameras, either. *Easiest trespassing I've ever done.*

"What do you think Lukkan wanted us find?" Edgar asked.

"Something fucked up, probably," Corman said. At the far end of the garage was a back room full of equipment. Power saws, power sanders, hammers, screwdrivers, WD-40. And a metal door with AUTHORIZED PERSONNEL ONLY stenciled across it. "Ten reichsmarks says this is what we're looking for."

Unfortunately, there was an electric keypad underneath the door handle. Corman stroked his chin. *I need an idiot.*

Fortunately, the entire garage floor was full of them.

One of the Sons closest to the back room, a lanky, skinny guy, looked cowardly enough to fuck with. Corman slipped behind him and threw arn arm around his neck; he applied just enough pressure so he wasn't crushing the guy's windpipe.

"I'll make this quick," Corman said, just loud enough to be heard above the din of sparks. "I need the code for the door in the back room."

"T— there's n— no door there."

Corman tightened his arm. "I can snap your neck pretty easy, guy."

"I— I don't know what you're—"

Corman started to cut off his circulation. "Or I could suffocate you. Either one works. Just so long as you don't make a scene."

"They'll *kill* you," the Son murmured.

"It'll only take me half a minute to get out of here," Corman said. "You, on the other hand, will be dead a *lot* longer than that."

"You won't—"

He felt the Son's adam's apple against his elbow as he squeezed tighter. Then he let go, just enough to let the Son breathe again.

Coughing and sputtering, the Son collapsed to the ground with a hand on his throat. "One, eight, four, eight. Please, I gave you what you want. Don't tell me."

"Keep your mouth shut, and I won't," Corman said.

The code, to his surprise, worked. There was a click, and the door opened up to a concrete stairwell.

"They do love their secret bunkers," Corman said, peering over the edge of the railing. Seemed like it went on forever.

The further down he went, the quieter the power tools and the louder some strange ambient noise from below got. As he neared the bottom, he started to shiver; they must've had an air conditioner going. *In November?* he wondered. The stairs led to a single metal door identical to the one on the surface, with the same authorization warning.

"You think that guy won't sound the alarm?" Edgar asked as Corman unfolded the scythe.

"I figure we have about five minutes before he does," Corman said, opening up the door. On the other side, he found some sort of operating table, complete with bright overhead lights, an EKG machine, and about five Sons in medical scrubs and surgical masks. On the table itself was a body covered in a sheet, its exposed midsection missing organs; the removed organs sat in steel sheets.

The surgeons didn't move. All they had were scalpels, medical saws, and surgical knives. Nothing that could cut more than a few inches into him. To emphasize that, Corman laid the scythe's blade around one of their necks.

"Bag it up and get it to a morgue," Corman instructed.

None of them moved. *Godfuckingdamn it.* Corman pulled the scythe toward him, and the surgeon's head slipped off of his neck. Blood splattered onto the other surgeons' legs as the skull cracked against the tile floor.. They all immediately got to work wrapping the cadaver into a black plastic bag.

"Once you're done with that," he said, "show me where you keep the flammable shit."

IX
GÖTTERDÄMMERUNG

All told, they doused the room with thirty liters of formaldehyde, turpentine, and paint thinner. In exchange for their cooperation, Corman allowed them to live.

"Count yourselves lucky," he muttered as they all scrambled for the door. No doubt they would sound the alarm the moment they got back up to the garage. He heaved the cadaver onto one shoulder. *And this corpse probably isn't going to make it past the parking lot.* Didn't matter. He needed to get it the hell out of here.

From his pocket, he fished out a Zippo he'd had since at least 1949. It was a good lighter, and reliable. Sad to see it go, he flicked the ignition wheel and tossed it into the pool of flammable liquid at the base of the operating table. Flames burst forth and slowly started to overtake the operating room. Corman walked up the stairs.

"You think the Sons are in on it, too?" Edgar asked.

"Maybe, maybe not," Corman said, feeling the weight of the body now. "Can't imagine what they'd see eye to eye on, though."

"The organ market has to be lucrative."

"All the better if I can swindle these fucks out of a couple million," Corman said. Below, he heard the snapping and cracking of small explosions. Above, he heard the clicking and sliding of gun metal. "So they have us trapped."

"How many are up there, do you think? Twenty? Thirty?"

"We'll see when we get there."

Turns out there was a good many more, all waiting for him to appear. Some fifty Sons gathered together near the entrance to the back room, shotguns and pistols and submachine guns in hand.

"You guys planning on overthrowing the Bolivian government again?" Corman asked.

One of the Sons pointed his .44 magnum revolver at his forehead. "That doesn't belong to you."

"I'm not well versed in postmortem property rights," Corman said, adjusting the corpse's position over his left shoulder. "But I *am* in killing fuckers like you."

The first shot rang out as Corman flung the scythe out and deflected the bullet. It ricocheted against the walls of the garage; he sliced the Son in half at the waist and charged headfirst into the crowd. More shots fired. More bullets were deflected. Corman cut through the swath of bodies in wide arcs, slicing bodies from side to side, waist to shoulder. Guns clattered to the ground; blood and organs plopped beside them.

A Son tried grabbing for him but he ducked and spun the scythe around, stabbing him in the back. Another rushed in as Corman ripped the blade free, just in time to send it through the chest of the newcomer. Bullets fired all around him, cutting across his arms and legs. One got lodged in his shoulder muscle as he flipped around to the other side of the Son. Shoving him off the scythe, the body slid down and collapsed to the ground. He deflected a few more shots.

Two carrying wrenches charged him. Corman raised the blade up and as it landed inside one of their skulls, he felt a bullet graze his abdomen. Yanking the blade back out, he took with it the Son's skull and a good chunk of his spinal cord. He sent it flying toward the other one, and the skull exploded as it collided with a nine millimeter bullet.

Under the falling debris of bone chips, Corman sliced open the other Sons' chest, and then booked it for the parking lot. Bullets soared past, and he felt the familiar sting inside of a calf muscle and across a shoulder. Stumbling, he landed hard on his right hand, cutting it open on the asphalt. With his slick, bloody hand, he picked up the scythe and started running again.

Back at the car, he slid the cadaver into the backseat. A thunderous crash roared through the still night air; the ground rumbled and shook violently. A gigantic wall of fire reached out from deep within the earth and consumed the garage. The bright oranges and yellows of the flames whipped and crackled, its dominance asserted over the fragile, weak beings that had brought it into existence. *Did they pour nitroglycerine in it, too?* he wondered as he got into the driver's seat. As soon as he sat down, Corman felt lightheaded and dizzy. Wet warmth spread across his torso. Pressing two fingers to his shoulder, he felt the bullet in there. Another one was stuck in his leg, and his gut was leaking.

"So you clearly didn't think this through," Edgar said.

"Yeah, don't— don't remind me," Corman said weakly.

"You haven't reached the critical stage in blood loss yet, but you're running out the clock," Edgar told him. "You can't be driving like this."

"I'm... I'm fine." His eyes started to flutter and hazy spots appeared in his peripheral vision. "I just need to—"

"Hold on, I need to figure out what you've done to yourself," Edgar muttered.

Through the blazing inferno came armed silhouettes, approaching the car with increasing velocity. Corman gulped down blood.

"What can you do about— about all this?" he asked, fading fast.

"Not nearly enough," Edgar told him. "You've got internal bleeding and puncture wounds in your liver and stomach. I can jumpstart the proliferation of your fibroblasts and double up on your myofibroblasts in the affected areas. As for the missing chunk of flesh in your abdomen, I can't do much. Even if I induce accelerated hemostasis, it won't be enough."

"So..." Corman's head lolled to the side. "Any ideas?"

"I'm going to flood your endocrine system with adrenaline. Just enough to get you out of here and back to Lukkan's. But you gotta keep moving once I do. I can't replenish the supply while I'm keeping you alive."

"Ready when..."

"Yeah, yeah, just don't do anything stupider than you have already," Edgar muttered.

His veins lit up neon blue as the adrenaline came flushing in. Instantaneously, his heart rate doubled, his blood pumped harder than it ever had before, and his body temperature exploded. Corman threw the car into drive and slammed on the gas. He *had* to, else he just might blow up himself. There was no pain, no sting of the bullet wounds, no thoughts in his head. Only the fiery night and whatever fell in front of him. The car blasted down the street, crossing red lights and stop signs alike. There couldn't be any stopping. If he slowed down, he'd explode. He had to keep going. *Go go go go go.* Cars in the opposite lane swerved out of the way as he took out a street sign. It went flying behind him. Guns and explosion might've been going off, but he couldn't tell and couldn't care. Hell, if he smashed this thing into a wall, he wouldn't give a shit. Let things go the way they would. Everything else was secondary.

Lukkan's bar appeared on the horizon. But why stop? Why not keep *going*? So he did. Corman drove right past the intersection and onto the Lowry Street Bridge. In the wrong lane. A semi-truck's headlights appeared out of nowhere, and someone other than Corman hooked an abrupt right. Next thing he knew, he was sailing out of the windshield and over the bridge. Water then enveloped him, and in the murky blackness, he felt himself lose breath. Flailing about, he wasn't sure how to resurface. There was so much water it felt as if he'd never see dry land again.

So when he opened his eyes to the morning sun, he was certainly surprised at the revelation that he wasn't dead. Water came up his windpipe and he coughed it, along with some vomit, onto the grass beside him. An ice cold wind cut through him; Corman shivered as he sat upright, his head throbbing.

"I think I OD'd last night," Corman murmured, rubbing his temples.

"So it would seem."

The hood of the car was scrunched up and and shattered. Checking under the hood, Corman found that most of the components were busted. The engine kept turning over, and the battery seemed to be dead. So he put into neutral and pushed it down the bridge and into the parking lot behind Lukkan's office. He'd figure out what to do about his travel situation later. Right now he had a debt to collect.

Lukkan sat alone, the only patron in the bar. Still a wreck, with none of the glass or debris cleared away. Only the dead were gone, though their stench lingered in the cold, dry air. As he went over the case documents, he drank a Bloody Mary. Corman took the stool next to him. Lukkan glanced over.

"You look like shit."

"You looking in a mirror?" Corman asked as he poured himself a whiskey. The burn on his throat felt good. Cauterizing.

"The wiemca are looking for the Horsemen, by the way," Lukkan announced.

The whiskey glass froze in place, halfway to his lips.

"It's not Lilith," Lukkan assured him. "I checked with Mordred. They have her dental records. Death certificate and autopsy reports, too. She's dead and gone. But whoever's pulling this stunt, they have a pretty clear inspiration."

Corman took another drink, winced at the pain. "That doesn't make sense. The wiemca are *opposed* to revelation. Why would they help cause the apocalypse?"   "Maybe not all of them," Lukkan said, handing him a few pages. "Some of these women didn't have their body parts pulled out. Autospies showed that these women had some sort of illness. One had hepatitis C. Another one was doing chemo. A couple had asthma. Three or four had an iron deficiency. And get this, thirteen of them had a history of mental illness. Depression, anxiety, PTSD, bipolar, schizophrenia. There was a gambling addict in there, too, and one with I think a heroin addiction. So it wasn't just diseases of the body. I think they were looking for anyone they considered corrupted to play Pestilence."

"Jesus," Corman murmured. "Did any of them not fit the bill?"

"Only three," Lukkan said, sliding over the appropriate documents. "But it looks like they just got cut up and thrown out. No organs were missing."

He frowned at the pages. "They've always had a propensity for clinical efficiency."

"The fuck does *that* mean?"

"Means they're assholes." Corman took a drink. "Chew you up, spit you back out. Standard operating procedure."

"I thought they did rituals," Lukkan said. "That must take time."

"They do," Corman told him. "They like to play with their food. Maybe they can rationalize it as a sanctification process, but it's like giving a sermon in a slaughterhouse."

"Speaking of slaughterhouses, what'd you find at that garage?"

"Some kind of organ harvesting ring." He finished the glass, set it on the bar upside down. "I took care of it."

"Judging from the bullet wounds, I'll say you did."

"What stake did you have in all that, anyway?" he asked.

"Why do you think I left in the first place?" Lukkan replied as he turned around in his stool, rested his elbows on the bar.

Corman rubbed his eyes. "So you used me as a third party to air out your dirty laundry. I was a fucking pawn."

"I needed to distance myself from it," Lukkan said. "And you hate them, anyway. What's the big fucking deal?"

"The big fucking deal is you *used* me, dickhead," Corman spat. "Used me to settle your personal bullshit."

"Yeah? And you wouldn't have?"

Corman poured himself another whiskey, took a drink. "Next time you get the brilliant idea to use me as a proxy cell, fucking tell me."

"I'm giving you a discount off my services. Twenty percent."

"And that still leaves me at what?"

"Two hundred."

"Two hundred my left nut," Corman growled. "I nearly got *killed* in there, you jackass."

Lukkan crossed his arms. "Yeah? You pissed because you didn't do it for free?"

"Fuck you," Corman spat.

"You're always knee-deep in shit, anyway. This hardly makes a difference." Lukkan checked his fingernails. "You default on your debt, and I might have to send a couple of them after you, tell 'em what you did."

"So I can point them in the direction of the guy who orchestrated it?"

Lukkan frowned.

"It's a zero-sum game, you fucking gorilla," Corman grumbled into his glass. "Besides, once they find out you let the mooncalf who had the audacity to walk on *your* property and disrupt *their* business, *live*? You'll be flayed alive, too. So we're even.

"The hell's a zero-sum game?"

Corman rolled his eyes. "You got anything else for me, or are you gonna make me inhale your stench all day?"

"Watch it, goatfucker," Lukkan snapped.

"Well? Do you?"

"No, that's it. The wiemca are looking for candidates for the Horsemen. Why, I don't know. Who's telling them to do it, I don't know."

"You wanted me to pay you two hundred dollars for *that*?"

"Look, I'm just telling you what I gleaned from these," Lukkan told him. "It wasn't much to go on. Honestly, if you want a better conclusion, bring better paperwork."

"Well I'm definitely not paying you *now*," Corman said, sliding off the stool. He downed the rest of the whiskey. "Unless you figure out something actually fucking *useful*."

"Unless you get your head out of your ass, I ain't doing shit."

"I suppose that ends our professional relationship, then."

Holding the car door in one hand, Corman stared down at the corpse in his backseat. If there was an answer, maybe this thing held it. Then again, maybe not. If the Sons and the wiemca were colluding together, what could the other possibly have to gain? Their individual missions were incompatible. *Seemingly, anyway*, he thought, slamming the door shut.

"I need to get this body to the morgue," he said.

"How are we gonna do that without a car?" Edgar asked.

"Same way I got this one," Corman told him, walking over to a mid-sized sedan across the lot with the lockout tool he kept in his trunk. He popped it open and ripped open the panel underneath the steering wheel. Fiddling with the wires, he got the engine going.

From his own car's glove box, he retrieved the title and registration. Then he unscrewed the license plates off and attached them to the hotwired one. Finally, he got into the driver's seat and closed the door.

"I was sort of hoping you were done stealing stuff."

"Of course I am," Corman said. "I'll even file the paperwork once I'm done with it."

"Call me naïve, but I was hoping I'd never have to see your ugly ass again," Nathan said as Corman laid the corpse on the autopsy table. Both of them were wearing scrubs, masks, and sterile gloves, at Nathan's insistence. "And perhaps even more naïvely, I hoped if I ever *did*, it wouldn't be with a fucking dead body."

"That's not naïve, Nate, that's being delusional," Corman said, unzipping the bag to the corpse's neck. "All right, watch it. The guts are gonna be loose."

"Jesus, Ryan."

Corman pulled the zipper down little by little, trying to keep the organs relatively in place. Worse came to worse, he'd just make sure the bag got the stragglers. As the bag opened up to the corpse's legs, the miasma of death filled the room. All of its insides stayed in place, except for the intestines, which spilled out over the sides.

"What do you make of it?" Corman asked.

"Whoever did the incision was sloppy," Natahn said, poking around with some metal tool. "Like a pig rooting for truffles. Whoever the Sons have doing this, they need to seriously consider firing. Look at all these unnecessary cuts. It was as if they were *trying* to damage the body. Even with an open chest cavity like this, you can sew them back up for an open casket. Not this one, though. Although their teeth are perfectly intact. That'll help figure out if they're even getting a funeral."

"You must be fun at parties," Corman said.

"Ha ha." Nathan closely examined the area around the corpse's larynx. "Seems like everything above the clavicles is intact as well.

The incision, though... It was done with some crude instrument, not meant for medical use. It's too jagged... like they did it with a modified buzzsaw. You say you found the body in an autoshop?"

"In its secret underground medical lab," Corman said.

"Wouldn't surprise me if the Sons cheaped out on proper lab equipment," Nathan said, shaking his head. "Cut this poor bastard up like a lemon."

"Can you figure the time of death?"

"If I had to place it, I'd say about two weeks ago. There's some evidence of cryopreservation, but the black putrefaction already took place. You can see the discolorations. Maybe it it's from being frozen for two weeks, but the tissues haven't softened. The face is still recognizable, too. There's not a ton of decay either. But that's most likely from the freezing."

And how many more ended up like this one?

"None of this is consistent with how the wiemca do it," Corman said.

"That much is true. They're much messier," Nathan said. "And as far as I can tell right now, all of the organs are here."

"Goddamn it," he muttered.

"You can't save everybody, Ryan," Nathan said. "I mean, if you did, I'd be out of a job."

Corman glared at him.

"Bad joke. Sorry."

"If you find anything during the autopsy, let me know," Corman instructed.

"I'll have to see if they have a next-of-kin first," Nathan told him. "Find out if they're even allowed to have one."

Back at his apartment, Corman slumped onto the couch and lazily dangled a finger over the voicemail button on his answering machine. He sighed, then clicked it.

"Hey, so, what's up with not telling me you're back? You think you can visit Mom and not *me* and get away with it? Get your ass over to the Hound's Tooth tonight, big brother. Or I'm telling Mom on you. Say hi to Ed for me."

He immediately erased the message.

"She knows *you* hear these too, right?" Corman asked Edgar, who was relaxing on the windowsill.

"It's the polite thing to do," he said.

"Christ," Corman murmured, feeling the bullet wounds. They were still painful and he still felt like he needed to empty out his guts. All in all, he was sore, exhausted, and had absolutely no inclination to move from his spot. Edgar had, as usual, done a good job of patching him up, but even so, the lingering aches and pains lingered much longer than they used to.

"You ought to ask Rowan about what's going on, anyway," Edgar told him. "Maybe she'll know who the wiemca are supposedly working for now."

"No one," Corman said. "Whoever it is, they're a ghost."

"Do ghosts know how to make Seals of Solomon? And so many of them, at that."

Corman's eyes shot open. "They know. Whoever this is, they *know* how to work Seals. How to work the wiemca. And we've probably arrested that kind of person a hundred times over. The Knights have to know *something*."

"You're not suggesting *that*. Please tell me you're not."

Corman smiled at him.

X

A SISYPHEAN EFFORT

A WELL KNOWN, IF slightly infamous, Minneapolis institution, the Hound's Tooth Tavern served the city's population of cambions, demons, and other unwanted, lonely freaks faithfully for sixty-five years. It wasn't advertised as such, but it was notoriously less apprehensive about its clientele than just about any other bar in the Twin Cities. Even if its patrons weren't almost exclusively the dredges of society, just the decor was enough to turn away the more respectable crowds: the interior architecture was damnably Gothic, full of sharp edges, gargoyles, and grotesque death masks. On the walls were images made in the style of German woodcuts, featuring Fasutian scenes of deals with the devil and the disemboweling of forest animals. Half-finished skeletons hung from the corners in the ceiling. Drinks were served in glasses shaped like skulls, the mouths of serpents, or the bellies of dragons. At the front of the place, just before the dip into the bar proper, were two stone Cerberuses. Not a lot of sensible, normal folks would descend into Hades for a beer. Which was more than fine as far as Corman was concerned.

"Goddamn," he muttered as he walked past the Cerberuses. "Smells like an orange's asshole in here."

"It's the incense," Rowan said from behind the bar. Stout, short, and covered in tattoos, she had her father's blue eyes and aquiline nose. She'd let her chestnut hair grow down to her shoulders. "Not my fault you have no taste in anything."

"So this city's turned you into an asshole, too," Corman said as she rounded the edge of the bar.

"You're still a bastard," she said, embracing him. "What the hell's been so important you can't see your own family?"

"The end of the world," Corman told her as they split apart.

"Oh, please. Even that takes a few days. You can say 'hi' in the meantime." She patted him on the shoulder and went back behind the bar. Bright yellow lights illuminated the dozens of bottles of low-end liquor. "Night crowd's not in yet, so you have my absolute, undivided attention. Now, where's Ed?"

"Right here, ma'am," Edgar chirped, taking his cat form on the bar. "You even kept the Seal open."

"Just for you, little man," Rowan said, smiling at him. To Corman she asked, "What're you having?"

"A long, metal pole rammed into my eyeballs," Corman said, getting up on a stool.

"Things have been that bad, huh?"

"Well, they haven't been great, I'll say that much."

"Ed, what kind of shit has our dumbass brother been dragging you through as of late?" Rowan asked, mixing whiskey with bitters into a glass skull. In lieu of a brain, the skull got an orange peel garnish.

"Chasing after the wiemca," Edgar said, munching on a bowl of beer nuts. "Blowing up Nazi organ harvesting rings."

"Might as well slit your wrists then, big brother," Rowan told him, sliding the old fashioned over. "Word is the feds are gunning for you, too. You add the local goon squads to that, and your life expectancy suddenly plummets."

"I'm a hundred and sixty, sis," Corman said. "The numbers don't concern me."

Rowan shrugged. "Maybe they should. You could live three lifetimes if you don't wind up getting yourself killed. Which is sounding increasingly likely."

"I'm onto something," Corman protested. He took a drink, grimaced. "You might want to start figuring out how to a mix a decent cocktail."

"Shut the fuck up," Rowan said, snapping a dishrag at him. "What are you onto you?"

"Like Ed said, the wiemca. All those women who've gone missing in the past six months? Twenty-five were wiemca vics. I've got the coroner's reports right here." He patted his chest.

"To what end?"

"I have two theories at the moment," Corman told her, holding up both index fingers. "One happens to be mine. The other belongs to Lukkan."

"*That* creep? You went to *him* for help?" Rowan frowned. "I can already tell that's gonna bite you in the ass."

"That's what I told him," Edgar added.

"*You* were the one who gave me the idea in the *first* place."

"That was *before* you decided to—"

Rowan cut him off. "What's this theory of his?"

"That they're looking for Pestilence," Corman replied. "This whole rash of kidnapping and murders is in service to bringing together the Four Horsemen again."

"That's sort of played out, isn't it? I heard some crazy bitch tried that eight years ago."

"Evidently someone else thinks it's a pretty good idea," Corman murmured, squeezing a bit of the orange rind into his drink. "Then there's my angle, which is that the wiemca are trying to create a philosopher's stone and they're using these women to do it. I'm not sure about the validity of either."

"But either way, they're doing it on behalf of someone else."

"Right," Corman said. "That's what got me at first. None of this makes sense for the wiemca. This whole business goes against their central ethos."

"Any ideas who they're reporting to?" Rowan asked.

"None whatsoever," Corman said with a heavy exhale. "The wiemca don't listen to any authority, perceived or otherwise. The only thing I can think of is that they for some reason think the Void itself has instructed them to do all of this."

"The Void?"

"Sentient dark energy," Corman said. "A physical manifestation of chaos."

"Talk about a mind fuck," Rowan said. "Glad I'm not the idiot who got themselves involved in this."

"Yeah, what an awful thing *that* would be," Corman grumbled. "Anything else you got to say to the idiot?"

"Plenty," Rowan said. "But I can see you're already pissed. I can hold off."

Corman rolled his eyes. "Oh, how gracious you are, sweet sister."

"So what's up with you and Mom?"

"Jesus Christ," Corman muttered. "I don't want to go there. Not here, not now."

"But I'm making you go there," Rowan said. "Look, I get it. You're a grouch. A cranky son of a bitch. Just a real unpleasant dude to be around. A cantankerous—"

"Get to the point."

"So you need time to yourself, alone and away from other people. But Mom's not like that. It wasn't fair of you to do that to her," Rowan explained, one hand on her hip. "Her only son comes back from what was supposed to be a life of exile, and he doesn't even bother to so much as *call* her? That was shitty, big brother. Real shitty."

"In case you haven't been listening, I've been busy," Corman spat. "Busy with important stuff. More important than Mom being too goddamn sensitive. As fucking usual."

"Hey, don't go getting all testy on me," Rowan said. "I'm not the dick who froze his own mother out of his life. I'm just pointing it out. You sure weren't gonna come to that conclusion on your own."

"What makes you say *that*?"

"Considering all the bullshit you've been up to as of late, I can only conclude that you've left sense at the door," Rowan told him. "Racked up quite the tab on criminal charges, as I understand it. And now you got that look on your face."

Corman narrowed his eyes. "*What* look?"

Rowan leaned over the bar conspiratorially. "The look that says you're gonna start throwing shit. But! Family or not, nobody breaks shit in my bar without paying for damages incurred."

"*Your* bar?"

"Yeah, I own the place."

"Since when?"

"Three years ago," Rowan said, smiling. "Old Mister Herschel's syphilis finally rotted his brain. More than it already was, anyway.

Shit, he put *me* in his will. Don't know why, but I'm not complaining. Gives our people a place to go."

"In that case, think I'll just throw one or two bottles," Corman said. "Just the most expensive ones."

Rowan gave him an incredulous look. "Most expensive thing we've got in here is a sixty dollar bottle of champagne. You'll have to settle for bottom shelf tequila. I know you'd hate to waste good whiskey.

"I wouldn't call this *good*," Corman said, examining his old-fashioned.

"You'd rather drink the swill they have at the Iron Door?" Rowan asked. "They water their shit down and mark it up forty percent. Not that it matters, considering their policy on clientele."

"They let cambions in."

"Reluctantly, and not for very long," Rowan said. "Anyway, you need to go see Mom again. Make nice, apologize for whatever nasty shit you said to her. She won't tell you how much it hurts her, but that's why she has me."

"Why should I fucking bother?" Corman asked. "The moment I step through the door, and she's on my ass. Nothing but a fifteen minute lecture about how I'm fucking my life up. Just because I'm her son doesn't mean I have to put up her bullshit."

"And just how *much* did you put up with, big brother?"

"Enough," he said.

Rowan crossed her arms. "Ed?"

"He started it," Edgar said, crunching into a beer nut.

"*Ed*," Corman hissed.

"What?"

"Don't know why you bother lying to me," Rowan said. She leaned onto her elbows and offered him a sympathetic look. "Look, I get it. You've always put a lot of pressure on yourself. That's just what you do. Which I get it. You feel like you have to make up for what you've done. That has to weigh on you. But don't take it out on Mom. She missed you like you'll never know. You're her baby. For life. There's nothing you can do about that."

Corman took a drink.

"I missed you too, but I know how you are."

A deplorable piece of shit, sounds like.

"We're all she has, big brother," Rowan continued, pouring more whiskey into his glass. "We're all *we* have. You know how lucky that makes us? That we're still together like this?"

"I'm sure the two of you got on just fine without me," Corman grumbled.

"Shit, *I* got used to it," Rowan told him. "I had to. But Mom? She was a wreck. Always on edge, always angry. And it was a divine, righteous anger. Not like yours. A mother's anger. A mother's grief. If you bothered to see it from her perspective, you might realize how cruel you're being."

"Shame I'm only half-angel," Corman said, "and she's far beyond my meager human intelligibility."

"You know, that's what really gets me about humans," Rowan said. "You're all slaves to instinct. That's what all this boils down to, really. You're all too goddamn impulsive. You feel angry in the moment and you just *have* to act on it. I swear, once you get an idea in your head..."

He raised an eyebrow. "Yeah?"

"Everything else just falls off. Like it's the single best idea in the whole entire world. And if that's true, then how could it possibly go to shit?"

"Sorry I was born to a fallible species," Corman said. "What do you expect?"

"For you to be better," Rowan told him. "You're still an angel. You have the capacity to conquer all of this shit, and you keep falling prey to it."

"Part of my nature, unfortunately," Corman said. "Hubris and all that."

"Is being a cunt part of your nature, too?"

"No, that's purely genetic. I get that from my old man." He took a long drink. "I swear, half the time I think I'm not even Mom's kid."

"Apparently our family's absolutely riddled with assholes like you," Rowan told him. "Our grandfather Hamish especially."

"How'd *he* fuck up?"

"You know Satan?"

"Rings a bell."

"Took his side in the war."

Corman drained the rest of his glass. "Like grandfather, like grandson."

"You need to reconcile your humanity with Mom's lack of it," Rowan told him. "She'll never fully understand you. But you have the opportunity to understand *her*. It's the one thing humans have going for them."

He held up his left hand. "I know a lost cause when I hear one."

"No you do fucking *not*," Rowan said. "You think this stupid crusade of yours is *smart*? That it *won't* end up with your head on a spike?"

"I never said mine wasn't lost," Corman said. "But if I give up, let this keep happening, the wiemca win. Who knows how many more dead bodies they're gonna leave in their wake before then? Doesn't matter if the whole city wants me dead. They've wanted me dead for eight years. What's a little more enmity between us?"

"That should probably tell you something."

"I need to finish this and get the hell out."

Rowan shook her head. "You're hopeless."

"I keep trying to tell him that," Edgar said. "In one ear and out the other."

Corman swirled the ice cubes around in his glass. "You don't what you're talking about. You haven't seen what they do to these women. What the Sons were doing before I put the torch to their operation. Nobody has lifted a *finger* for these women. Not the cops, definitely not the Knights. Half the fucking department's at each other's throats, the other half's looking the other way. And both halves are too busy killing our people.

"So the wiemca and the gangs are free to murder and pillage and kidnap and rape all they want. But for some reason, *I'm* the asshole for trying to stop them? *I'm* the asshole because I don't let this shit slide? Tell me how *that* makes sense. Tell me how *you* would go about fixing things."

Rowan studied walls around them, her eyes moving from gargoyle to woodcut to bas relief. "You're not Atlas, big brother. You're Sisyphus."

"You think *that's* gonna stop me?"

"No," Rowan said quietly. "No, because the rock always comes tumbling down. And you, being you, will always roll it back up again. But at some point, you have to realize how pointless it is. You did, once, and you saved us from Lilith because you did. You gotta realize, big brother, that doing this alone is just pushing that boulder up the hill every day. You can keep doing it, but it'll never stay. Instead of rolling it back up, you should find a way to keep it there."

Corman slammed his fist onto the bar. "That's not fucking *possible*. No matter what preventative measures you can take, *somebody* will find *some* way to break it apart. Besides, it's just me. Nobody else is getting hurt by me doing this."

"Are you kidding me?" Rowan spat. "You know how much *shit* people have had to wade through for *your* sake? Did you know that cambion hate crimes went up two hundred percent because of you? They say *your* name when they beat the shit out our people. You bother reading all the graffiti? It's *you*, Corman. Humans blame *you* and they take it out on the rest of us."

"I'm not responsible for any of that. They'd do it anyway."

"What about Sasha and Yue? What about Mom?" Rowan snapped. "You've done nothing but make all their lives hell just so you can satiate your bullshit martyr complex."

"If I didn't—"

"And how many of these women have you actually saved, Corman? Just the one?"

"One is better—"

"You're going to get yourself *killed*," Rowan yelped, slapping the bar with her palms. "Where's that gonna leave us, huh? What do you think that'll do to Mom? To me? To *Ed*?"

Corman slid off the stool and held his hand out. Edgar looked from him to his sister, hung his head, and went back into Corman's palm.

"I have work to do," he said. "Doesn't matter if the world's against me. Doesn't matter what happens to me. I need to fix things. There's no other way. I have no intention of dying, either. Not until I've fixed this."

As he walked toward the exit, he heard Rowan ask, "You're not gonna do something stupid, are you?"

"What do you think?"

He stood outside the bar, hands in his pockets, and felt the cold wind bite into his skin. *She doesn't get it, never will*, he thought. Nobody despised her, called her a monster. Their family hadn't nearly disowned Mom because of her birth. She knew where and to whom she belonged. Corman had no such luxury. All of his kind went extinct centuries ago. They were wretched abominations, nephilim, scorned by angels and humans alike. Colossal, bloodthirsty creatures with no knowledge of what was good. So that left him, alone. In a way that nobody could ever know.

"She was just trying to get through to you," Edgar said. "Help you."

"She did a shit job of it," Corman told him. "She doesn't get it, Ed. Mom doesn't, either. They never had to straddle the line like this."

"What line?"

"I don't belong anywhere," Corman said. "I don't have a people. Not like Rowan, not like these cambions. Fuck, not like Abigail. So where does that leave me? In between this and that. Somewhere between God and the devil. There's no place for me anywhere. I have to carve it out myself. And nobody knows how much blood I've had to shed doing it. So fuck that. Fuck anyone saying I haven't suffered for this."

"Are we still going to Camelot?"

"I'm finishing this one way or another," Corman said. "The world be damned."

"Take a minute to reconsider," Edgar suggested. "Take a breather. You're planning on storming the heart of the enemy with nothing but me and a gardening tool."

"Hasn't stopped me before."

"No, but it probably should have. Ease up on the gas a little. Just for tonight. Your wounds haven't even healed all the way yet."

"I'm gonna get shot at no matter what," Corman said. "Might'll as well do it with a few bullet holes left in me. Saves you the trouble of sewing them back up."

"Hey, here's an idea. Go to Abigail's show tonight," Edgar advised him.

"And why would I do that?"

"You could use another friend that's not your left hand," Edgar said. "Plus, you get a rush of oxytocin when you see her."

He's bullshitting. Has to be.

"You keep that between us and I'll go," Corman said, sighing. "I'm fucking exhausted, anyway. But as soon as my scar tissue heals, I'm going back out."

If it gets everyone off my fucking back for a night, fine. He was sick to death of everything anyway. Six hours without any of that might be a nice change of pace. Unless, of course, that sneaking feeling of being worthless snuck up on him. Which if he was honest, was probably going to happen.

Per Edgar's urging, Corman went back to the apartment for a quick change of clothes before heading over to the Trismeg. Once he got there, he wished he hadn't bothered. Everyone there was older and richer, dressed in formal wear much nicer than his simple sport coat and tie. These were the people who could afford to see shows; Corman didn't spot a cambion among them.

"This is what happens when I let you talk me into things," Corman muttered, pushing through the throng of the elderly to the main auditorium. "I feel like an idiot."

"A night of theater is never wasted," Edgar told him. "Even on the likes of *you*."

"It's actual idiots prancing around on stage like the world outside isn't falling apart," Corman said, shuffling down row F. "Talk about completely fucking pointless."

"Art nourishes the soul," Edgar said. "Life would be pointless without it."

"So Mom says," Corman grumbled as he plopped into his seat. "Great use of your time, making up pretend situations about people who don't exist."

"You should take your ire up with Plato," Edgar said.

"Don't get me started on philosophers," Corman muttered.

"You do that fine by yourself." Soon the rest of the crowd filed in to fill up the house. A speaker over the announcement system informed the audience that no flash photography or recordings of the performance were permitted, and that all cellular phones should be silenced. *Wonder if Ed qualifies.*

The house lights dimmed and the stage lights went up. And just like that, Medvedenko and Masha entered from stage right, discussing the monochromatic color scheme of her wardrobe. Corman held Edgar out on the armrest, keeping his fingers stretched out.

It was a rather unremarkable rendition of the play, Corman thought. He'd seen plenty better than this. At least, until Abigail and the guy playing Trigorin got on stage. They were electrifying in their portrayals, succinctly honing in on the insecurities and anxieties of their characters. There was a palatable chemistry; his eventual betrayal of her love and loyalty to him hurt all the more. As the final curtain fell and the cast came out for bows, Corman found himself as part of the applause.

Then the lights came back on and it was over. Corman could feel Edgar giving him a smug grin of satisfaction.

"You liked it," he said.

"Can it," Corman muttered.

"No, you're right. It was okay. Nothing special. What you liked was seeing Abigail."

"Arkadina and Trigorin were good, too," Corman said.

"No extra hit of dopamine from seeing *them*, though," Edgar pointed out.

Corman shoved him into his pocket. He kept him there all the way from his seat and back out into the lobby, where the actors milled about talking to the audience members. Though he saw Abigail near the box office, still in full costume and makeup, Corman kept walking. She was talking to a bunch of people, and besides, she didn't need to know he was there, anyway.

Just as he laid a hand on the door, he felt Edgar pinch him.

"Say hi," he urged.

"No," Corman said.

"You don't have to 'talk' to her, all right? But go say hi."

He's not gonna let up until I do. Edgar could be adamant about the weirdest shit. Exhaling out his frustration, Corman turned around and stood outside Abigail's circle. Then she spotted him and her eyes went wide. But there was no excitement in them. Merely recognition.

"Corman?"

"Yeah," he said, moving in a little closer.

"Wow, I didn't think—" She shook her head, then motioned to the three girls she was talking to. "These are my roommates. Roommates, this is Corman Ryan."

"Wow," one of them said.

"Thank you," said another. "That was brave of you, to do that."

"We'd have to pay her half of the rent without you, so thanks," the third said. The other two gave her disapproving looks. "Joking, joking. Jesus. We love Abby."

"You, uh, didn't have to—" Corman murmured. "No problem."

"Abby said you're a Knight," the first roommate told him. "Is it true? Out from D.C.?"

All she knows about you is a lie.

"Yeah."

"Your life must be so exciting," the second roommate said. "I have the *most* boring job *ever*. Like, I think it might be killing me boring."

"Oh, uh, sorry," Corman murmured.

"You're all she talks about, you know," the third one told him. "Couldn't get her to shut up for like, a week."

Abigail, blushing, waved her hands in protest. "That's not true."

"Maybe it's me that can't stop," the third one said. "Never known a guy who could cleave a wild animal in half before."

"*That's* true," the first roommate said. "You really took down a chimaera, all by yourself?"

"Yeah."

"Hey, so," Abigail piped up, "I never got the chance to actually thank you. Maybe I could buy you dinner or something. I mean, if you wanted."

Corman felt Edgar pinching him again.

"Yeah, sure."

So Corman found himself at a diner sitting across from a woman he rescued from the jaws of death. There'd been plenty of far more bizarre situations in his life, but for whatever reason, this was the one that made him feel like throwing up.

"Is that all you're getting?" Abigail asked after the waitress brought him his pot of endless coffee.

Corman shrugged. "I have a small stomach."

"It'll be hard to sleep, won't it?"

"My sleep's been messed up since I can remember. There's no salvaging it."

"You know," she said, "I figured you were a black coffee person."

"That a good or bad thing?" he asked, looking over the rim of the mug.

"Neither," she said. "How you take your coffee tells you something about the person is all. It's... well, it's not an original observation."

"What does drinking it black say?"

"Official," Abigail said with a nod. "Businesslike. You have places to be."

"This sounds suspiciously like astrology," Corman told her. "Which is bul— bucolic."

"Bucolic?" She considered that for a moment. "Because it's not scientific?"

"Sure, only rubes believe it," Corman said. "You know, the uneducated."

"Oh, and are *you* educated?" she asked, smiling.

"No," Corman replied. "But I know nothing is written out beforehand. It's all... there's no grand plan or anything."

"So for you it's all free will," Abigail said. "No signs or omens or anything?"

"Determinism is just an excuse to refuse accountability for your own actions," Corman explained. "You're responsible for everything you do. Shifting the blame just makes more problems than it solves."

"So, what about systematic problems? You know, in the law and at the federal level? Most people can't do anything about those."

"You're responsible at the micro," Corman said. "If everybody understood that, then it'd reflect back on the macro. Every little thing flows into the bigger picture."

"As above, so below," Abigail said.

"You educated?"

She laughed. "Not really. I have a degree in theatre arts, which is completely worthless. At the time, though, it seemed like a good idea."

"Better than me not having a degree in anything," Corman said.

"So you've been a Knight since day one?"

"Since I could be, yeah." Corman resisted the urge to sigh. He settled on exhaling through his nose. "It's all I ever wanted to be."

"The only thing? You didn't entertain any other possibilities?"

"Maybe, but if I did, it was so long ago I can't remember," Corman said. "Acting been your only thing?"

"Nah, I've done other stuff," Abigail told him. "But acting is what I'm good at. At least, I used to think that. Now, though, I don't know. Five years out in New York and I barely booked any jobs. Just a few plays here and there, but it never went anywhere. You get discouraged."

"I know the feeling," Corman said before taking a drink. "Before I got transferred, I didn't have a lot of faith in my job performance. Guess I still don't, now that I think of it."

"Couple of frauds," Abigail said, smiling.

"I never thought of myself as a fraud, just..." Corman paused. Whatever he *had* thought of himself as, this was not the time nor place to say it. "I don't know."

That's what this is, isn't it? he wondered. *Constant hesitation? Not knowing what's okay to tell people? Never knowing if what I am is reprehensible to her?*

"It's normal to feel like that," Abigail told him. "That's what I've been learning lately. Everything's just so competitive. It's all designed to make you feel worse about yourself. It's all that stuff about systemic issues."

"Never put much thought into it."

"Really? I'm surprised."

Corman raised an eyebrow. "Why's that?"

"Well, you're going out there and fighting monsters," Abigail said. "By yourself. It doesn't sound like the rest of the Knights are all that interested in protecting people from them. You're working to fix the problems they just don't bother with. Maybe you don't think about it, but you do it."

"If that's the case, I'm doing a terrible job of it."

Her face didn't contort; she didn't seem disgusted by the self-effacement.

"Why do you say that?"

"Well, no matter what I do, it seems like everything just goes back to square one," Corman explained. "I take one coven down, save one person, and then the next day, I find out there's fifteen more I didn't even know about."

"That's not your fault, though."

"When you're the only one doing anything about it, it tends to feels like it."

"It's why I'm glad for the work I do," Abigail said. "Not just doing one-man shows. This way the show's success is dependent on everybody. The director, the set designers, the other actors. Everybody needs to prop the play up so it's good. It's a real... community effort. If it was just me doing everything, I'd feel bad about it too if things didn't go well."

Shame there's no money in doing that, Corman thought as he sipped his coffee. *King wouldn't piss on a burning man if it meant she couldn't get the life insurance payout.*

"That sounds a lot nicer than what I do," he said instead.

"There's a lot of politics in the bigger theater scene, but at the local level it's a lot less vicious," Abigail told him. "Once you get big enough, you start losing sight of what counts, doesn't really matter what you're doing."   "Yeah," Corman said. "Shame about that."

"So, I was kind of putting it off because it's embarrassing," she said, putting her utensils down, "but how'd you like the show? What do you think?"

Oh, Jesus, Corman thought. What *did* he think? He wasn't a fucking critic. What did it even matter what he thought? But he could hear Edgar already scolding him for bypassing the question. *No more goddamn lectures.*

He settled on, "It was good. Trigorin is a difficult character to get all the nuances right with, but I think your guy did a good job. I mean, that's sort of the deal with all of Chehkov's leads. There's a lot of layers to unfold in their characters. They're never just one thing."

Abigail smiled. "Wow, you didn't study drama at all?"

"My mom's... artsy," Corman said. "Made sure I was raised on it. I read Ibsen instead of Doctor Seuss, and I've read every Tennessee Williams play. Most of O'Neill and Miller, too."

"Your mom sounds awesome."

"I wouldn't go that far."

"Any other sophisticated art she forced you to appreciate?"

"The list of what she didn't is shorter," Corman said. "I can tell you how each note in each movement of Beethoven's Ninth moves the piece like it does. Why the turtle chapters in the 'Grapes of

Wrath' are important to its themes of personal progression. How the background composition of every Caravaggio painting progresses the drama of the scene. I know too much and there's absolutely no reason to know any of it."

"Sounds like your mom *really* wanted you to be cultured," Abigail noted.

"I hate art now," Corman told her. "Though according to her, that just means she did her job right."

"My parents are... well, they don't care much for any of that," she said. "They're very simple people with very simple tastes. We... never had much in common."

"Yeah, same with mine."

"Guess that's always how it goes, isn't it?" She let out a soft sigh. "Parents and kids never understand each other."

"I never understand anyone," Corman said. *And vice versa.*

"Even with your breadth of worthless knowledge?"

"Crazy how truly worthless that knowledge really is."

"Good thing you didn't go to college," Abigail told him. "Sounds like you would've hated it."

"I thank God for that every day."

"So, um, I know this is sort going back on the conversation, but what did you think of me tonight? My acting, I mean."

"You were really good. I liked how you played both sides of Nina's character. There's definitely a sort of selfishness to her that isn't necessarily translated into every performance, but I think you did," Corman said, with more honestly than he anticipated. "But it has

174

to be a certain kind of selfishness. The kind you have when you're a kid."

"You got all that just from seeing it once?"

"Your director is good at her job," Corman said. "So are you."

"Thanks," she said, blushing. "That's all any actor wants to hear. That and they're better than Olivier."

"He still the benchmark?" Corman asked. "Would've thought someone usurped him by now."

"A few almost did," Abigail admitted. "But before they stopped making movies, it was getting to the point where nobody had any real staying power. So the old guys are still up there."

"You'd know more than I would."

"You? After all that you told me, I don't know."

"I guarantee you, all of that knowledge is surface level," Corman said. "No way to apply any of it to a practical situation. Didn't help me at all as a Knight."

"What's it like?" she asked. "Is it much like being a police officer?"

"In the amount of paperwork we have to file, yeah." He sighed. "Most of it is just writing

reports. But I was on this thing called the Round Table here, which is twelve of the highest ranked officers, and we handled the bigger cases."

"Like with the wiemca?"

"Yeah. It's mostly when their chimaeras get loose, but yeah."

"What do you do out in D.C.?"

"Clean up other people's messes." That was, in a roundabout way, true. But even so, it felt wrong to lie to her. Especially now. She wasn't just some woman he would never see again now. Even if they never spoke again after that night, she was irrevocably more than that. She'd gotten to see some part of him he didn't know he still had. *Don't give her anymore of it.* Keep her on that side of the table, don't let her see anything more. "I investigate cold cases, basically. The stuff everyone else gave up on."

"By yourself?"

"I've... always worked without a partner. So I'm used to it."

"You don't mind the challenge?"

Corman shrugged. "I don't think of it like that. I think of it as just something to be done. Just another task to cross off the list."

"God, I *wish* I could think like that," she said. "Everything stresses me out. I mean, I'm trying to improve that, but it's been... well, a challenge."

"It's something you pick up in my line of work," he told her. "I didn't even really register it happening until a few years in. Besides, don't you need all that to act?"

"Oh, sure. But I mean in my real life. You don't worry about much, do you?"

God you have no fucking idea. I worry about fucking everything.

"Not particularly."

"Can you teach me how to do that sometime?" she asked.

"Yeah, why not?"

Some twenty-five minutes later, he pulled up in front of her apart-ment complex and threw the car into park. "It, uh, beats having to walk, right?"

"After... well, yeah. Yeah it does."

"Hope the rest of your shows go as well as tonight's," Corman said.

"Thanks," she said. "For, um, well, everything. You're too kind to me."

"Not really."

She got out of the car, then lingered in the doorframe. "It was nice seeing you again, Corman."

"Yeah," he said. She closed the door and walked up to the front entrance, bag swung over her shoulder. Corman stayed until she was inside, then drove away.

"So you do have it in you to be civil after all," Edgar said.

"Considering she's the only person who doesn't constantly bitch at me, yeah, I can be civil," Corman murmured. "Doesn't matter. All she knows about me is a lie."

"Which you can eventually turn into the truth."

"No, I don't think so," Corman said, pulling up to a red light. "That's the last time I'm ever gonna see her."

"What makes you so sure about that?"

"Because I'm gonna make sure it is. She doesn't need my mess of a life in hers, and I don't need anything else complicating mine." The light turned green. "I'm an angry, violent person, plain and simple. She'd be bound to piss me off eventually. I don't want her to be around for that."

"You could *change* that part of yourself," Edgar said.

Corman sighed. "People don't change, Ed. They never fucking change."

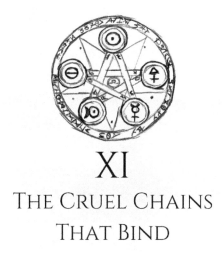

XI

THE CRUEL CHAINS
THAT BIND

"I STILL SAY THIS is a bad idea," Edgar said. They turned onto 1st Street South. Taking up nearly three city blocks, the Federal Knight Bureau's Precinct 7 Building No. 1485 stood where the Minneapolis post office once did. In 2023, once the USPS was officially declared defunct, it only took two months for the Knights to file the proper paperwork, get their permits approved, and move in. Little had its exterior and interior had changed, besides the phoenix insignia of the department taking the place of the post office's logo. It was still just another U.S. federal building, reeking of ineffective bureaucracy and efficient lobbying.

There would be upwards of sixteen Knights still in the building, plus another sixteen on call for the fourth shift. After normal public hours, a magnetic employee card was required to enter. Though his had been stripped and shredded eight years ago, Hermes promised him that his fake one had the same electromagnetic properties. Worse came to worse, he could just get in the old fashioned way. *Though I've never been at the best at burglary.*

"There has to be another way to get the information you're looking for without trespassing again," Edgar said as Corman, hood up, walked into the east parking garage. If his memory served correctly, there were security cameras just about everywhere they could be. He hurried to the elevators. "This *can't* end well."

"That's never been the goal, Ed," Corman said as he called the elevator down. "That's not the point of any of this."

"Has it occurred to you that your recent risks have far outweighed the rewards? Or are you ignoring that, too?"

"I'm choosing to ignore the fact that you don't trust me," Corman said as he stepped inside. He swiped the fake employee card; the reader lit up green. "I guess Hermes isn't entirely full of shit after all."

"You haven't exactly been earning my trust as of late," Edgar said. "Rowan was right when she said I can't protect you forever. One of these days, someone's gonna give you an injury I can't fix."

"We're not having this discussion," Corman told him. They ascended to the fourth floor, where the Knights' public records were stored; this included the archives, which required authorization from King for viewing, part of a "freedom of information" bill passed while he was away. Nothing inside the archives was allowed outside of the reading room, and each document had a barcode that would set off alarms should they be removed. Which meant Corman was going to have to copy longhand, and he had an increasingly small amount of time to do that; roughly fifteen to twenty minutes before someone realized he was inside the building.

"Of course we're not," Edgar muttered. "Why would we? It's not like we're partners or brothers or anything. What do I know? I'm just a stupid eyeball."

"We'll talk about this when I'm done here, all right? Keep your fucking voice down."

"If you don't get yourself killed first." The elevator door slid open; on the far side of the hallway was a dark wooden wall with a bulletproof glass window situated in the center of it beside a metal door. Corman started to walk toward it; Edgar pinched his palm.

"This is a set-up."

"And?"

"*And*?"

"If it is," Corman said, walking again, "I'll just fight my way out. Same as I always do. You seem to forget I've made it out of every scrap I've gotten into."

"Because of me," Edgar said. "But I can't keep up with you anymore."

"What are you talking about?"

Edgar sighed. "I'm tired, Corman. I really am."

Corman didn't respond; he just slid the fake ID into the card reader. The door clicked open. Dim floor lights gave the library a faint green hue. Made up of blocks of movable shelves, decades upon decades of information the Knights had to publicly acknowledge but privately resented lay within. The filing system was cryptic; serial numbers that meant nothing to him were posted on each shelf. *Goddamn it*, he thought as the shelves parted, flipping through a portfolio of rejected public works permits. It'd take up the twenty minutes he had just to find the right section.

As he slid the documents back into place, he heard the distinct sound of a footstep against linoleum.

"Shit," he breathed. "Shit shit shit shit."

On the other side of the shelves, he poked his head out to see a shadow move ever so slightly against the green light. He grabbed the billy club.

"We need to get the hell out of here," Edgar whispered.

"I can't come back, not if they have me on camera," Corman told him. "They'll be watching for me."

"Then *don't*," Edgar said.

"Where else am I supposed to find this information?"

"Somewhere that doesn't make you *fugitive* if you go there."

Corman stepped out from behind the shelves and flicked the scythe out. That satisfying click of the blade snapping into place caught the attention of a Knight.

"Holy shit, you *are* an idiot," the Knight said, unsheathing his rapier. "Guys, I found the intruder."

Three more Knights joined him, their swords already out.

"You didn't think we'd figure out it was you?" one of them asked.

"Of course I did," Corman said, sizing them up. All they had was that pitiful excuse for a sword. Not great odds, but ones he'd take. Had to, in any case.

"*Run*," Edgar pleaded.

And he did, swinging the scythe at the Knights. In one slice, he got them on the backfoot, only for them to use it to launch forward, swords aimed directly at his chest. Dropping the scythe, he slammed the rapiers down into the floor and flung himself over their backs into an aisle between shelves, grabbing for purchase with all four limbs. A rapier sliced down between his legs; he sent a kick into the Knight's face, hearing a crunch of bones. Someone grabbed his leg. Corman sailed straight down, bashing his head on the floor. Blood rushed out of his nostrils and mouth. Out of his peripheral, he saw a rapier poised to strike. Twisting himself at the waist, he kneed a Knight in the jaw and grabbed his shoulders, throwing him at the other.

Then he caught a rapier in the meat of his shoulder. The Knight responsible laid a boot to his back and slid the sword out. As Corman fell forward, a gauntlet met his cheek; blood splattered the shelves and the spines of books therein. This sent him spiraling into one of the other Knights, who twisted his arms behind his back. Another gauntlet launched into his ribcage, knocking the wind out of him.

"Oof," Corman yelped involuntarily.

This was promptly followed by a flurry of punches to the gut, each one bringing out another involuntary groan of pain. The blood running past his eyes blurred his vision. Eventually, they got the brilliant idea to take the scythe from him; they did this by breaking his wrist, forcing him to drop it. Before it could clatter to the floor, however, one of them caught it.

"Children shouldn't play with weapons," he said, smiling. Or at least, what Corman perceived as smiling.

"Like a mooncalf could even figure out how," another added. Then, into the radio attached to her pauldron, "Got 'im. Bringing him in now."

He was dragged out of the library and back to the elevators. Though he squirmed and writhed, it did nothing. One of the bastards would kick him in the back of the thigh or at the knee, sending a pulsating shock of pain up his body.

Barely able to see straight, he wasn't sure where they were taking him. When the elevators doors opened, he could just make out a plain white hallway made of bricks and stainless steel doors. *Oh, fuck*, he thought as they dragged him down the corridor.

Bringing him before one of the doors, one of the Knights knocked. Opening it was, as far as he could tell, the new Lancelot.

"Oh, you are *fucked*," Kyle Woods said with a grin. "All right, bring him in."

The Knights dragged him into the cell, a room with nothing but two chairs and a stained wooden table in the middle. The breaks between the soundproof pads on the walls were made of the same white bricks as the hallway, only these were stained with the dark maroon of dried blood. Woods sat across from him as the other Knights clasped handcuffs around his wrists behind the chair. Blood seeped down his forehead and onto his cheeks. Corman tasted copper.

"The great thing about idiots is that they're predictable," Woods told him. "And there's no bigger idiot than you."

Even through his swollen eyes, he could make out the gilded white and gold inlay of Lancelot's armor, the only set in the department besides King's made to be completely bulletproof, fire retardant, and shock absorbent. A useless cloak was attached at the gorget and hung down to the knees. It was supposed to be for ceremonial purposes, but Woods always wore it, even to something as degrading to his office as this. He had to make sure everyone and their mother knew who he was, and what his daddy had accomplished for him.

Kyle Woods was a legacy; his father had been the Lancelot before Sasha. And for those twenty-five years, Kevin Woods became synonymous with terror. Wearing that pristine white armor in his equally white and equally pristine cruiser, the senior Woods spent his days beating cambions, addicts, prostitutes, African Americans, Mexicans, Native Americans, poor whites, and everyone else he didn't like within an inch of their lives. Some had criminal records. Some were reported as resisting arrest. Some were suffering from delusions and paranoia. Some had their full mental capabilities.

Most of them died. By getting their brains bashed in, by getting fifteen bullets in the chest, by suffocating underneath his poleyn. The department was immensely proud of him; he was their trusted public affairs spokesperson. To allay any concerns regarding another dead body made at their hands. It never mattered the vic, nor the cause of death. They had deserved it, and the Knight in question was doing everything in their power to keep the city safe from people like them. When one of the victims who sued him actually managed to win their case, Kevin Woods was arrested for aggravated assault. A day later, soon after his bail was posted, he was found dead in his cell, which he had shared with five cambions. All five were later tried and executed for first degree murder. Corman, of course, reviewed the case. None of the testimonies added up, none of the facts presented to the judge withstood any amount of scrutiny. It was the fifth case like that just that month, only difference was this one had a renowned Knight on the docket.

Now his son, one of his five lovely white children, sat before Corman wearing not only the armor but the same self-satisfied grin.

"You *had* to know this is what would happen if you showed your face around here again," Woods said. "But still, even *King* didn't think you'd be dumb enough to try. You *do* know we have security cameras like, *everywhere*, right? We have your biometric data. Your face is on our digital records. There was *no way* we *weren't* gonna catch your dumb ass."

"You're uglier than I remember," Corman murmured, the cuffs already starting to chafe.

"Get your licks in," Woods said. "You won't be able to do much of anything once we're through with you."

"I'm serious," Corman told him. "You look like your mother fucked roadkill."

"Is that supposed to upset me?" Woods raised an eyebrow. "Why would I give a shit about what *you* think?"

"And your ass, you get that surgically attached to your neck?"

"Insufferable as ever," Woods said. "How we didn't kill you back then is beyond me."

"How many cambions you kill this month?" Corman asked. "You meet your quota?"

"Six," Woods replied without hesitation. "Drug dealers. Addicts. They opened fire on me and my team. I was well within my rights. Not just as an officer of the law, but as a private citizen. Even *you* have to agree that most billygoats are junkies. Junkies with itchy trigger fingers."

"Any chimaeras in your caseload? Or would you hate to kill family?"

"No, no, keep going," Woods said. "Try to make me angry. Because it's clearly worked so well so far. Or should I just go into what they're going to kill you for?"

"I've heard my record so many times these past couple of days I think I have it memorized," Corman told him.

"Your theft of the scythe is twenty years minimum at a federal penitentiary. The D.A. is going to make you for not only trespassing, but both burglary and breaking and entering. That's another ten right there. With your impersonation of a federal officer and obstruction of justice charges, that puts you at forty to life. Unless the judge decides to just have you executed and save us all the headache."

"You could just fine me."

Woods leaned in. "Do you know *how* many of my guys want you dead, here and now? I say the word, they rip you limb from limb and there's *nothing* anyone can do about it. No habeas corpus. No trial. No jury. Just your corpse, in this cell, decomposing in the next fifteen minutes."

Corman spat out blood onto the floor. "Takes longer for a body to decompose than that."

"You've not only made a mockery of this department, but the Knights as a whole, Ryan," Woods muttered. "All you've done for the past six months is wipe your ass with an honorable organization. An organization dedicated to keeping Americans safe. You took what you wanted, did what you wanted, *killed* who you wanted.

Without so much as a slap on the wrist. That ends tonight. King wants you alive so we can put you on the stand. Make an example out of you. prove to Arthur we're an effective chapter. Fortunately for me, however..." He stood up and waved to one of the Knights standing guard by the door. They moved the furniture out of the cell while the third Knight forced Corman to his knees, then onto his stomach. A metal chain was tied around his ankles. The Knight threaded the rest of the chain through a hook in the ceiling, then pulled. Corman was lifted into the air, upside down, and made to hang there with the blood rushing to his head. His arms dangled underneath him.

"...she didn't specify *how* alive you needed to be," Woods finished, adjusting his right gauntlet. "Keep in mind, Ryan, that you deserve *much*, *much* worse than this."

Then came the punch. Corman's ribs cracked. Wounds Edgar had just started to heal broke open. Blood seeped through his shirt and down onto his neck. Woods punched him again with his steel fist, then again, and again. Bile sloshed around in his stomach. Vomit built in his throat. Blood spewed out of his mouth as he vomited over himself. Haymaker after haymaker went straight into his stomach, his chest, and his throat. Blood and vomit splashed onto the concrete floor below, but not without first running down his arms and chest. He could barely see anymore. Dark red splotches appeared in the corners of his vision. Everything tasted like copper and burning shit. He was so light headed he could barely register what was happening.

From somewhere in that fog, he heard Woods call for help. A moment, or minute, or hour later, a cattle prod stabbed him in the sides. Electricity coursed through his body, burning through his nerves and muscles. Bruises blossomed all over his skin; his organs ruptured and started to bleed. Scorch marks were left behind where he was prodded. All the while vomit came rushing out of him and blood soaked through his clothes. Worse yet, he pissed himself. Every bone vibrated. Every organ screamed out for it to stop. His mind went blank.

"You need a wash," Woods said in the distance. Something metal appeared beneath him and then he was enveloped in water. No longer able to so much as squirm, Corman breathed in the water and started to choke. Seconds before he thought he'd asphyxiate, his head got pulled out and he could breathe again. Except he just kept on coughing, his lungs burning. Water dropped into the puddle of blood, urine, and vomit below.

"You can expect this every second of every day for the rest fo your miserable fucking existence," Woods snarled. "Know that you're finally getting what's coming to you. Know you're being put in your place. Always walking around like you were God's gift to Earth. You fucking pompous dick. You *jackass*." He punched Corman directly in the side of the head. There was a ringing sound and something that sounded like it cracked. "*Pathetic. Worthless. Arrogant. Asshole.*" With each new insult Woods hurled at him, he threw another punch.

A thin screen of bile hung from his mouth as he received the final punch right to the gut.

"Fucker," Woods spat. Then he and the other Knights left the cell; the door closed with a loud metallic clang.

In the dim light of the bulb above the door, Corman hung limply, unable to think and unable to move. There was a dull, pulsing pain everywhere in his body. It had shut down, refused to function. Except for Edgar.

"Don't fall asleep," he said. "You fall asleep and you're dead."

Corman gurgled.

"Now listen to me. I'm going to overload your hypothalamus so your wrists will be lubricated by the excess sweat," Edgar told him. "It'll consume most of the potassium and bicarbonate you have left, but I don't have any other options. Once your hands are free, I'm going to flood you with dopamine and adrenaline to give you enough energy to reach up for your feet. Then you'll unwrap the chains and free us. Overloading you... now."

In a matter of seconds, Corman felt his entire body heat up; the cell suddenly shifted into a sauna. Sweat collected on his forehead as the blood, without Edgar's physiological dam, rushed to his head again. His hands were simultaneously drenched in sweat. With as much force as he could apply, Corman slipped his wrists out from the cuffs. They clattered in the puddle below.

"Hitting you with the hormones now," Edgar said. Just as his neurotransmitters fired up and his enzymes balanced out, the door swung open. Corman's vision suddenly became clear in time to see the door open. *For fuck's sake.*

In stepped Bors and Kay.

"Woods wasn't shitting us after all," Kay said, smiling. "We actually *caught* the bastard. Hey Ryan, how does it feel to be on the other side for once?"

"Great," he croaked.

"Jesus, it looks like you got hit by a bus," Bors observed. "I'm surprised he's still breathing. It sounded like Woods gave him the Max Baer treatment."

"Shame he didn't finish the job," Kay said. "Hey, you think Woods would be pissed if we did it for him?"

"What the hell do you think?" Bors asked.

"Yeah, I'd hate to be screwed out of my prize, too," Kay chuckled. "This is getting bin Laden *and* Huessin in the same day."

"Jesus," Bors said.

Kay crossed his arms. "What? Am I *wrong*? Oh, *shit*, he *pissed* himself. Hey, you ever piss yourself once you were out of diapers?"

"Will you shut the fuck up?" Bors snapped. "Don't tell me you feel *sorry* for him," Kay said. "After all he's done?"

"It's called due process, you fucking idiot," Bors said. "You can't just beat the shit out of someone because you feel like it."

"Uh, yes you can," Kay argued. "Especially if you're Lancelot. Honestly, Sasha was a complete waste. Never did *anything*. But look! Woods finally got the bastard. Gave him *exactly* what he deserves."

Kay strode up beside Corman and pressed a finger into his side. "That hurt, Ryan? You feel that?"

"Not really," he mumbled.

"Jesus man, leave it alone," Bors told him.

"You *do* feel sorry for him," Kay yelled. "I knew it."

"I feel sorry for *me* for being stuck with a goddamn stupid piece of shit for a partner," Bors shouted back. "You don't understand *anything*. You're intellectually incapable of understanding anything beyond fucking whores in parking lots. You wanna know something, Ryan? They're *cambion* whores."

"Hey, *hey*!" Kay raged, grabbing Bors by the shoulder. "You fucking *asshole*. You said you'd never tell anyone!"

"But it's *Ryan*," Bors said, imitating him. "Nothing he hears *matters*. He's a *dead man* anyway."

"You motherfucker—!" Kay punched him across the face; Bors stumbled into the wall, hand on his cheek. "Come on, you son of a bitch! Come on!"

The two ran at each other. They collided; they toppled to the floor. Bors was on top of Kay, slamming him with one punch after another. Kay wrapped his hands around Bors' throat and managed to throw him off.

"Now," Edgar whispered.

Corman swung himself back and forth; he gained enough momentum to reach up and grab hold of the chains around his ankles. The rush of adrenaline allowed him to tear at the metal, pulling it apart until it loosened up; he went sailing to the floor, right into the puddle of his fluids and the chains themselves. Once he stood up, he saw the Knights still pummeling each other. He went over and pressed his boot onto Kay's face. Both Knights froze in place; Corman applied pressure to his right foot.

"Give me your rapier," he said quietly.

Bors stared up at him, mouth agape. "But you were just—"

"I know," Corman said. "Give me Kay's sword."

"Don't—" Kay muttered from beneath the boot. "Greg, *don't*—"

But Bors did exactly that. He slid the rapier out from it sheath and and pointed the blade at Corman's chest. "You give me a reason not to kill you first."

Corman grabbed the rapier's blade and ripped it away; his hand was slick with blood.

"Probably should've."

He sliced Bors' legs at the opening between the thigh and knee plates; Bors toppled over Kay and collapsed onto the floor; blood spilled out onto his legs. Corman lifted his boot from Kay's face and headed for the door.

XII

AM I MY BROTHER'S KEEPER?

A TRAIL OF BLOOD ran from his broken body back to the cell. Leaning against the wall, both hands on the rapier's grip, he wasn't entirely sure he'd be able to make it out. For one thing, two lesser Knights guarded the elevator doors. Unlike the ones on the Round Table, they didn't wear armor and didn't have the same degree of combat training. Normally, they'd be easy enough to take out. For another thing, he was bleeding out and probably dying. *It'll be more than just them in about five minutes*, he thought. *Sooner, if—*

"Stop him!" Kay shouted behind him. "That's Ryan! Fucking stop him! He stabbed Greg!"

"Dickhead," Corman mumbled, pushing himself off the wall. The lesser Knights bolted down the hallway, hands on their holsters. About ten feet from him, they got down to one knee and aimed their revolvers. Blood dripped down Corman's wrist onto the rapier blade.

"Put the sword down," one of the lessers commanded.

"This?" Corman raised it, pretended to inspect it. "Shit, I just cleaned my teeth with it."

He heard Kay click his revolver's hammer into place. "Drop it." Corman glanced over his shoulder and shrugged. "All right, all right."

"Now kick it over," Kay demanded.

"You sure about that?"

"Shut up and *do* it."

So he did, giving it a gentle little nudge with the side of his boot. As it rolled over to Kay, Corman threw himself behind Kay, landing hard on his shoulder. The Knight turned around, eyes narrowed, and Corman kicked his feet out from under him; a moment later, he had Kay's revolver in hand.

"I asked if you were sure," Corman said, wrapping his arm around Kay's neck. Standing, he propped Kay up as a human shield. "You two, go check on Bors. See if he's bled out yet."

"You bastard," Kay snarled.

"For the record, I hope he hasn't," Corman said, moving forward. "I'm not in the business of killing people."

"But you'll take them hostage," Kay growled.

"Which doesn't necessitate taking your life," Corman told him, hitting the elevator button. "Was the archives a set-up?"

"No, you're just an idiot," Kay grunted as the doors opened. "We had no idea you were gonna show up tonight. But even you had to it was fucking stupid to come here."

"Sure," Corman said. *Though delusional might be more appropriate.*

As they ascended to the tenth floor, Kay did his best to break Corman's grip; since he still had all that adrenaline in his system, however, he was essentially trying to wrestle his way out fo a crocodile's mouth.

"You're suffocating me," Kay gasped.

"You're lucky that's all I'm doing."

Once the doors opened again, Corman dragged him into the top floor offices. It looked exactly like it did eight years ago. Dutifully reporting every morning at seven, he would walk over to the Round Table conference room, a glass cube with one giant table taking up the entirety of the space. There he would receive his assignment if he wasn't working on a major case, and there he would do nothing to solve any of the city's ills. *We were an office full of murderers*, he thought. *And I was stupid enough to go along with them.*

He took Kay's handcuffs and locked both of his hands to a desk.

"You're not leaving here alive, Ryan," Kay told him.

"Oh, I will be," Corman said. "It's *you* I'd be worried about."

Directly adjacent to the conference room was King's office, whose windows were bisected by frosted glass. No time to be delicate about this. He wrapped his ruined jacket around his right hand and broke through a pane. The shards crashed to the carpet. Corman stepped over them and immediately started rummaging through whatever drawers were unlocked. All he found in her filing cabinets and three-ring binders were municipal reports, copies of permits, tax records, and meeting minutes. *Fuck*, he thought, tossing aside another irrelevant folder.

"Have you find anything?" Edgar asked.

"If I was trying to get them on tax evasion and bank fraud, sure," Corman murmured.

"What about her computer files? She has to have something on a hard drive."

"Maybe," he said as the floor lights turned a bright red. An alarm blared over the public announcement system. "Goddamn it."

After Corman booted up her desktop, he was given a prompt to enter her password. "Shit."

"She's old school, isn't she?" Edgar asked. "She must have her password written somewhere. Check the drawers again."

"Already dumped everything out, but..." Corman perused the milieu of shit on the floor. Opening up a black notebook, he found a collection of nearly one hundred passwords.

"She's on a *lot* of dating sites," Edgar noted as Corman punched in the login password and was brought to her personal desktop. He pulled up the filing system. The folders and the document therein must've been written in some sort code.

"Fuck," Corman said. "D-U-R twenty? One-zero-five-six-seven? Zero-zero-five-one?"

"Try using quick search," Edgar suggested.

He entered a number of key phrases through the operating system's search function; alchemy, wiemca, Seal of Solomon, chimaera, immortality, and finally, philosopher's stone. "No good. None of the files have the key words in the name."

"She must have a codex somewhere," Edgar said.

"We don't have time for that," Corman muttered.

"I'm here! I'm here!" he heard Kay shout over the alarm.

"Get a flash drive and take what you can," Edgar told him. "We need to go."

"Where'd you see one?" Corman asked.

"Bottom left drawer." He inserted the USB drive into one of the computer's ports and pulled up the document library, started transferring the files. Looking over the screen, he saw Knights flood into the office, assault rifles at the ready.

"Fuck," he said.

"What?" Edgar asked. "What's out there?"

"Assholes with guns," Corman said. Less than one third of the documents had been copied over to the drive. "How much time left on my adrenaline?"

"Four minutes, unless you overexert yourself," Edgar said. "I only calculated enough to get you out of the building. I didn't anticipate you taking a detour."

"You didn't?"

"We just escaped getting tortured to death," Edgar said. "I kind of assumed you weren't gonna be pulling this shit."

The Knights were closing in on him. *Six assault rifles versus a stick.* A profound disadvantage. Worse yet, Knight rapiers were just another part of the uniform. As far as effective weaponry went, they were about as useful as a butter knife. *But you can still stab someone if you know what you're doing.*

"Ryan!" one of the Knights shouted. "Surrender now or we *will* open fire."

"Not exactly an appealing proposition," Corman called out, eyeing the progress bar.

"I could give a rat's ass. Get out here *now*."

"Honestly I'm surprised you haven't shot at me already," Corman said. "Seems like the thing you guys would do."

"You were one of us once," the Knight told him. "I'd say that's bought you ten more seconds than usual."

"How generous," Corman said, sliding under the desk. To Edgar, he asked, "You see a Walther or thirty-eight special anywhere?"

"You think you could get us out of here with a stapler?"

"I'm not John Wick," Corman said.

The first rounds of gunfire burst overhead. "That's your time, Ryan. We are authorized to use lethal force and trust me, we *will* be exercising that right."

"How much time we have left to go?" Corman asked, holding Edgar up to the screen.

"We're at forty percent."

"It'll have to do," Corman said, ripping the drive out of the USB slot.

"You're supposed to eject it before you take it out!" Edgar said. "You might've corrupted the files."

"*Now* you care?"

"If you're risking our lives for this, then yeah, you should've ejected it properly."

"It's fine," Corman said, pocketing the drive.

"Yeah, but what if it *isn't*?"

"Meliant, Morholt, take point," the Knight said.

Delta squad? So they'd sent the d-tiers. That'd buy him some time. Corman rammed his shoulder into the desk, tipping it over onto its side. He heard the computer burst apart as more gunfire erupted.

Heavy footsteps approached on either side; Corman held the rapier tightly. *Less than two minutes*, he thought as Meliant and Morholt flanked him. Whoever stepped in on to his right, he launched himself at them, thrusting the rapier through their side. Corman rolled away, hand wrapped around their rifle's shoulder strap, and ripped it off. He fired at the other four Knights as he slid behind another desk.

He checked his ammo count; sixteen rounds left in the clip. *It's enough*, he thought himself, popping out from the desk. Nothing left to do but make a mad dash for the stairs. Over his shoulder, he fired blind at them. Halfway there, a bullet cut across his thigh, and another went into his left shoulder muscle. Corman stumbled, nearly dropping the rifle, but made it to the stairwell. He slammed up against the wall and fired off the remainder of the clip. Opening the door, he was met with the business end of a shotgun. On the other side was Kay.

"Bastard," he said.

"No arguments here," Corman said, ramming the butt of his rifle into Kay's forehead. This sent him tumbling backward. Droplets of blood followed. On the next landing, Corman ripped the shotgun away and hurried down the stairs. As he reached the eighth level, however, he began to feel sluggish. His legs were heavy and his vision started to blur.

"Thirty seconds," Edgar said.

"No more... nothing left in my system?"

"I used what little potassium and bicarbonate I could without killing you," Edgar told him as he slumped against the wall. "You were dangerously low on just about everything."

"You did... what you could."

"It's never enough for you though, is it?"

"What are you... talking about?"

"We just escaped death. *Twice*. But somehow, despite all that, we're still gonna die. That's how it always goes with you. I'm so sick and tired of being so close to death. I'm so fucking tired, Corman. I can't protect you like you need me to anymore."

"Then use up everything else," Corman said, his words starting to slur. "Put me into a coma after this, if you... if you have to. But— get us... out of here."

"There's nothing left for me to use!"

"Oh." *So that's it.* "Fuck."

Out of the corner of his eyes, he saw two dark figures coming for him. They spoke to each other, though as well as Corman could hear them, they might as well have been a hundred miles away. He felt them pick him up by the arms as everything went dark.

Something in that darkness reached him; his heart shrieked in pain. His eyes bolted open and he sat up so quickly he doubled over. The floor underneath him rumbled. All around him were the sterile walls of the back of ambulance. An IV needle was stuck in his elbow joint. Sitting on either side of him were a couple of old coworkers. Safir was dressed in full armor, while Kalebrant only wore the armored pants, the pieces usually covering their standard issue mesh undershirts absent. In lieu of his ruined clothes, they dressed him in surplus military clothes; cargo pants, black undershirt, combat boots, and fatigue jacket.

"Good to know the morphine worked," Safir, a skinny kid with dark hair, said.

"What the hell is happening?" Corman asked, his mouth bone dry.

"We're saving your dumb ass," Kalebrant, big and bulky, told him. "Found you half-dead in a stairwell. You remember that much?"

"What about Delta?"

"How do you think you didn't die back there?" Kalebrant grunted. "We're part of Delta. Were. After this, we're definitely getting canned."

Corman frowned. "Why the hell would you do that?"

"Sasha told us you were gonna need help," Safir said.

"But she went dark on me," Corman told him.

"So she could set this up without being figured out. She figured you'd try to break into Camelot at some point. Said you'd eventually wind up in the hanged cells. So she planned to break you out. Took a while to get all the pieces in motion, but I think it went pretty well, all things considered."

"Except for you basically being dead," Kalebrant added. "Sasha only figured you'd get shot a couple of times. Riding in the back of this thing was last minute. You got to pay her back for the van rental."

"She tell you why she bothered with this?" Corman asked.

"I imagine she had her own reasons," Safir replied. "I certainly do. What you've been doing... I have a little sister, and I— I can't imagine what those families are going through. Without you, I don't know. Maybe I would've lost her."

"I only saved one person," Corman mumbled.

"But you took out a lot of the wiemca," Safir said. "I've checked the records. They're not as active as they were six months ago."

"What's your excuse?" Corman asked Kalebrant.

"Fuck King," he said. "Fuck Woods too, for that matter."

Good enough.

"Whatever's happening, though, she was certain you'd be the only one who would

stand a chance against it," Safir said. "Nobody hunts chimaeras quite like you."

"Where are we going?"

"To a safehouse. Only Yue knows where it is."

Corman frowned. "Yue?"

She turned around in the driver's seat. "Hey, Ryan."

"Sasha roped you into this, too?" he asked.

"That *would* be the word for it."

"Tomorrow you're gonna be put on a charter plane to Alaska," Safir told him. "Sasha suggested you stay up there for the foreseeable future, given that there's a federal manhunt for you. Arthur wants you dead now, too."

"Did he put out a kill order?" Corman asked.

Safir nodded solemnly. "Yeah."

"So we gotta get you the hell out of here before he gets all of our asses," Kalebrant said. "Gotta figure out some sort of plausible deniability."

It doesn't make sense, Corman thought. *What's Sasha playing at here?* What could she possibly stand to gain from smacking the hornet's nest?

"I need someone to let someone named Abigail Steward what's happened," Corman said. "Discreetly. I don't want them hunting her, too."

"She your girlfriend?" Kalebrant asked.

"She's someone I want safe," Corman replied. "My sister and my mother, too."

"No problem, we'll—" Safir paused, looked out the back window. "Uh oh."

Passing underneath the rows of streetlights behind them, a Sheridan tank was in pursuit. Corman glanced at the IV bag, then at the medical supplies behind the windows of the wall cabinets. *One more shot ought to do it.*

"Hit the fucking gas," Kalebrant shouted to Yue. "They brought out a tank."

"We don't *have* tanks," Yue said. Then she looked in the review mirror. "When the fuck did we get tanks?"

"We can't outrun *that* in *this*," Safir said.

Corman ripped the IV out of his arm and wrapped his elbow in gauze. Rummaging through the cabinets, he found a adrenaline needle bag. "I got a plan."

"Ryan, what the hell are you doing?" Kalebrant asked.

He ripped the bag open and jabbed the needle into his arm.

"You're gonna fall into a coma," Safir told him. "Your body won't be able to reach homeostasis."

"You wanna get blown up?" Corman asked. "Yue, I'm gonna jump out the back. Don't stop driving. One of you give me your gun."

"Fuck you I'm doing that," Kalebrant said.

Safir poked him with the muzzle of his rifle. "I hope you know what you're doing."

"It'd be ungrateful of you if you died," Yue called out. "Considering how much trouble we went through to save your sorry ass."

Corman strung the rifle around his shoulder and pushed open the doors. The frigid night air cut across his flesh, stinging the bruises and half-healed cuts all over his body. His stumps itched something fierce. *All right. Try not to die.* He leapt out of the ambulance and smacked into the asphalt, absorbing the kinetic energy through his shoulder and somersaulting for a few yards before finally slamming into the tank treads.

The launcher, likely operating on an automatic tracking system, remained focused on the ambulance; the hatch popped open and a D.C. Knight, the red-and-white eagle insignia gleaming in the light of the streetlights, lifted himself out. Rolling away from the ensuing hailstorm of bullets, Corman went underneath the tank. *Wish I had C-four*, he thought as boots hit the ground by the treads. Going prone, he fired off a clip into into a collection of ankles. Bodies dropped, grasping their bloody legs. Corman rolled out from under the tank, rifle at the ready, and climbed up the ladder to the hatch. He fired into the air.

"Everyone out or I'll send a couple of ricochets your way," he shouted. Instead of obliging him, the ones still inside blasted shotgun shells at him. Corman tumbled backward onto the street, where a slug slammed a mere inch from his foot.

As he hurried to the back of the tank, he heard sirens blare down the street. Peeking out from behind, he saw the ambulance barreling toward the tank at full speed. *What in the fuck—?* The launcher clicked into place and fired. The missile screeched through the still air, colliding with the ambulance. In its place a moment later was fire and smoke, bits of metal and plastic falling to earth.

"Hands up!" he heard Safir say. Looking up, he saw all three of his rescuers on the tank, their weapons aimed down into the hatch. Yue nodded at Corman.

"That's not gonna be cheap to replace," he said.

"Not my fucking problem right now," Yue said; the D.C. Knights removed themselves from inside the tank one by one until they were all lined up neatly, at gunpoint, with their arms raised.

"We can take this thing," Kalebrant said, one leg dangling off the treads, "as long as we borrow the driver."

This is just gonna keep happening as long as you're with them, Corman told himself, feeling the USB drive in his pocket. *Plausible deniability.*

"I appreciate what you did for me," he said. "But I'm not going."

"What?" Safir asked.

"You are *not* pulling this," Yue spat. "Not *now*."

"I can't leave things like this," Corman told them, taking hold of the rifle grip. "The last few pieces are about to fall into place. I need to see that they do."

"Let us worry about that," Yue told him. "You're in deep enough shit as it is."

So why not go deeper? He pointed the gun at them.

"Don't be an asshole, Ryan," Kalebrant said.

"I'm going. I'm ending this. I never asked anyone to risk their lives for me. So don't pretend like *any of you* did me a favor." They would all be better off with him dead, so what did it matter? *Let's be done with it. Let me die. Just let me do what I need to do first.*

"We did this for Sasha, you idiot," Yue said. "And this is a pretty shitty way to repay her."

"Then you won't mind telling her she put her faith in the wrong person," Corman muttered, taking a few steps backward. "She should've known that in the first place. All of you should've."

Slowly, he backed away into the darkness, leaving behind the destruction already wrought for his sake. All that remained of it was the burning visage of the ambulance and the ugly, sickly feeling in his gut.

Doesn't matter what you feel, he told himself. *You're seeing this through.*

"I don't think this needs saying," Edgar said, "but we're fucked."

"We were fucked from the jump, Ed. Nothing's changed since day one. Not a thing."

XIII
RUBICON

S NOW STARTED TO FALL again by the time he was a block from the Minneapolis Central Library. It had been a long, exhausting walk in the cold; Corman could barely keep himself awake. The adrenaline was wearing off again. Once he was inside, though, he could wait for Edgar to do the necessary repairs. Get his body warmed up.

The fake ID unlocked the entrance underneath the elongated, inverted pyramid. Its floors were separated by a large open space, giving it a spacious, modern feel to its design, with wood and glass comingling with the necessary steel that bound them together. Despite this, Corman felt the walls closing in on him.

Every floor had a collection of six sectioned off tables for computer use. Corman climbed to the topmost floor, hoping that should anyone find him, which was more than likely, it'd give him some time before his inevitable arrest. Though his pace was sluggish, each step knives inside his feet, he made it. Sitting down in a chair in front of a desktop, he let himself feel the briefest sense of relief.

"How— how low are we?" he asked.

"The reserves are empty, Corman," Edgar said. "You're out of everything."

"Do what you can."

Besides the emergency lights and Corman's computer screen, it was dark in the library. Like the shadows of his mistakes were all around, inching closer. *Ignore it. Do what you need to do.* He plugged in the drive and pulled up what documents he managed to copy. It wasn't much, only about a hundred and ten files out of maybe a thousand, all of them falling under the same cryptic naming conventions. Clicking them open, he found more of the same information that was on the paper copies. *Taxes, taxes, permit applications, subpoena requests... Goddamn it, don't tell me I have nothing. I can't have nothing.* A ways down the list, however, was a file named "2006projectJKe.pdf."

"Two-thousand six?" he murmured. "What the hell happened in two-thousand six?"

ATTN: BARBARA OLSEN
10/18/06
Barbara,

As I'm sure you've heard by now, progress on "Holy Grail" is coming along quite nicely. The particulars are, at the moment, of little importance. I'll explain everything in detail once we're further along in the project timeline. I assure you, however, that the Knights as an organization will benefit immensely from my work here. Once Adam sees what my research has been able to produce, that grant will immediately follow. Your confidence in me has not been taken for granted. I will pay back that loan as soon as the grant money starts coming in, and like I said, it's a but a certainty that it will. In the meantime, I encourage you to come down to R&D and see for yourself what we've been cooking up.

John Kelley – "MERLIN"
Employee No. 15650781
Federal Knight Bureau, Minneapolis chapter, R&D Division
"*That* John Kelley?" Corman said.

ATTN: JOHN KELLEY
10/23/06
John,

Thank you for giving me that look into your division's work. Mighty impressive. That said, you will eventually have to file a report that includes all of your progress up-to-date and then some, including a comprehensive, itemized list of all your expenditures. Adam will not accept the work without it having gone through the proper channels. You might also have to apply for a patent before he accepts it for widespread use. Check with HR before you take any of your work outside the laboratory. My confidence in you and your team's abilities has been more than earned. I look forward to further progress updates. Again, be certain to have one of your team members file the right paperwork before you move too far into the project and details begin to slip by you.

Barbara Olsen – "KING"
Employee No. 61678205
Federal Knight Bureau, Minneapolis chapter, Round Table Division
ATTN: BARBARA OLSEN
11/08/06

Barbara,
As much as I appreciate the department's overall enthusiasm for the project, I must object to the more, shall we say, "invasive" measures that have been implemented. To be perfectly honest, it has begun to worry my team despite your assurances that the other Knights' presence is to simply ensure the project's secrecy and safety. They've all been burned before by unnecessary seizure of intellectual property, and I have done my best to assure them that this will not happen in any FKB lab setting. It is becoming increasingly difficult to convince them of this. If you

could perhaps decrease the visits from daily to once a week or less, that would be a great help to their workflow.

John Kelley – "MERLIN"
Employee No. 15650781
Federal Knight Bureau, Minneapolis chapter, R&D Division
ATTN: JOHN KELLEY
11/16/06

John,

I would accept your terms if it were up to me. Unfortunately, Adam has mandated that your project be surveillanced to such a degree. This is, as he mentioned to me an email earlier this month, one of the single most important undertakings made in this department's lifetime. He believes that any information leaked to the public will result in disastrous consequences. I must admit I agree with his assessment. I hate to remind you yet again, but you must start to file your progress reports in a more timely fashion starting immediately.

Barbara Olsen – "KING"
Employee No. 61678205
Federal Knight Bureau, Minneapolis chapter, Round Table Division
ATTN: BARBARA OLSEN
11/27/06
Barbara,

I'm afraid I must insist on the issue of "increased security" once more. It has been nothing but a complete detriment to my team's productivity. Simmons and Clairmount have taken temporary leaves of absences due to frayed nerves because of this, and I fear more of my team will follow suit if this continues. The nature of the great work is already a highly pressurized one, and by adding to that pressure, you threaten to shut down the project entirely. This work of ours is to be used by all of humankind, and not just to serve the department's private interests. Though I'm sure you agree with me, it seems increasingly likely that Adam only has the latter in mind when he implements these sorts of tactics. I speak to you on this for not only the project's sake, but for my team as well. I will follow up with a report shortly.

John Kelley – "MERLIN"
Employee No. 15650781
Federal Knight Bureau, Minneapolis chapter, R&D Division

ATTN: JOHN KELLY
12/01/06
John,
I will be traveling to the D.C. office soon to discuss certain matters with Adam. I will do my best to bring up your concerns. In the meantime, I will be out of the office from 12/04–12/08. Please direct any grievances to Cynthia in HR.
Barbara Olsen – "KING"
Employee No. 61678205

Federal Knight Bureau, Minneapolis chapter, Round Table Division

ATTN: BARBARA OLSEN
12/11/06
Barbara,

I don't know what Adam has asked of you, and even though I am certain it was great importance, I must admit my disappointment with the proceedings. My team is gone. Those who haven't been transferred have quit, and the project remains unfinished. We only had around twenty-five to twenty percent left to go according to our numerous estimations. This is little more than an insult to not only my life's work, but also to my team's dedication to the project. They were a group of talented, hardworking scientists and researchers, and the past five years have been unceremoniously dumped in the garbage. Excuse my terse language, if you will, but I must admit I am deeply frustrated and concerned at what has transpired. At one time, I felt as if the FKB allowed science its due and allowed it to flourish naturally. Now I feel as if it is constrained to allow for private interests and agendas to dictate progress. I am afraid that should things continue down this path, I will be unable to continue my work with the Knights, a thought I have never entertained before and which brings me great sadness to consider.

John Kelley – "MERLIN"
Employee No. 15650781

Federal Knight Bureau, Minneapolis chapter, R&D Division

ATTN: JOHN KELLEY
Notice of Termination
12/26/2006
Mr. Kelley, designation "MERLIN,"

It is with great reluctance that senior leadership of the Federal Knight Bureau, Minneapolis chapter, have decided to officially terminate your position as Deputy Director of Research and Development, effective immediately. This decision does not come lightly, and was made with the overall interest of the bureau in mind.

We hope you find meaningful employment elsewhere.

Federal Knight Bureau Senior Staff
Minneapolis Chapter, Round Table Division
101 1st St. S, Minneapolis MN, 55401

MINNEAPOLIS STAR TRIBUNE OBITUARIES (January 2, 2007)
JOHN ROBERT KELLEY

John Robert Kelley was born on August 7, 1960 to Robert and Miranda Kelley of Saint Paul. Kelley was a longstanding member of the Federal Knight Bureau and bore the designation of "Merlin" and acted as their deputy director for their research and development department for eight years, previously having served with distinction as "Percival" for the previous eleven. He died on Jan. 1 of a self-inflicted gunshot wound. He was 46 years old. He is survived by a brother Calvin, sister-in-law Marcie, two nephews, and one niece.

Funeral services will be held on Friday, Jan. 5. at 10:30 a.m. at Saint Bonaventure Church with Rev. Charles DeVine officiating. Interment services will be held at 3 p.m. the same day.

"Did— did King *kill* him?" Edgar whispered.

"Took his life's work first," Corman said. "Seized it and made sure nobody else could replicate it."

"So is the Holy Grail the philosopher's stone?"

"Has to be," Corman said, opening up the subsequent files. "Both are instruments to induce immortality. The alchemists who originally studied the Seals of Solomon were trying to find a way to reproduce the effects without having to actually go through the arduous process of creating one. They never could. Sounds like Kelley was picking up where they left off. And that he found a way to do it."

"Do you think the Knights figured out the other twenty-five percent of the equation by themselves?"

One of the documents he pulled up were photocopied pages of a notebook, with symbols, sigils, and inscriptions identical to the ones in his own. "Not that I can see. All the chemical compositions here are incomplete. It looks like they had a hard time decoding

Kelley's notes into something useful. They only have the easiest symbols to translate here. Salt, ammonium, platinum, and then the quintessentials."

"What about these here?" Edgar asked, looking to another incomplete equation near the bottom of the page.

"Potassium, hydrogen, and oxygen," Corman said. "Alone, they don't mean anything. They need other chemicals to make anything useful. Even if they *did*, they'd still need to denote which stage in the transmutation process they were being used in for clarity's sake."

"Aren't human bodies composed of all these?"

"We have them, sure, but there's eight other primary elements, plus a little extra," Corman said. "There's no place in the equation for, say, the incredibly small amount of lithium or copper in the body, and we need those. They're small, but vital components."

"It looks like that's what they were going for," Edgar noted.

"The philosopher's stone is the soul made material," Corman said. "It demonstrates the mastery of the art of alchemy itself, but over the individual's soul too. Kelley must've done the groundwork for a practical way to transpose... the soul."

"What?"

"If you could somehow devise a way to transpose a human soul into an inert philosopher's stone through something like a horizontal gene transfer, then you could theoretically cause the catalyst to collide the particles of the body inside the stone, making an entirely new chemical composition."

"So the stone is like a hadron collider?"

"That's why alchemists were unable to make one before modern scientific discoveries," Corman said. "It would require more advanced knowledge than what was available to them. I think Kelley found a way to synthesize ancient findings with his own."

"But the soul would need a lot of energy to do that," Edgar said.

"And it'd have to be mostly kinetic energy," Corman murmured.

"So whoever they hired to finish Kelley's work had to know all of this, right?"

Corman opened up the last document on the file list, "2007an lv.pdf." It was a two hundred and six page legal contract involving ownership of intellectual property and patent rights. All the way at the bottom were a collection of signatures, including Barbara Olsen, Adam Norton, and... *Lilith Valentine.*

"Lilith?" Edgar said. "She was... they—"

"Hired her to finish Kelley's work," Corman finished. *She tried sacrificing me to open up the portal to Hell... whose infinite population would contain enough energy to activate the stone.* "The soul itself is the catalyst. But you need more to keep it operational."

"So by sacrificing all those women, the wiemca were trying to open Hell to get her back?"

"The stone is thought to reverse death," Corman said. "If given enough souls as fuel."

"You don't think—"

The familiar sound of a helicopter's blades thundered through the still air. A floodlight filled the library through the glass windows. Glass shattered onto the floor below. An armored division of Knights entered through the shattered panes, assault rifles at the ready. In orderly fashion, they marched through the building.

Corman was just about to take the drive out from the computer when Edgar pinched his palm. "Properly, this time." As soon as he properly ejected the drive, he heard the heavy footsteps of the Knights come up the stairs. Corman crawled under the desk as flashlights scoured the floor.

"We're going back to the hanged cells," Edgar said. "Goddamn it. God*damn* it Corman."

He waited until all of the flashlights were among the bookshelves, then bolted out from under the desk for the stairs. But his movement was clumsy and slow from the fluid imbalance in his system. Just as he reached the stairs, he tripped and slammed into the railing.

"Your vasopressin levels are severely depleted," Edgar told him. "Pretty much every function of your hypothalamus is out of sync."

"Thanks for... the head's up," he mumbled as Knights swarmed him.

Then he heard Woods' voice. "Lower your weapons. She wants him alive." He crouched beside Corman and smiled. "Would've been smarter to just let the tank run you over."

His vision was getting blurry; the bile in his stomach was churning around again. "You don't say."

"If you thought what *I* gave you was bad, you're *really* gonna hate what she has for you," Woods said.

"What does King... h— have for me?"

Woods offered him a mirthless chuckle. "Oh, no. The woman I'm taking you to is an entirely different breed of bitch."

"Bigger of a bitch than... than you?"

"By a landslide."

Knights grabbed him by the underarms and lifted him to his feet. As they dragged him down the stairs, Corman couldn't help but think that maybe he should've listened to Edgar on this one.

XIV
KATABASIS

OVER THE COURSE OF a hundred and sixty years, Corman had given plenty of consideration to how he would die. Every possibility that presented itself as the conclusive cause, he had managed to skirt around. Now though, as Woods and a bandaged Kay dragged him out of a Stingray, he finally had the definite answer. Whatever lay inside the Trismeg Theater, it would kill him.

Though it didn't matter who sold him out now, he couldn't help but wonder. Could be anyone. Safir, Kalebrant, and Yue were the most obvious. But Sasha herself just as easily could've thrown her hands up and handed him off. It would make all of their lives easier if they turned him over, and he couldn't blame them for taking the opportunity. *You had this coming, you fucking idiot*, he told himself. *Should've listened to Ed. You should've listened*.

Inside the lobby, Woods threw him to the floor and kicked him in the tailbone; Corman collapsed onto his stomach.

"So much for hospitality," Corman murmured.

"I've recently gotten intel that you're on the verge of your bodily functions failing you. That won't do. Not for her. So you're going to give it your all before she takes it from you."

"Where— where did you get that from?" he asked, getting to his knees. Kay slammed a boot down into the small of his back.

"None of your goddamn business, goatfucker," Kay spat.

"I made them... They were coerced—"

"Even if that's the case," Woods said as he produced a sealed medical bag, "they still cooperated with a traitor." From the bag, he pulled out a hypodermic needle. "They've all been charged with aiding and abetting a known criminal and international fugitive. Hope whatever you bailed on them for was worth it."

"You motherfuck—" The needle was jabbed directly into his jugular. The flush of adrenaline sent him into convulsions.

"You'd think a mooncalf would be able to take a needle or two," Woods said, shaking his head. "But then again, you're a prescription pills guy, aren't you?"

Corman's eyes flashed open. He leapt up to strangle him, but was met with the butt of a rifle. Blood spilling into his face again, he glared at the two of them.

"She's waiting for you, Ryan," Woods said. "Can't postpone it forever."

No doubt his body chemistry was beyond fucked now. All he felt was a white hot rage at everything in front of him. The veins across his arms and neck bulged; he felt heat spread through his entire body. His fists shook. His teeth ground together.

"You attack me, and you still won't die," Woods told him. "We'll just take some fingers and toes. Then we'll wait a while before we take the rest."

Corman spat at him, then turned toward the doors. He burst them open as he stormed down the center aisle to the stage. *So be it.*

The stage was lit up for a performance, the backdrops and props all still there, albeit knocked over and at various stages of disrepair. His stomach dropped.

Standing directly center stage was Abigail. Her eyes were red, her hair a mess. Cuts and bruises lined her arms.

"No," he said. "*No.*" He ran the rest of the way and leapt onto the stage, took hold of her by the arms. "Who did this to you? *Who?*"

"I thought it would be a nice surprise for you," an unearthly, raspy voice said from the wings.

He turned to see a limping, pallid creature in a black robe enter from stage right. The skin was pallid and yellowish, the hair thin and dirty and falling in loose strands down to the bony shoulders. There were obvious stitch marks over joints and sections of bone. And the face... It was little more than a skull with a thin veneer of flesh stretched over it. Its yellow eyes were sunken, hollow, and bloodshot. The crooked, broken nose and its misshapen jaw didn't match the rest of it. So much of it was mismatched and disproportionate; one leg was longer than the other, and its upper left arm was thicker than the lower half. It was neither man nor woman, human or demon. It was *her*.

"Hello, Corman," Lilith said.

"You fucking—" Corman growled, letting go of Abigail. "She has *nothing* to do with this. None of those people had *anything* to do with this."

"If you had just done as I asked all those years ago, none of them would be dead," she told him. She examined her awful body. "And I wouldn't have had to reconstruct myself. I used to be so *beautiful*. And now look at me, Corman."

"You murdered those women for *this*?" he screamed.

"I needed a body. This was the only way."

"You could've stayed *dead*, you fucking—"

"Oh, no, I couldn't have done *that*, Corman," Lilith said. "Then I couldn't have made this little beauty." She pulled out a small, misshapen red gem from her robes and held it out. "I just need a few more souls to amplify its power."

She did it. She fucking finished it.

"Use mine instead," Corman said. "Leave her out of this."

"Oh, no no no, I'm afraid that's simply not *possible*," Lilith said, trying to shake her head; her neck was far too fleshy to move naturally. "I need you alive. I can't kill you *yet*. It would be such an inconvenience. You see—"

"Shut your mouth," Corman spat. "Let her go."

"Also not possible."

He looked over his shoulder at her; she was shivering, shrinking into herself, hands clutching her arms. *You have to end this. Now.*

"Fine," he said. "But you get anywhere near her, and I'll kill you."

Lilith's crooked, sewn-together mouth moved to form something like a smile. "You're still a little idiot."

"Who're you calling little, you rotting old bitch?"

Lilith retrieved a billy club from inside of her robes and flicked it out into the scythe. "I can see why you liked this little thing so much, Corman. It has a real weight to it."

She glided across the stage, almost gracefully, and sliced at him. Corman grabbed the hilt and bashed his head against hers, knocking Lilith back. As she regained her composure, he glanced back to Abigail.

"Go!" he yelled at her, rushing at Lilith. "Run!"

Lilith met his charge, scythe outstretched. And he caught it, in his right hand. Blood gushed over the sides of the blade as it cut into his skin. Through the straining, the sweat dribbling down his forehead, and the pounding of his heart, he couldn't see Abigail; she had to have escaped. Or else... *Else what, you idiot?* It would all be in vain? Wasn't it already?

The lifeless, yellow eyes occupying Lilith's sockets stared at him; he met her gaze.

"Careful now," she rasped. "You don't want to lose that hand of yours."

"This ain't the important one," he grunted.

"No? Then why am I bothering with it?" she asked, jerking the blade to the left, slicing his palm down to the bone. Corman, now without his support, tripped. A charred, skeletal foot bashed him in the back of the head. Again, he stumbled. Yellowed, rotting finger bones grabbed his shirt collar while another set of them broke his nose. Then he was on the ground, his body buzzing from the adrenaline and morphine cocktail coursing through his veins. *Won't reach homeostasis... Need to—*

Those same finger bones wrapped around his neck and forced him to his knees.

"You were never going to win, Corman," Lilith croaked. She bent to be eye level with him, and licked the blood oozing out between his lips. "Such a shame. You were so close to catching up to me."

"Was... was I," he mumbled.

A sharp fingertip scratched the scars of his burgeoning horns. "Still shaving them down, are we? And where did it get you? What did it do, Corman? What did it do?"

"If all you're gonna do," he sputtered through a crushed esophagus, "is monologue at me... Just kill me already."

"But it's been eight years, don't you want to catch up?" she asked, tightening her grip ever so slightly.

"You're... you're still a bitch and I'm still an idiot," Corman told her. "What's there to... to discuss?"

"You're a wretched creature, aren't you?" The pressure around his throat released, and he collapsed to his side. Lilith faced the seats, her robes flowing around her legs. "In this impossibly grand show, you think yourself a tragic hero. A beleaguered warrior, brought down by those around him... But it was yourself, Corman. You were always going to be the one to destroy yourself. Consider me the spotlight which illuminates your downfall."

"If I say... Macbeth, think the roof will fall in on you?" Corman gulped.

"In your final moments, and all you have to offer are jokes," Lilith said, shaking her head. "Still the little idiot."

"National— national average," Corman said, managing to get up to one knee. "But at least it's my body."

"This *is* my body now, fool," Lilith said. "And it will be until the final resurrection. Until all things rise up again in my glorious—"

The scythe slashed in a backwards arc, just as Corman was about to grab it. As he leapt back, he saw those discolored spots again, lost his sense of place. The scythe came back down on him; Edgar tugged his left arm out of its socket. And then there it was, severed at the elbow, squirming on the stage in a pool of blood.

"Ed?" he whispered. "Ed?"

Then the pain hit him. Corman shrieked, grabbing his stump with his sliced-up hand. It was too much to bear; he fell to his knees once more. As tears welled up, blurring his vision, he screamed out for Edgar, screamed for him to come back. The scythe pierced his left hand, right through the eye. A convulsive shock spread through the arm, and it was still. With a trembling hand, Corman reached out for him.

And that's when the blade went through this chest. Underneath his gaze was the shimmering steel alloy sticking out of him. Glaring down, Lilith twisted it and raised him to his feet, dangled him off of the scythe.

"You didn't have to die like this," she told him. "You could have died with glorious purpose. But you chose them over me. You chose your tormentors and your persecutors and your enemies. You have chosen to forsake me *again*, like the idiot you are." She held him close to her decayed, mutilated face; her teeth were crooked and out of place and her nose was sliced down the middle. "You disgust me. You prostrated yourself before humanity, and you let them *crucify* you. You are *nephilim*, yet you crawled around in the dirt with the worms. Begged them to take you in. Where has it gotten you, Corman? What good has it done you, to bow to your lessers? You were born to conquer, and you chose slavery. A slave to the slaves. Disgusting."

"Ed..." Corman gurgled. "I'm sorry. I'm sorry, I'm sorry I'm—"

The blade slid out of him, and the stage came up to crack him across the skull. Not only blood, but spinal fluid, leaked out. Though everything was faint, he could still feel it, all around him. The hot stage lights, the blood under his fingernails, the prickling of his missing arm. He had lost. *Oh*, he thought.

And then the blade entered his heart.

Why hadn't he listened? Why had he done this? Run, run, run. Into the chimaeras. Into exile. Into the blade that killed him. That killed Edgar. Why had he run? Why didn't he listen?

Where was his mother? Rowan? Edgar? Where was he? Was he there, or here? Was there even a place to go now?

So how was he aware of this, this nonexistence? This... nothing? He was a thought, a brief glimpse of a memory before it faded away. But how could he know? Where had he gone? The outline of himself started to crack. Crack, crumble, and turn to dust. His insides froze. And then he burst into flames. Try as he might, he could not scream. The pain, the pain, the pain. Muscles snapped apart, his skull broke open, and a lead weight replaced his stomach. His left arm prickled, a thousand needles all jabbing him in the same spot. Salt filled his mouth, and then copper, and then bile scorched his throat. Something grabbed him and tore him in half, both halves of him equally aware they were separated. That something let his halves go, and as though magnetic, they collided with each other.

Fireworks went off inside his brain, inside his thoughts, and he felt that prickling again. His whole existence was pins-and-needles, his whole person. Bones solidified, blood clotted, tissue and muscle grew back, organs burst forth to life, and skin stitched itself over all of it, just as his eyes popped back into their sockets. A fiery ache grew from his reborn forehead, two ebony horns clawing their way to the back of his ears. Wisps of flames licked his head as they did, until they reached their full length, and then there was Corman Ryan again, naked and alone in a white void.

Am I really here? He waggled his left arm at the stump. Was it really missing? When he looked up again, he saw a great bronze gate before him, another solitary figure in the pure nothingness. Twenty feet tall, its vicious, violent scenes loomed over him. Carved into the bronze were the souls of the damned, in the throes of their eternal torture. Their eyes were open wide with fear and knowledge, their mouths unhinged in silent screaming. Heat emanated from the other side, and this hot wind blasted past him as the doors opened. Shrill voices accompanied it, begging to be released.

There was nothing on the other side. Only blackness. A thin, hollow voice told him to enter, to join it there.

Slowly, with shaking legs and a fluttering stomach, Corman did as he was bid. He stepped past the gate, into the dark. The doors slid shut behind him, and all was that same emptiness.

Then the lights came on. Blue candles, sitting in wall sconces, illuminated a forum bordered by ivy-laden columns and marble statues of gods. Wine dark skies above crackled with thunder; lightning cut through them. In the center was a small end table made of driftwood. On it, a three-piece suit and a note. It instructed him to dress before walking out the front door. Sure enough, a scale model of the gate had appeared on the other side of the forum. It opened as soon as Corman finished tying his windsor knot.

Outside was a jagged, rocky outcropping above a vast, desolate wasteland of scorched earth and ash born of it. A blood red sun hung in the putrid yellow sky, seemingly bleeding. Standing next to him was a tall, gaunt figure dressed in a simple, undyed robe, a string of hemp rope tied at the waist. It turned to him with its death's head of a face.

"Hallo, Sohn," the shade said. "Willkommen in der Hölle."

PART III
CINRINITAS

XV

THE LONG SCOURING
OF THE SOUL

BEYOND THE OUTCROPPING WAS a wide, translucent green river that stretched for miles; it tapered off as it neared some sort of conical rock formation that stretched down into a vast pit of black nothingness. A strong gust whipped up thick clouds of dust that obscured whatever was inside of it. Overhead Corman heard the squawking of carrions despite not actually seeing any.

With a wave of its hand, the shade led him down a staircase carved into the rockface, step after step detailed with bas reliefs of the damned: skeletons, ghouls, monsters, all screaming.

At the foot of the stairs was a rickety old pier, made of both wood and bone. Standing inside a gondola made of the same materials was a giant, gaunt ghoul with a wrinkled, punched-in face; its facial features were not so much body parts as they were gaping holes. It stared down at them. The shade presented two silver coins, which the ghoul gently accepted with long, bony fingers. It motioned for them to step onto the boat, then ripped off a bone from its hip and dipped it into the water.

The river stunk of sulfur and rotting meat, like they were paddling through a septic tank. Dead things, pieces of mutilated bodies, bobbed up and down in the water. Maggot-like creatures crawled over them and burrowed inside. A waterfall awaited them at the river's end, which dropped off into that pit below. The only thing separating them from the abyss was a narrow plank bridge. As Corman and the shade disembarked, the clouds parted, revealing a massive city built upon rings, each layer shrinking the further down it went. All of the lower rings were shrouded in darkness.

Another wind, cold and sour, billowed around them; the shades' robes and Corman's left sleeve flapped about wildly. He grabbed the sleeve tightly between his fingers.

"Jetzt kreuzen wir. Folgen sie genau," the shade said, placing its hands on either side of the bridge's ropes.

Corman followed his example, albeit down a hand. The bridge rocked back and forth, and Corman stumbled forward. Another gust of wind howled by, and Corman slid toward the edge; he felt a hand grab him by the collar. "Vorsichtig, Junge," the shade said, setting him upright.

He peered over the ropes, straight into the abyss. Corman had never seen anything quite so pure in its darkness. Quite so devoid of light. Like some sort of black hole, only... Maybe this place was somewhere outside of spacetime? Or maybe this whole dimension existed within a sort of rip in the fabric, a pocket dimension. Then there was the possibility that maybe there wasn't any logical explanation behind it at all. That it existed beyond the limited scope of his understanding.

"Beeilen Sie sich jetzi," the shade called from solid ground. "Du darfst nicht zögern."

Hurrying along to join him, Corman realized he was speaking German. *The first language I knew*, he thought. *And the first one I forgot.*

There, the two stood on the precipice of the ringed city, with every building, step, and additional adornment carved into the rock walls as the ground beneath their feet went around and around, spiraling all the way down into the darkness. Though from there, Corman could just make out some shimmering lights amidst the nothingness. Though the path seemed to disappear here and there, it always returned to what must be its center. It had to exist outside of his reality; no physical structure could work like this. Not in the universe he knew.

"This is Hell, isn't it?" Corman asked the shade.

"Nein. Das gibt es nur in deinem Inneren," it replied, taking a step off the edge of the rim. Just as its foot fell, steps moved out from the rock to catch it, and descended smoothly from there. Corman followed. "Kommen Sie mit."

As soon as he touched the ground below, the dust clouds rolled in once more. This time, however, they came accompanied with thunder. A wind bellowed through the clouds, and then another wind joined it. They collided. A tornado arose from the clouds, hurling debris into the walls of the city. Bits of rock scratched Corman's face and clothes; he bled from the cheek as a light shone from within the cyclone. Floating in the eye of the storm was the scythe. But his eyes had welled up from the dust. Could just be what he wanted to see.

Upon blinking, he found that the scythe really was there. The shade stood perfectly still beside it. *It works on this world's logic,* he told himself. *Not mine.*

"Am I supposed to get it?" Corman shouted over the storm. The shade said nothing.

But if he was supposed to, then how? There was nothing that could be used as a foothold. Just empty space and a funnel of wind and dirt. Corman took the first tentative step out over the ground. His foot landed on something unseen. *Maybe I do, too.*

There were physical laws to dictate how he might proceed, only they weren't his. So be it. Corman took another step out into the nothing. Once again, he had not plummeted to his death. But the winds were growing stronger and angrier, and his feet began to slide backward; the shade remained motionless, rigid. *He's showing you how to do it.*

Slowly, carefully, he inched ahead. His overcoat twisted and flapped about wildly behind him, but Corman's footing was sure.

A large chunk of debris barreled toward him; it smashed into him, knocking him down and toward the edge of the invisible bridge. With only one arm, haggard breaths aching in his chest cavity, he managed to hold on while the rock smashed into a wall below and exploded into pebbles. Corman's arm burned from the strain of holding his entire body; he swung his legs up onto the underside of the bridge and pushed off. Though he gained a little ground, another violent wind hurled itself at him. With one more, immense push, he flopped his torso back onto the bridge, legs kicking against the edge. He rolled onto his back just as another rock flew over his nose.

Instead of getting back to his feet, Corman crawled to the tornado. This close up, he could hear the sounds of sharpening blades, a cyclone made of buzz saws. He got to his knees and raised a shaking hand up to the wall of the tornado; the wind ripped his arm from the socket. Corman, crying out in pain, stumbled forward, right inside the cyclone.

All around him, instead of walls of dirt and rock, he saw Lilith. He saw her everywhere. Dressed in a pantsuit, and stripped down, and fully naked and covered in blood; she murdered Edgar, murdered him. Above them all was just her face. Her pale, lily white face. Her beautiful blue eyes. Those rosy cheeks. The soft curvature of her jaw. Crimson lips curled into a smile.

Corman stood, his one arm hanging limply. He couldn't get the scythe like this. Not down two arms. No other choice. Positioning himself beside the tornado's buzz saw wall, he braced himself. Then he thrust his arm in. He screamed as his bones clicked back into place; before they got ripped off entirely, he pulled himself away. Though his shoulder felt as though it'd been lacerated to the bone, his arm was back in the right place.

With it, he reached out and grabbed the scythe. As soon as his fingers wrapped around the shaft, it began to melt into a sticky white liquid. Corman wrenched his hand back; the liquid pooled at his feet into a fleshy, bright red creature. Two rudimentary horns stuck out from its head; its three eyes blinked open. One of its arms was limp and unfinished. Cyclops grew from its bottom half, writhing and bubbling.

Corman felt vomit rising into his throat.

"Warum ekelt Sie Ihr eigener Körper an?" the shadow, who appeared beside him, asked. "Das ist dein Saman, der in die Dunkelheit verschüttet wurde."

The thing gurgled and bobbed for a bit, each one of its eyes looking directly into Corman's. Then it shrieked before melting into black sludge. It bubbled up and disappeared. The tornado slowed and swirled one last time before dissipating, revealing not the city but a dark corridor supported by the same columns as the forum. In between each column was a black, glistening wall that held a sconce full of bright green flame. Corman and the shade walked down it together.

After some time, they eventually came onto a wide open chamber, with a singular statue placed therein. It was of himself, dressed in the Lancelot regalia. His horns were fully grown, reaching over his head and crooking behind his ears. His left palm was raised and his right hand was pointed down. A Seal of Solomon was carved into his bare chest. Only instead of the usual sigils in between the points, there was only the symbol for God.

At the foot of the statue, Corman read its inscription. "Here lies the one He made through His infernal wisdom."

Corman stared into the statue's eyes. They were ugly, twisted things, like blocks of dull amethyst. A sinister look spread out over the face, pleased with itself. Its eyes snapped down to meet Corman's as the ground began to shift and crack open. Beneath the shimmering marble floor, magma churned and hissed, bathing the room in a bright orange hue. The statue broke free of its base to tower over him. Corman hurriedly glanced around for the shade. It appeared behind the statue, scythe in hand.

"Fangen, Junge," it said, throwing the scythe to him.

Catching it, he felt the weight of it immediately and nearly tipped over into the magma; he used the momentum to leap over the crack in the floor instead. The statue pounced at him and crashed into the floor, sending chips of marble flying as it swung its massive stone fists at him. Corman blocked them with the scythe

Undeterred, the creature punched again, and again, and again. Each time Corman deflected the attack, but with each block felt a greater strain. Tired of throwing fists, the statue tried a kick. Corman rolled out of the way, but got the other foot in the back. He smashed into the floor and slid over one of the cracks. The heat from the magma burned the right side of his face. Corman screamed; the statue grabbed him by the legs and dangled him in the air.

It started to laugh at him; the laughs boomed throughout the chamber, shaking the walls. Through the reverberations, Corman could make out cracks underneath its horns, where blood ran down its now-burned face.

Flinging himself up, Corman raised the scythe. On the downward arc, he rammed the blade into the statue's burns. A scratchy, raw scream erupted from the statue; it kicked and flailed, shaking Corman in its fist before finally dropping him to hold its stab wound. When Corman slammed into the marble, the statue grabbed its back and promptly lost its footing, taking a tumble right into the magma. It shrieked as it boiled to nothing, until there was no more life to cry out for.

A door appeared in the wall behind where the statue had been; the shade waited for him there. *I ought to kill him, too*, Corman thought as he walked through. The door slammed shut, leaving the two of them in complete darkness.

Lights blinked into existence, one by one. As they solidified, Corman realized they were the bulbs of streetlamps. Snow fell from a gray sky onto the streets in front of a dilapidated Hound's Tooth Tavern; the rest of the block was destroyed, but the Hound's Tooth still stood. But even it hadn't gotten out of whatever disaster befell it unscathed. The furniture was moldy, ripped apart, and gnawed on by rats. More vermin scurried across the shelves of broken bottles and sour liquor. The air was rank with the stench of decaying flesh, stale urine, and dried feces.

Standing behind the bone-dry bar was Rowan, half of her face missing flesh and her jaw hanging on by a thin strand of muscle.

She poured a black liquid into a glass decanter.

"In the back," the dead Rowan rasped. "In the back."

"Rowan?" he asked. "What happened to you?"

"In the back," she said again. "In the back."

Corman rounded the bar to where the storage room was supposed to be, only instead finding a door marked with an "X" in dried blood. The handle shook and rattled before opening on its own. Inside, hanging amongst intersecting yards of black rope, was a bloated corpse full of blisters, pustules, and festering wounds. Thin strands of yellowish-black hair hung limply from its puckered scalp. Its head lolled to one side, all seven of its eyes trained directly onto him. Its jaw abruptly cracked off from its skull, black ooze dripping onto itself.

"Bastard," it croaked. "Bastard, bastard."

"Mom?" Corman asked.

"Ungrateful! I do everything for you. I gave everything for you. What did you give *me* in return?" she shrieked. "Ungrateful little *bastard*!"

"Is this how I see you?" Corman murmured, taking hold of a bit of rope. It was corded, rough, and cut his finger as he touched it.

Retracting his bleeding hand, he saw that the rope was made of small hooks. "How did you get like this?"

"He traded himself for you!" Mom snapped. "I wanted him, not you!"

"Ed? Are you talking about Ed?"

"Bastard! Bastard!"

Corman looked over at the shade, who was leaning against the scythe. "Do you know what she means?"

"Nur zu gut, Junge," the shade said. "Aller Hass ist Säure. Die Seele korrodiert."

The ghost of his mother started to scream, twisting and turning in her ropes. Then the screaming was replaced with gurgling, and black ooze seeped from her throat. Black as pitch, it coated her body until it began to shake and froth, like the small creature before. She writhed, her eyes wide in agony, as she melted. Soon a tar-like puddle was all that remained of her.

A simple wooden door had appeared in her stead. The shade pointed with its skeletal finger. Corman opened it to reveal a dark forest full of twisted undergrowth. Stepping into it, he found the trees impossibly tall, their branches dozens of miles above him. There was no sky, no light, beyond the pale illuminations from candles in the tree trunks. Above each candle was a face, twisted and deformed, in the middle of an agonizing pain.

"Diese gewalttätigen Vergnügungen haben ein gewalttätiges Ende," the shade told him. "Was bleibt, ist Ihr Tod. Stirb, und werde wiedergeboren, Junge."

"So you're finally here," a cold, raspy voice said. Two trees leaned close together, their warped trunks forming faces.

"Sorry it took so long," the second tree croaked. "I had some other stuff to—"

The first tree's branches tickled the second's.

"Are you ready?"

"I— I don't know. I've been, you know, going over everything, and—"

"You haven't told anyone about this, have you?"

"No, no, that'd be—"

"You can't *trust* them."

"And I don't. I just think that maybe we need to, you know, reconsider the impact this is going to have on—"

"There's no *time* for that. We have to do this *now*. I can't wait any longer."

"You— What?"

The ground rumbled, and from the dirt branches burst forth, so lean and sharp that they could be fingers. All around him, these branches grew. Then they lashed forward, tightly squeezing his arms and legs like wooden manacles. Their bark dug into his skin, cut down to the bone. And then they started to return to the dirt.

The eyes of the first tree burst into flaming crimson petals. "I have *waited too long* for you to turn your back on me. I thought you loved me."

"I wouldn't— I'm not. I do. I'll do this. Please, don't think I don't. I do."

Earth began to swallow him. The sharp, jagged branches dragged him further and further down. He didn't care.

"What are you doing?" Corman cried out to the second tree. "What are you fucking *doing*? Stop it! Don't listen to her! *Think, you idiot! Think!*"

"I'll do it," the second tree said. "For you. For us. I love you, Lilith."

"She's using you, you stupid bastard! Don't do this! Please! Think!"

Then everything fell away, and he began to fall. Down, down, down, into an unknowable void, and he was once more nothing but a thought. How quickly, or how slowly, he fell he couldn't say. But he knew he was falling. Somehow. And somehow, he began to see color again.

The darkness gave way to a bright sheen of ice, and Corman found himself in his body again. Giant stalactites pointed down toward a frozen underground lake. There was nothing between him and shattering into pieces. Unless he crashed through and drowned. Or froze to death. But what did any of the particulars matter, anyway? He was already dead. Whatever pain reached him, it wasn't any more real than any of this.

So when he crashed through the ice and water enveloped him, he felt nothing. Not the cold, nor the shards that cut him up from head to toe. Until, that is, he realized he was running out of air. Flailing about underwater, the cold seeped into him and the ice sheet flipped upside down, and as he swam toward it, he saw light. The ice cracked, burst open, draining him out from underwater and back to the surface.

With frozen fingers, he clawed his way onto the frozen surface of the lake. Yet above him wasn't the ceiling of a cave, but the endless expanse of the sky. Stars dotted its deep purple hue. Mountains and their peaks poked into the smooth canvas, and Corman realized he was back in Antarctica.

A wind cut across his numbed face, and his horn stumps burned. There was nothing except snow, an endless sea of white. A pain stabbed him in his left arm. *I can't tell*, he thought, *is this mercy?* Broken, frozen, and soaked. Maybe this is where he actually died, where his soul or whatever qualified for consciousness now, finally passed on. Was that why he was here? To endure a final suffering? One last long scouring of the soul before it all faded away?

It was too unsatisfactory of an answer for him.

Move, he told himself. *You have to move.*

So he did. Despite the aching in his bones, the strain on his muscles, the adamant refusal of some part of his brain, he moved. Got up. With his weary and tired body, Corman moved from the ice onto hard packed snow, one laborious step after another. Like he'd been put back together wrong, everything felt out of place. Like his entire body was just one big ulcer. A headache brewed underneath his stumps. That throbbing pain stayed in his left arm.

Under the shadows of the mountains on the snow, he felt small. So very, very small. A gnat on a polar bear. How could he have ever thought he was anything but? This small, wretched creature that he was, dreaming of one day resting atop the world. *You deluded yourself. You deluded yourself into thinking...* Oh, what did it matter what he had thought? Nothing mattered now. Only that he walk.

Out some ways in the distance, that ugly gray compound came into view. Surrounded by barbed wire and electric fences, HADES stood its lonely vigil. His home for the past eight years , that ugly scar on the face of the frozen desert. For those eight years, he'd been just as he was now: a ghost, waiting to pass on. It was said that if the cold didn't get you, the loneliness would. Corman, having been born equipped to survive both of those things, had the unfortunate fate of staying alive.

His body could withstand subzero temperatures for weeks without succumbing to hypothermia, and should he ever get there, he had Edgar. The only thing that could've killed him was hidden away in the gun locker. But calling a HADES prisoner suicidal was redundant. There was on average ten inmates at a time, and within a year, seven of them would be dead. Most would try to make for a research station, despite the fact that only one was still in operation, and on the other side of the continent. What none of them knew, or chose to ignore, was that the researchers had orders straight from the UN to shoot on sight. Harboring a prisoner from HADES was likely to cause an international incident. It was better for everyone if they died.

So for those eight years, Corman never contemplated escape. No point in it. He would survive the cold, sure, but even he would die of starvation or dehydration. The only way out was to die, and the only way to die was painfully drawn out.

Instead, he cleaned the latrines and deiced the snowmobiles and knocked down icicles. Only other thing to do was to sit in his cell and patiently wait to lose his mind. There was a library, but an embarrassingly paltry one; there was a Finnish dictionary, faded nature magazines, manuals for snowmobile maintenance, and a copy of *A Two of Two Cities* with the back half ripped out. He read all of it five times before the end of the first month.

The food was worse. Inmates received two meals a day: gruel in the morning and gruel in the evening. It tasted like nothing and filled him up the same amount. The wardens ate pitifully small servings of salted cod or sardines. Rumor was the wardens were prisoners themselves that had gotten upgraded by proxy of being there long enough.

Yet here, in whatever plane of reality this was, Corman was the sole occupant. The metal corridors were just as barren and empty as they always had been, but without the humming and drumming of the pipes underneath the walls.

It didn't take long to reach his old room in cell block C. Unit 89 was identical to every other cell in his block, and to every other cell in the compound: four gray walls with a cot and a sink. Yet when he opened the door, it wasn't the claustrophobic concrete box, but a lavish foyer wallpapered with a cheery rose pattern and a grand chandelier hanging from the ceiling. Even the staircase, with its gilded gold inlay, was in the right place.

Just fifteen miles from Munich, the old family estate had stood proud for centuries, withstanding countless peasant uprisings, plague, and even the First World War. So when the SS scoured the Bavarian countryside for plunder, they naturally claimed it for their glorious fuhürer. It took some five hundred years, but in the end a couple of Panzer tanks did what the entire Prussian army couldn't. As Corman had heard it, nobody in the family lived past the first couple of days. During the final days of the war, the whole place had been burned to the ground to prevent German soldiers from retreating there. What remained had been a smoking pile of ash, the phoenix of a gas station arising from it.

But here was, walking through its warmly lit corridors, its muted reds, greens, and yellows that swam in seas of off-white. The furniture just as ornate and melodramatic as during his childhood. His feet led him through the wings, from the stately library to his grandmother's quarters, which took up at least three separate rooms. When he stepped inside the east drawing room, he saw a small boy with horns sitting on a chaise lounge, staring up at oil portraits of feathered abominations; his ancestors, in all their incomprehensible glory. His younger self wore a vest and heavy coat, and a fire was crackling in the nearby hearth. Corman walked over to the gilded window; the grounds were pure white against the dark green treeline some two miles away.

Must be here for the solstice, Corman thought. He sat down on the lounge beside the boy and looked up at the portraits with him.

"You know who they all are?" Corman asked.

"Great-great-great grandfather A'ymothaol," the boy said in a quiet voice; he had curled into himself, though not from the cold. "That's great-great-great grandmother Marlemcytha."

"I'm surprised you remember all that," he said. "I sure as hell don't."

"Mother says not to curse," the boy told him. "Did she change her mind?"

"No, but you decide to start anyway," Corman said. "Part of you getting to make your own decisions. Though I don't think you ever make a good one."

"Why not? Am I not smart?"

"Reckless is the better way to put it," Corman said.

"Is that how you lost our arm? Is Edgar okay?"

"No," Corman told him. "Edgar's dead."

"Asking how doesn't change that, does it?"

Corman sighed again. "No, it doesn't."

"You look tired," the boy noted. "And your head's all weird. Where'd your horns go?"

"You shave them down when you move to the States," Corman reported, clasping his hands in the space between his knees. "After you become a Knight."

"Where's the correlation?"

"They hate you," Corman murmured. "So you decide that it's better to blend in."

"Wait," the boy said, "why would I work for people who hate me?"

"Because *you* hate you."

"I don't follow."

Corman closed his eyes for a moment. *This really is Hell, isn't it?*

"Has Mom remarried yet?"

The boy tilted his head to the side. "Yeah. Do you not like Ruh-nah'alal?"

"No, I like him fine," Corman said. "It's everyone else I don't."

"What did they do to us?"

"Blamed us." Corman rubbed the fabric of his left sleeve between his fingers. "It gets to the point where you feel like everyone's against you, so... you decide they all must be right."

"Aunt Sophie says I shouldn't worry about what people think," the boy told him. "Even though I keep telling her nobody else likes me. Not even Mother."

"What does she say about that?"

"That Mother loves me very much." The boy waggled his feet. "So why doesn't it feel like she does?"

"Bad memories, I guess."

"Do I ever feel differently?"

Corman turned to face the boy for the first time. Those little features, so soft and innocent still, that eye in his left palm, it made him weep. He rested his face in his hand to keep the boy from seeing. But the tears came just the same, his eyes welling up far too quickly to prevent it. Corman cursed himself under his breath, but even his self-effacement drowned in his sorrow. How could he have done this to this boy? How could he have maimed him like this? *I cut off his arm, I mutilated him, day after day, year after year. I damn near killed him.*

"Quite the strange homecoming, isn't it?" a deep, authoritative voice said behind him. Corman turned swiftly to see a gigantic, burly man dressed in a tailored three-piece suit. Atop his head were two fine horns sticking straight up from his forehead. His legs were bent backward and ended in hooves. In his mouth, he piped on a cigar. The man extended a hand. "Satan Beelzebub the Seventh."

Corman wiped his eyes with the back of his hand, then shook the man's. "Satan?"

"It's the title I share with my forefathers," Satan told him. "Welcome to Kelzjah, C'ymaerlothyan."

So the man knew his real name. *A name only pronounceable in the tongue of angels.* "I thought this was Hell."

"Not in the sense most understand it, no," Satan said, putting a hand in his pocket. "What people see when they come here is what they hate and fear most. They torment themselves here because they tormented themselves back on Earth. You manifest all of these tortures yourself. I'm merely in charge of where they go from there."

"Where's that?" asked Corman.

"Until they come to peace with themselves, nowhere at all," Satan said. "When they do, also nowhere. But in the case of the second, it's a peaceful nowhere. The uglier their imaginations, the longer it takes. Those who have committed heinous sins, as it were, almost never leave. They usually fail to acknowledge the truth of the matter."

"And the reward is nonexistence?"

"Not quite. It's a, shall we say, realm of bliss. No misery, no pain. Nothing at all. Life is defined by its proximity to suffering. Which isn't to say life isn't without its benefits. But it is, as it were, a balancing act."

"Does everyone comes here?"

"On their way that other nowhere The ones who have an extended stay go further and further down," Satan said. "Down into that endless abyss you saw around that city. In most cases, however, this is where they take their leave. The cold has a way of waking you up."

"And Ed?" Corman asked. "He has to be here, right?"

"He's in the room next door," Satan said. "Shall we pay him a visit?"

Satan led him there, a wide open room with a grand piano, a magnificent fireplace, gilded cupboards, and a glass chandelier. Sitting in a rocking chair beside the fire was something Corman could hardly call a man; more like a skeleton with the skin still on. His eyes bulged out of their sockets. His white hair was so fine Corman could only see it when the light from the hearth moved in just the right way. He was missing his left hand.

"This is Johann Twardowski," Satan introduced him. "Your father."

"My—?" Corman grabbed his left sleeve. "You said it was Edgar."

Satan nodded. "I did, yes."

"Then—"

"Allow me to show you something, C'ymaerlothyan," Satan said, walking over to Johann. Placing a hand on the side of the man's head a cold blue light appeared in Satan's palm. He placed it into the fire, and it began to dance. "Look into the flames."

Corman knelt before the fire, his hand on the hearth, and leaned in to see a small cottage in the middle of a thunderstorm. Then something pulled at his brain, like it was trying to rip it from inside his skull. His entire body burned up, and he squeezed his eyes shut. When he opened them, he was running. Or, more accurately, he was in the body of someone who was.

He burst through the door, thunder behind him, absolutely soaked. Standing in the middle of the kitchen was a beautiful blonde woman holding a baby in swaddling clothes. She looked to him with soft brown eyes. *Mom?*

"Where have you been? I was getting worried."

"Gretchen, gather your things," he told her. "We have to go."

"Go? Go where?"

"I'll explain everything once we're safe," he said. "But for now you have to trust me. Get Corman ready."

"Safe? Where could we possibly be safer? Napoleon hasn't come back, has he?"

"Gather your things," he repeated, rummaging through cabinets. The only things he took was glassware. Rushing down a narrow hallway, he hooked a left into what looked to be a laboratory. There, he gathered together scientific equipment and books into a rucksack.

"I need to know what's happening, Johann," Mom called out from the kitchen.

"Just pack your things," he instructed.

"I need to know *why* I'm packing," she protested. "For Corman's sake."

"Gretchen," he said as he returned to the kitchen, "*please*."

There was another crash of thunder; Johann jumped.

"You've been nothing but nerves lately," Mom noted. "Tell me what's going on. You've been in and out for months now, and—"

"Gather your things. *Now*," he demanded. "We haven't much time."

"Tell me *why*, and I *will*."

"Damn it, woman!" Johann spat, throwing down a large book onto the kitchen table. "If you did as I asked, you'd have your explanation by now."

Mom pursed her lips; she laid Corman in his crib. "Fine. But I expect you to tell me *everything* when I'm finished."

"Yes, yes, just *hurry*."

A wind beat against the cottage as the thunder roared. A flash of lightning filled the room, and the door burst open once again. Rain drove past the dark figure standing in the doorway. It stepped inside; instead of a foot, it was a goat's hoof. The hooves gave way to a goat's lower body, which in turn became the naked torso of a man. A cloak flapped behind it, alongside its tail. Two large horns extended from its forehead.

Satan?

"Johann Twardowski," the figure boomed alongside a clap of thunder, "I have come to collect my payment."

"No, please, I—" Johann yelped as the figure shoved him aside. It heading straight for the crib. Mom threw herself in front of it.

"You stay away from my son," she told it.

The figure turned and glowered at Johann. "You didn't tell her."

"How— you can't imagine— it was—"

Mom, body pressed against the crib, began to shake. "*What* didn't you tell me?"

The figure stood before Mom, towering over her. He placed once clawed hand on her shoulder and lifted her into the air without so much as bending his fingers. Mom dug her own fingers under them in a vain attempt to pry herself loose. She kicked at the figure's stomach in vain. "Leave him be!"

"The child is mine by rights," the figure said, bending over the crib to scoop him up.

"Don't you dare *touch* him!" Mom screamed, beating on the figure's arm. This didn't bother the figure; it held Corman in one hand and shook her off with the other. Mom started to cry. "Don't you *touch* him! Johann, please! What is *going on*?"

"Go on, then, Johann," the figure said. "Tell your wife."

"I— I— Gretchen, you have to—"

"The child's soul belongs to me," the figure told her. "In exchange for boundless knowledge, your husband gave me the child's soul."

"You— You... *bastard*," Mom screamed through tears and snot. "You *gave away our boy*? *You sold my baby*?"

"I thought— I thought since you were an angel, that—" Johann stammered.

"No living human soul is exempt from a devil's contract," the figure said. "Your husband knew that when he signed for the entropy clause."

"But he's only *half-human*," Johann protested.

"Does that not make him human, fool?" the figure barked.

Mom looked up at the wall beside the door. Hanging from a chain was a scythe. Unbeknownst to the figure, she crawled toward it.

"You shall now reap what you have sown, Twardowski," the figure told him.

"So will you," Mom said, slicing the figure's head off with the scythe's blade. Its head rolled off its shoulders and cracked against the floor like a melon. She grabbed Corman from the figure's arms and clutched him to her chest. "Oh, my sweet. My sweet."

"He'll come back to life," Johann said. "Even if we run now, we won't—"

"Then *fix this*," Mom spat. "Save his life."

"There's no possible—"

"Use that knowledge you sold your son for," Mom snarled. "*Do something.*"

Johann rose to his feet. "There's no point in trying. He's—"

"I don't give a damn *what* he is," Mom snapped. "Or what he can do. You're saving my son's life."

"Your son—?"

"*Save him*, Johann."

His father looked down at his hand, made a fist. "There... I don't know if it'll work, but there *might* be a way. I can— I can try to create a homunculus and attach it to Corman. He can't take him if he houses a part of another's soul."

"Then *do* it."

"We'll have sever his hand and replace it with mine."

"Will it save him?"

"Yes, Maybe. I—"

"*Then do it.*"

Johann retrieved his equipment from the rucksack and began to work. For an hour, he mixed, diluted, and purified chemicals. At the end, he had a green, bubbling liquid in a flask. He held his left hand over the flask and a knife to his wrist. He dug into his flesh. Blood spurted out of him as he cut, bit his tongue to muffle his screams. Finally, he sliced through the bone and his hand splashed into the mixture below. Howling, Johann collapsed to the floor, grasping his bleeding stump. The hand, meanwhile, began to move inside the flask.

"Sever his hand," Johann instructed Mom. "Dip his wrist into the flask. The hand will... will attached itself. I'm going into... into shock. I don't have..."

Mom laid Corman on the table and held the knife over his tiny hand. Tears fell from her cheeks. "It'll be over soon, little one. I promise."   Closing her eyes, she cut her baby's hand off. Corman wailed, kicking his feet. As he wailed, Mom lifted him up, whispering soothing affirmations, and submerged his left arm down into the flask. The chemicals bubbled and popped, sizzled and hissed, and Corman shrieked. Then, all at once, he calmed down just as the chemicals did. Mom lifted him up again, and there on his wrist was his father's hand, now the exact proportion of an infant's. An eye opened up in the palm and looked around.

"Hello," it said.

Mom looked down at Johann.

"It's a new being," he explained. "One that... will take care of him. That's... all he wants. That's the entire point of... he has no other purpose."

"No," Mom said, holding the hand tenderly. "He will be more than that. More than *you*."

The decapitated head began to shiver. Mom held Corman tightly as it rolled back to its body; the figure picked it up and screwed it back on. It cracked its neck left and then right, and rolled its shoulders.

It turned toward Mom and reached for Corman; its hand was still outstretched when its eyes widened.

"A homunculus," it said quietly. Then, to the parents, "His soul is still forfeit."

"But he has his father's—" Mom began.

"Should he lose his hand, their souls will be severed once more, and ownership of his soul reverts to me. Should I die before then, then ownership passes to my son." It stared down at Johann. "And *you*, Twardowski, shall live precisely until then. You will age, but you will not die. Your body will fail you, but you will not perish. You will wish for death, but it will not come. As the original owner of that hand, you cannot cut it off again to save yourself. His life and yours are now linked until death."

The figure then promptly walked out the door and disappeared as thunder rolled.

Mom scowled once more at her husband. "And you will live all that time alone. You will *never* see your son again, nor me."

"Gretchen, you have to—"

"He is no longer your son," Mom said. "And I am no longer your wife. Now get out."

"Gretchen, please. I—"

"Get. *Out.*"

"I— I— I'm sorry."

"Get out!" Mom shrieked; her voice echoed through an abrupt cut to black.

Corman threw his head back and wound up on the floor. *I— He— Ed...* Propping himself on his elbow, he looked up at Satan, who was leaning against the hearth, smoking his cigar.

"Your father, by signing a devil's contract as a human, willingly accepted the terms of the standard entropy clause. And we have to have that, because, well, you know how humans are. Fickle, indecisive, unsure of what they want until they don't have it anymore. So should a human try to nullify any of the conditions set forth by the contract, they automatically forfeit their soul. The clause acts a safeguard. Should they violate it, per the terms of the agreement, everything they've gained likewise becomes forfeit. Now, there *are* alternatives to this, namely, transferring the debt over to a blood relation. Naturally, it fell to you, his firstborn and only remaining family by blood."

Naturally.

"In short, if you're found guilty of breach of contract, you lose everything and gain nothing. Then you're sent here, where your soul withers for eternity. You remain in a constant state of death, never fully ceasing to be. That is what became of your father. Only, since he was tied directly to you, a living being, he felt the physical effects of constantly dying as well. Until, that is, your death. I gave him temporary respite to guide you here, whereupon he reverted back to his... original state."

Corman crouched beside the skeleton in the rocking chair. "What happens now?"

"My father, the Satan your father made his deal with, passed only a few years ago," Satan continued, "and I gained possession of all his belongings, your soul included. I am, however, willing to relinquish ownership and return it to you should you grant me a favor."

"What sort of favor?"

Satan placed a hand on his shoulder. "I want you to bring my daughter home."

"Daughter?" Corman frowned. "You want me to bring Lilith here?"

"Find her, and bring her back to Kelzjah for sentencing," Satan told him. "She will stand trial here, before a jury of her peers. She must answer for her crimes, but in the proper way."

"How do I do it?"

"Kill her physical body," Satan said. "That will send her soul back to me. Then you will be free once more. Your soul will finally be your own."

Corman studied his father's skin-tight face, felt his empty sleeve. "All right."

"Before I have the contract made up," Satan said, "what would you have me do with your father?"

"What?"

"His fate is bound to you. As I see it, it should be decided by you. Either he stays here, bound this perpetual suffering, or you can release his soul into the void, where he will cease to be. Once your soul is yours again, whatever you decide will take effect."

Corman looked into his father's eyes. They were nothing more than glass spheres now, no life or light behind them. *A man enslaved to its instincts*, he thought. *Who lost everything and gained nothing.* What was there to say to a man who sold his only child? What was there to be said at all? He stood up and walked away without looking back. In the doorway, he stopped for a moment.

"Set him loose."

"Are you sure?"

"I don't care to see anyone else suffer for my sake," Corman said. "Set him free."

In the end, the contract in question came out to two hundred and sixty pages. Satan went over the details with him in the study that once belonged to grandmother G'awathini. Using ink made of his own blood, Corman initialed and signed until they came to page two hundred. There, written out as a bold letterhead, was the entropy clause.

"An unfortunate necessity," Satan said. "A nephilim you might be, you're still human."

"Yeah," Corman said, signing his name at the bottom of the page. "Unfortunate."

After the final signature was written out, Satan rolled the document up and stuck it in a pneumatic tube on the side of the desk, where it was sucked up and sent away. "Modern technology has made this process a bit less arduous than it was in the time of our fathers."

"You're still about fifty years behind," Corman said.

"Time moves slower here," Satan conceded, shrugging. The canister returned to the desk, and Satan unfolded it, nodding approvingly. "It's just been officially notarized. You're clear to return to Earth."

"Maybe not *fifty* years, then," Corman said.

Satan led him out onto the estate grounds, the only sound between them the crunching of their feet in the snow. Across the vast expanse of dull gray and white, Corman smelled a bonfire.

"That's sulfur and brimstone," Satan explained. "Further down, even further from here, the experience becomes increasingly more unpleasant."

"The torment is exponential," Corman said.

"Quite so." He removed a Luger pistol from under his coat. "The way out is like the way in, I'm afraid."

Corman gazed at the gun, nodded. It might as well be.

"Before I go," he said, turning his back to him, "what happened to Ed?"

"He returned to your father," Satan said. "Their soul is one again."

So that's that. "Does it hurt?"

"Only as much as you think you deserve," Satan said.

Like a bitch then, Corman thought as the bullet entered his brain.

PART IV
RUBEDO

XVI

ANASTASIS

H E AWOKE IN DARKNESS. A suffocating, plastic darkness. Icy shrapnel dispersed through his chest as his lungs took in oxygen again. His first breaths were ragged, bloody things; his throat was chafed raw. Every part of him pulsated with pain. His blood was flowing, but as if in the wrong direction. He flexed his hand muscles.

"Ed, I need..." The phantom of his left arm prickled. "I need you back."

But he was gone. *Because of you.* Because of his father. His wretched, pathetic father. A man who sold his only child. *A goddamn—*

Corman squeezed his eyes shut and took a few deep breaths, despite the pain. No. Now was not the time to fly off the handle. Only way out of this mess, he knew, was to take things one at a time. First and foremost, he needed to get out of this bag.

There was nothing in his pockets. Nothing to help him... *They took it.* He sighed, tried to hold back tears. Edgar had died so he could get that damn drive. And now *they* had it. That familiar rage bubbled under his ribs and reverberated down to his fist. A burning sensation burst from his horn stumps. Corman twisted and turned, the pain overcoming him again. *No, no, no. Think. You need to think, goddamn it.*

He prodded the tip of his horn. Still dull, but if he applied enough force to the plastic, maybe he had his way out. Ramming his horns through the top of the bag, he punctured two holes through it and pulled it back, plastic flakes snowing onto his shoulders. He stuck a hand out and pulled the zipper down, releasing himself from his artificial womb.

Studying himself under the dim lights of the autopsy room, Corman realized he wasn't even naked. *I wasn't dead for very long*, he deduced. Though his body probably already went through every stage up until livor mortis, the fact that he hadn't putrefied was an encouraging sign. At least, his abdomen didn't feel swollen. *My larynx still works, too.* Decomposition hadn't set in. If that was the case, then he'd only been dead for, at most, two days.

It was time to get the blood flowing. He sat up straight and stretched his sides, his arm, and his legs; they'd also taken his socks and boots. Sliding off the table proved more laborious than he anticipated, and he nearly collapsed as he touched the floor. The linoleum was freezing, and as he retracted his foot, his twisted sense of balance sent him careening into the walls. *One step at a time.* Climbing up using the mortuary lockers, he held position until the feeling returned to his legs. The pins-and-needles erupted into an uncomfortable explosion, and he had to bite his tongue to prevent himself from yowling.

Outside the glass walls of the autopsy room, he was surprised to find it wasn't guarded. *Maybe upstairs*, he thought as he crept up the steps. But as he poked his head out over the railing, the whole building was in the dark, save for the red glow of the exit signs. Completely empty. *Then again, who'd go stealing my body?* Mom?

The thought of her gave him pause. He needed to make things right with her, as soon as he could. But how was he supposed to atone for so many years of accumulated resentment? *Think of an apology later.* He might not even get out of here in the first place. Not without shoes, not in this weather. He'd have to find somewhere to lay low for the night. There was only one office whose occupant wouldn't immediately turn him in. *Wishful thinking.*

Nathan's office was the very end of the northwestern corridor, forcing Corman to round the front desk and brush against the bone chilling cold of the outside. *I wouldn't last thirty seconds.*

Hanging from the door was a plain, dull plaque proclaiming him the Mortuary Liaison of the Federal Knight Bureau, Minneapolis Chapter. The doorknob didn't move. So Corman punched the window in. Blood ran down his hand from where the glass shards stabbed him. Leaning over the shards still in the window frame, he unlocked it.

A pathetically small office, Corman wouldn't have been surprised if it was originally a supply closet. A low, narrow room, it had only enough space for a single filing cabinet and a desk. A mop stood inside of a bucket by the door. *Stuck the poor guy in storage*, Corman thought as he shut the door. Sitting at the desk, he examined his injured arm. *Can't keep doing this*, he thought sadly. *No one's here to save you anymore.* He leaned back in the chair and stared at the ceiling fan. *No miracle cures, no twenty-four hour stitches, no tissue repair.* He sucked on his teeth. *And no fucking common sense.*

So where did that leave him?

You just came back from the dead. Everyone still thinks you are. A pain shot up his left side, and he clutched his stump. *You lost Ed. You lost the only friend you ever had.* Why did Mom keep it from him? Did she tell Edgar? Did Edgar *know*?

No. He shook his head. *It'll have to wait until morning.* So would sleep. As soon as they discovered his sudden reversal of mortality, they'd turn around to undo it. Staying here, even if it was just until morning, wasn't a viable option. *The hearses should be all here*, he thought. *So must the keys.* They had to be in some sort of shared locker.

The only place that could be was in the break room. It was likewise locked. He looked at his mutilated arm and sighed. *I'm gonna be missing both hands by the time this is over*, he lamented as he punched in the glass.

A dreary, undecorated room with simple gray cabinets and a plastic table in the middle, it was as depressing as Nathan's office. Underneath the CRT television hung up in the southwest corner was a metal box attached to the wall. It required a passcode to bypass the lock, and after his third failed attempt, it warned against a possible lockout until an administrator could fix the problem.

Footsteps scuffled against the tile floor outside.

"What the hell...?" Nathan wondered aloud. Before Corman could scurry away, the door swung open, and the two stared at each other in the darkness; Nathan flipped the lightswitch on.

"You know the passcode for this thing?" Corman asked, pointing to the box.

Nathan jumped, slamming his knee into the table. Staring wide-eyed at Corman, he absently rubbed his leg, most likely trying to fathom what the fuck he was looking at, how he was talking to a corpse. How said corpse was talking at all.

"How the ever loving *fuck* are you not *dead*?" Nathan blurted.

"I made a deal with the devil," Corman told him. "He's real, by the way."

"You defy the laws of *nature* and the only thing you have to say is some stupid fucking joke?" Nathan held his head in his hands. "What the fuck is happening right now?"

"I'm serious about the devil," Corman said. "I'm here on assignment."

"How?" Nathan demanded. "How are you *actually* alive? Were you never dead?"

His resurrection carried three serious implications, and Corman wasn't entirely sure Nathan was in the right place to learn about all of it.

"No, I definitely died," Corman answered. "I guess to simplify all of it... Souls are real, the devil is real, and a version of Hell exists."

"And you just... *happened* to come back to life."

"Not really. There's plenty of expository details to it."

"Jesus fucking Christ," Nathan mumbled, slumping into one of the chairs. "It's too goddamn early for this shit."

Corman joined him, on the other side of the table. "It's all connected to a long, painful family history that doesn't warrant explanation right now."

Nathan ran a hand down his face. "Of course. Your whole existence never made sense to me. Why should it start now?"

"Speaking of, I need to stay dead to the world for the moment," Corman said. "Think you could keep this between us?"

"Since when do *you* ask people for things?" Nathan asked, folding his arms. "Not feeling up to being a total cunt today?"

"Not exactly," Corman said. "I need a key to one of the hearses."

"Hold it," Nathan said. "This... biologically impossible feat aside, you were in Knight custody when you died. You'll have to stand trial now. And *I'm* not going to be the one to take that away from King."

"You think custody extends to the posthumous?"

"I don't know *what* to think," Nathan murmured. "But I *do* know I'm not getting any more involved with this than I already am. I mean, I'm talking to a *corpse* right now. This shit's not natural."

"Neither is King's grip on your balls," Corman told him.

Nathan scowled. "You're not making a case for yourself."

"Would it make a difference if I did?"

"No, I don't think it would." Nathan stared at the tabletop, hands balled into fists. "You want to know what your problem is, Ryan? Why nobody in the department ever liked you?"

"Not really," Corman said.

"Ever since you waltzed into that fucking office, from day fucking *one*, you thought you were better than everyone else. You can talk a big game about nobility and honor, and doing the right thing until your throat fucking bleeds, but at the end of the day, you were nothing but a gaping asshole.

"Every time you killed a chimaera, or smoked out a coven, or did whatever, you would come back, the self-satisfied dickhead you were, and we could all tell how *superior* you felt. It was in your walk, you know. How you carried yourself, like you were God's gift to Earth. And *oh* were you fucking *saintly*. Never hurt a cambion, did you? Never so much as hit a civilian, right? You were hot shit, all right. Weren't you? But *everyone* knew you were full of it. And you knew we knew. And you *hated* us for it. Because *who* could possibly have the balls to criticize the great *Corman Ryan*? We were nothing but insects to you. Just *things* to step on."

Corman gave him an incredulous look. "You done?"

"You aren't special, Ryan. You never were. You're a pathetic, narcissistic *jackass*."

"Yeah, I got it," Corman said.

"And just when we thought we were rid of your for good, you come strolling back on in like nothing even happened."

"*I got it.*"

"Just so you could make everyone's lives hell *again*—"

Corman slapped him across the face; Nathan glowered at him.

"I *know*," he said. "I *know* I was an asshole."

Nathan frowned. "What?"

"I was an asshole," Corman barked. "All right? I was a big swinging dick. I had a martyr *and* a God complex. So will you *shut up*?"

"Jesus, all right, all right," Nathan said.

"What I said earlier is true," Corman told him. "The devil brought me back to life so I could kill Lilith. She's back, and she's been working with some of the Knights for God knows how—"

"I know," Nathan said. "Everyone does. She has full control of them."

"In a *day*?"

"Two, actually," Nathan said, consulting his watch. "Technically three now. The whole city's under martial law."

"And King?"

"Who do you think gave her the keys?"

"Of fucking course." Corman strummed his fingers on the table. "I still need to borrow a hearse."

"You want to add *another* charge to your record?"

"Why do you think I would give a shit?" Corman asked. "This? All of this? It goes beyond me. Beyond me trying to fix my own fuck-ups. This is about stopping more innocents from getting butchered. I'll do what I have to."

"In service of killing her."

"It's in my contract."

Nathan screwed his face up. "You didn't *really* make a deal with the devil, did you?"

"No, I just wished *really* hard, and the blue fairy made into a real boy," Corman said, standing up. "Yeah, I did. If you're gonna help, hurry up and do it. I'm on a tight schedule."

Nathan entered in the passcode to the locker, took out one of the keys. He looked over at Corman for a moment, then held out his hand.

"If anyone asks, you coerced me."

Corman snatched the keys up. "Yeah, yeah, and I put a gun to your head, too."

His bare feet slapped against the asphalt of the parking lot, each step puncturing his nerves with freezer burn. An icy chill blasted out of the vents as he switched on the ignition. *I gotta get out of this fucking state.*

Driving with one arm proved troublesome. He couldn't use the turn signal and the hearse was an unwieldy motherfucker. On his way over, he ran over more than a few curbs and his turns weren't exactly clean.

Only when he pulled out in front of Mom's apartment building did the heat finally kick in. Grumbling, Corman unbuckled his seatbelt and prepared to step out into the cold again. *Fuck fuck fuck fuck*, he thought as he raced into the lobby. Took more than a few tries to get the elevator gate shut, all the while the stinging cold of the metal burned his fingers.

What do I tell you about, first? he wondered as the car shuddered its way up. *Dad? What you did for me? Ed?* He sighed, rested a fist against the wall. *Ed's gone, Mom. He's fucking gone and I couldn't save him. I couldn't pay him back. I couldn't save him. I fucked up, Mom. I fucked up. What do I do?*

It was deathly quiet in the hallway. No music, no light, no evidence to show someone lived there. Still, he knocked on the door. No answer, either. He opened the door, his mother staring out the window as the moonlight bathed the apartment in a grim off white. Her wings hung limply past her rings, which spun slowly. No flame was lit.

"Hey, Mom," he said, still standing in the doorway. All seven wings spun around at once, knocking him off his feet. "I'm not a ghost, in case you were wondering."

She flew over to him, all ninety-eight eyes open wide, and held him in a rough, feathery embrace. Though the metal of her rings was cold to the touch, he could feel it beginning to warm.

"You're dead," she said quietly. "You're *dead*."

"Was," he corrected her.

"How did—? Corman, how are you—?"

"I met Dad," he said.

All of her eyes looked into his. "Your... You weren't... Corman, I—"

"It's okay. Mom, it's okay."

Yet all ninety-eight eyes cried; steam rose from her rings the tears fell. "I never wanted you— You must think I'm a terrible mother."

Corman took hold of a wing. "No, Mom. I don't."

"I *butchered* you. Cut your hand off. I *failed* you. I let... I let that *bastard*—"

"You saved me, Mom," he told her. "That's the long and short of it."

"How could I have let that happen to you? My boy? My only boy?"

"It wasn't your fault," Corman said quietly. "Plus, I... I never would've gotten Ed if you hadn't."

"The poor dear," Mom whispered.

"Did he ever know?"

She shook her head. "I didn't want either of you to... He's back with your father?"

"Yeah."

"Oh, God," Mom cried.

"Everything you did... that you've done, I mean, you did because you were scared," Corman said. "I never understood that. I never could have."

"I should've told you. I'm so sorry, Corman."

"Maybe, maybe not," he said, shrugging. "That's not for me to say. But I'm sorry, too. You did all that for me, and you wound up with the world's shittiest kid."

"You aren't," Mom protested.

"Six months," he said. "I was back six months and I didn't even try talking to you. I didn't listen. Not to you, not to Ed, not to Rowan... Not to anybody. Well, I listened to myself. And all I had were bad ideas and a death wish. So. I'm sorry, Mom. I was an asshole."

"You're my son, Corman," Mom said. "You never have to explain yourself to me. I know."

"Maybe, maybe not," he said.

"But how did you come back? Even within the terms of the contract..."

"I signed one myself," Corman told her; the eyes began to well up again. "To take my soul back."

"Satan offered you your soul?"

"There's a new one now," Corman explained. "Pretty nice guy, actually."

"How do you know he didn't deceive you?"

"I read the whole thing. I bring him Lilith, and he gives me my soul back." Corman held up his hands as her bristling wings stretched out.

"He sent you here as his personal bounty hunter?" she yelped.

"Well, he couldn't just give up a soul for nothing," Corman said. "That's strictly against his office's code of conduct. Article one, section nineteen, subsection a. A soul cannot be released without proper reimbursement."

"You really read it," Mom said, sniffling.

"It was less tedious than the Knight handbook, actually. Shorter, too."

"But she's *dangerous*, Corman. She— she was the one who—"

"And I was the one who brought myself back." He went into the kitchen and put a kettle on. As he rifled through the cupboards, he said, "She killed Ed, Mom. No doubt killed all those women. I have to make sure she sees justice."

"And this contract, it outlines punitive measures?"

"She'll be put on trial before a jury of her peers," Corman said. "What she's planning, it ruins how things work down there, too."

"So Satan was working for his own best interests," Mom muttered.

"Everyone does, Mom." He pulled out the tea set. "Even me going after the wiemca, that was self-serving. Rowan spelled it out for me, even though I wasn't exactly receptive to the idea at the time. I wanted everyone to forgive me. To forget. Put what I did behind them. But that won't happen. Can't. I know how humans are. But... I was acting like Dad. A slave to my instincts, losing everything over and over again to gain nothing. I thought I didn't have a people, so I needed everyone to accept me. 'Course, now I know I don't need that. I got you and Rowan. I don't need anyone else to accept what I am."

"And now?"

The kettle whistled. "Now I rectify those mistakes. I just... don't know how." He turned to her. "What do I do, Mom?"

"First, we have our tea," Mom said, floating over to the stairs. "Then we go see your sister. She'll have a few ideas."

XVII
SKÅL, CAMBIONS

T HOUGH HE'D BEEN THERE hundreds of times, he'd never seen the Hound's Tooth so full as he did that night. Cambions traveled discreetly for the most part, taking back streets and sidestepping humans, on their way anywhere. They didn't like being around each other or around humans for the most part. Hanging above their horns were the inevitable beatings, the being left for dead, the hanging onto life by a thread. Traveling together wasn't safe. Every cambion knew it; the more of them there were, the worse it got for everyone. Corman had seen it play out, had to break it up plenty of times. Their terrified, bloody faces would stare at him in his armor, already anticipating further terror. *I'm not them,* he wanted to tell them. *I wouldn't do that.*

Putting on the armor made him them, though. Going into Camelot every morning meant that he would. It would never matter to them who he was. That they were kin. All that mattered was who he was with, what he wore. How had he never seen that before? How had that never crossed his mind? All that time he fought to stand apart from the rest of them, and all it did was cement him as something worse. One of them, but one of them who lied. To himself, to the cambions, to the world. He touched a fingertip to the horns. *That was all I had to do.*

He had them back, now. They were still just nubs, only an inch or two tall, but they were the longest they'd been in years. *It doesn't matter who knows what I am anymore.*

The truly bizarre thing about the Hound's Tooth that night was not that it was at maximum capacity; it was that for the first time in its history, it had humans inside of it. Humans from nearly every gang in the city. Even the ones that fucking despised each other. Somehow, Rowan had pulled it off. On the phone with Mom, she promised she would gather the strangest menagerie the tavern had ever seen.

"Better turnout than I thought," Corman said, back to the liquor shelves and beer in his hand. "Figured everyone would be hiding under their beds."

"They were," Rowan told him, "until they heard you pushed the boulder out of the way. Your pentecost begins now."

"These are my disciples?"

They were a sorry sight; racked with nerves, all of the folks she managed to congregate shared looks of paranoia and mistrust. Moreso the humans, but thus far none of them had lashed out. *Give it five minutes*, he thought.

Rowan shrugged, then got up onto the bar.

"Dear, are you sure that's sanitary?" Mom asked.

"It's called soap, mother," Rowan replied, grabbing a bottle of vodka and pouring out a shot.

"But will soap get those scuff marks off of the maghony?" Mom murmured as Rowan called for the attention for all those present.

"Hello, hi, thank you all for coming," she said. "I appreciate you all braving the streets to show your support for my dear big brother. In case you were wondering if he was truly dead, well, here he is in the flesh. The world's a strange place, and the world outside of ours stranger still.

"For those of you who don't know, a former Knight commander named Lilith Valentine has taken control of the Minneapolis chapter, and with it, the city itself. You've all been loyal patrons of mine, or otherwise shown yourselves to be friends to my family. In return, I ask only one thing. Tell your loved ones, your family and friends, to get the hell out of the city if you can. Otherwise, tell them all to hunker down for the next few days, and to stay away from Loring Park."

"What's happening?" a woman blurted. "I don't understand."

This was met by a chorus of agreement; nobody else to understood any of it, either.

"How is he here if he died?"

"I saw his body on the news! That can't be him."

"Who's Lilith?"

"What's going to happen at Loring Park?"

"Please, just tell us what's going on!"

Rowan glance down at him, shrugged. *Whether or not they accept it as truth is out of my hands*, he thought as he finished his beer. Then he hopped on top of the bar.

"Lilith has the Holy Grail," he told them. "Only way to make it work is to sacrifice enough people's souls. To make herself immortal, she has turn pretty much everyone else into wights. Which are, like, uh, zombies." This in turn was met with another outroar.

"The Holy Grail? How does she have *that*?"

"What do you mean, zombies?"

"She's gonna kill us?"

"I still don't know how the hell Lilith is!"

"All right, all right, just calm down," Rowan yelled over the clamor. "My brother will take care of everything. All you folks have to do is *stay away* from Loring Park and tell all your loved ones to do the same. That's *it*."

"But what if she finds us anyway?"

"That won't happen," Rowan assured them. "The park is going to be the place she tries to, uh, tries to..."

"Drink from the Grail," Corman finished. "I'm not going to get into the specifics, but as long as you stay *away* from the park, you'll be fine."

"And *you're* gonna be the one to stop her?" someone demanded. "*You*? You were the Knights' lapdog! You *worked* with her!"

All eyes silently fell onto him.

"I did, yeah," Corman admitted. They started yelling again before he could get another word in. He crossed his arms and waited. *Christ, and I'm putting my life on the line for these people?* When the excitement finally died down, he cleared his throat. "Are we done?"

Seemed like they were.

"Yes, I worked with her. Eight years ago. She almost got me to open a portal to Hell. But I didn't. I refused. She almost killed me for it. And a couple days ago, I refused to help her again, and that time she actually *did* kill me. To make a long story short, I have no love for this woman. The Knights chewed me up and spat me out when they found out, then sent me to die at HADES. I have no love for them, either. Oh, and—" He held out his stump, let his sleeve hang from it. "She cut off my arm. That good enough for you?"

"So how are you alive?" someone called out.

"Call it a miracle if you want," he said. "Call it a blessing from God, or Allah, or Adonai. Reincarnation. I don't care. The particulars don't matter. I'm alive, and I'm here to stop Lilith. That's it. Whatever you think of me doesn't matter, either. Just protect your families. Protect yourselves. Stay out of Loring Park until you get word that Lilith is dead. And for the love of God, warn people about it. Don't trust the Knights, or the cops. Trust each other."

"Trust *you*?" someone barked.

"Trust the fact that I didn't have to tell you any of this," Corman growled. "Trust the fact that I'm a mooncalf out for blood. Trust the fact that this woman killed my brother."

He closed his eyes and took a deep breath.

"Trust my sister. My mother. They're good people. So was my brother. I know you all have people like that. For their sake, tell them what I'm telling you. Stay out of Loring."

This left a heavy silence.

Rowan took up the torch. "My brother has fought and bled and *died* for the lives of everyone in this city, even when every person who knew his face wanted him dead. He's a good man. Unpleasant and cantankerous as he may be, he's dedicated his life to protecting the weak and defenseless from chimaeras, and the wiemca, and everything else we can't fight against for ourselves. He's made mistakes, but he's doing what he can to help now."

A cambion with a half-formed eye on his temple raised his glass. "Corman Ryan!"

A few of his fellow cambions did the same. "Corman Ryan!"

Soon, every cambion in the bar was toasting him, stomping their feet and chanting, "Ryan! Ryan! Ryan!"

The humans stayed put, though some quietly rose their glasses to him.

"Skål, cambions!" Rowan cheered, to the delight and applause of the cambions. Behind him, he caught Mom smiling.

"World's shittiest kid, huh?"

"So she was the one who finished it?" Rowan asked. Most of their gathered supporters had departed to spread the news. Some remained, including, strangely, some of the humans.

"Yeah," Corman replied, sighing. "Only there was an intellectual property rights dispute, and it never went to trial."

"They must've settled out of court."

"No, not with something of this caliber. King and Arthur would've fought tooth and nail to keep it for themselves. Imagine the amount of funding they could get by leveraging it over Congress."

"They'd really use the key to immortality as a bargaining chip?"

"Kill seventeen hundred civilians without it, it's a casualty of war," Corman said. "Kill seventeen hundred *with* it, it's an investment. Imagine how much support they'd get with the public knowing they can go to war without deploying as many troops. Add *that* to these soldiers being immortal, and they have a stranglehold over any country they invade."

"So America becomes the world's only government," Rowan said. "Under Lilith's discretion."

"You don't think there'd be some sort of détente? Someone else might capture one of these soldiers and reverse engineer the formula."

Corman shrugged. "Maybe. But I don't want to take the risk. Right now, it's in America's hands, and that's dangerous enough as it is. Lilith won't let it go without a fight. Might start a war to get that one soldier back."

"Goddamn," Rowan said, taking a swig of her beer. "I don't envy you, big brother."

"Get in line," Corman told her as a middle-aged human woman approached him.

"Excuse me," she said, "I'm— I wanted to thank you, Mister Ryan. For what you did for our girls. My daughter, Sarah, she... I always thought it was the wiemca, but I couldn't be sure. But everyone I asked here told me you were trying to put an end to it."

"Tried, yeah," Corman said. "Can't say I was successful."

"But you tried," she told him gently. "That's more than most can say. So I wanted to say thank you. Stay safe, Mister Ryan."

Corman watched her as she left, dumbfounded. *That's a first.* And then, just as she opened the door out to the street, two members of the Sun Kingdom walked in, dressed in kimonos and dou. Which meant they were there to negotiate. *And that's another one,* he thought, raising an eyebrow at their entrance.

"Corman Ryan," the taller of the two envoys said, "we represent Emperor Wukong. We have come to discuss terms with you."

"Be my guest," he said, picking up his beer bottle. "Have at it, gents."

"His Majesty requests an alliance be made to combat Mistress Lilith," the envoy told him. "Your actions taken against the Sons of Odin have not gone unnoticed, and you have been designated as a potential friend of the Sun Kingdom."

"Consider me honored," Corman said.

The envoy nodded to his companion, who retrieved a scroll, writing board, inkpot, and pen from his satchel. He laid the items on the bar.

"His Majesty has already signed the concordat," the envoy said. "Should you do likewise, your signature will be presented to his official notary, and our alliance against Lilith and her allies will be cemented."

"Anything I should know about, in terms of repayment?" Corman took a drink. "Hate to think I'd be in his majesty's debt."

"Merely that you will look the other way when it comes to our own dealings."

"Never been an issue before," Corman said. "Unless you're into human trafficking now."

"It is best we do not discuss such matters now," the envoy told him.

He couldn't take on an entire army of samurai. *Maybe I could have, once upon a time*, he thought. But whatever reservations he might have now, they would have to wait. Diplomacy was a different sort of beast, but a beast nonetheless. He'd find a way to deal with it, should he disagree with what they were up to. *If I come out of this alive.* Corman signed the treaty.

"Much thanks," the envoy said. "When you have need of it, do not hesitate to call for aid. His Majesty will oblige you."

"Appreciate it, boys," Corman said. As they left the bar, the implications of their visit hit him. *If they know, then...*

"Think they're actually into that kind of shit?" Rowan asked. Then, as he got off his stool, "Hey, where you going?"

"We're being watched," he told her.

How did he not see it? He hadn't recognized most of those humans, hadn't so much as glimpsed their faces before. *She's got eyes on the inside.*

"Wait, Corman, hold on—"

He slipped on his coat as he stepped outside, the night air frigid. All around him the streets were quiet, no traffic coming down South Ninth Street. Nothing down Marquette, either. All was quiet. That set his teeth on edge. Foshay Tower loomed overhead. *If the Sons wanted a Kehlsteinhaus...* It's observation deck would be an ideal hide spot. Especially if he was dumb enough to step out into the open. Corman swung back inside, bumping into Rowan as she knotted her scarf.

"What's got you all riled up?"

"If the Kingdom knows where I am, the Sons will too soon enough," he said. "Wouldn't surprise me if the Knights get dispatched."

"What's going on?" Mom asked, joining them.

"I'm running interference," Corman murmured, poking his head out.

"You're letting in the outside, man," Rowan griped.

"I'm going for Foshay," Corman announced. "Anyone comes asking for me, you tell them that."

"Corman," Mom said, "just hold on a minute. What are you planning?"

"Lilith's gonna know where I am, if she doesn't already," he told her. "The longer I'm here, the higher the probability she firebombs it."

"You expecting a fight?" Rowan asked.

"Not if I can avoid it. I need to lead them away from here." He scanned up and down Ninth Street. *Where's the one place they won't be expecting you?* "Then I'm going to Sasha's. I'll call when I get in."

"Not sure that's a good idea," Rowan said.

"What if she turns you in?" Mom asked.

"She didn't before," Corman said. "I'm trusting that she'll look the other way again."

Rowan frowned. "And if she doesn't?"

"Then at least I'll get my one phone call," Corman said. "She'll give me that much."

Mom took hold of his stump. "What about your arm?"

The phantom pain prickled. "Like I said, I'm not looking for a fight. I don't need it to run. That's all I'm gonna be doing. Anyone comes in, you tell them exactly where I went. You don't need to stick your necks out for me."

"You haven't learned anything, have you big brother?" Rowan asked.

"No, probably not," he told her. "See you when I see you."

He hurried down Ninth, keeping to the exteriors of the adjacent businesses. It was a clear night, the moon brightly shining down on the streets. Without cloud cover, he'd be in the sniper's line of sight for a good twenty seconds. Fortunately, he'd also be at an almost ninety degree angle. *Ten seconds. Make 'em count.*

Corman took off in a dead sprint across the street; a round winged a stoplight. As he ran, he heard the sizzle of neon. *Why do I always have to be right?* Now underneath the tower, he passed an old steakhouse as another round smacked into the asphalt of the intersection. *Optimistic.* Cold air billowed into the building as he broke the glass in the doors. *Let 'em know I'm coming*, he thought as he bolted through the lobby.

Nearly pitch black besides some mood lights in the ceiling, it'd be a good spot for an ambush. *Especially if they predicted this.* Not that it'd be hard to do; his failure at Camelot was proof enough of that. *They know how you work.* He dug his fingers into his stump to dull a sudden rush of pain. The skin underneath his horns burned. Avoiding a fight was paramount now. There was no way in hell he'd be able to stand on his own like this. *Talk about growing pains.*

As the elevator slid smoothly on up to the observation deck, he contemplated the viability of his next move. *Four snipers, at a minimum. And they know I'm coming*. How best to counteract that? The doors opened, but without reception. He stepped out into the vestibule that led out to the deck. *They're waiting*. Step by steps, he walked up the staircase to the exit door, and slowly pushed it open. A sniper round blasted through the glass; shards cut across his arm as he leapt back. Legs appeared in the doorway, and Corman bounced back to throw himself directly into them; he tackled the sniper as another shot went off. Corman kicked the sniper in the jaw with his boot as they grappled for the rifle. One precise slam of his elbow into their nose released their grip on the gun. He somersaulted backward, knocking over another sniper, and swung the rifle around. The remaining sniper had him in their sights, and them in his.

"You're not trained to use that, mooncalf," one of them spat.

"I learn quick," Corman said.

"You broke my fucking nose, you fucking *shit*," the first sniper bellowed.

"Keep talking, and I might break your jaw, too."

"You fucking *did*!"

"What can I say?" Corman said, lowering the scope a bit. "I'm efficient."

"Lower the fucking gun, Ryan," one of the others demanded. "You got one arm and just *one* of these rounds can rip your spinal cord out from this range. You really wanna risk that?"

"You wanna risk the recoil?" Corman asked.

"I can handle it. Worry about yourself, goatfucker."

"About that. It was a good idea to change the prefix," Corman told them. "Rolls off the tongue better than devilfucker."

"I'm giving you one more chance to shut your goddamn mouth and throw the gun out," the sniper barked.

"The fact that you haven't done it already means you have orders to keep me alive," Corman said. "Me, on the other hand…"

He threw the rifle around the neck of the sniper with a broken nose and pulled the gun toward his chest. "I was never one for rule following."

"Shoot this asshole!" the sniper with the broken nose croaked.

"Are you fucking stupid? I can't shoot at this range with *this* thing!"

"What I thought," Corman said, suplexing his hostage. Once he hit the ground, Corman charged the other two, bashing one in the gut with the butt of the rifle and smacking the other one across the head with the barrel. Then he crushed the latter's fingers beneath his boot and picked his rifle up; Corman tossed both pilfered sniper rifles off the side of the building. Keeping the remaining one, he held it like he would a pistol, and pointed it at the still-conscious sniper.

"So, whose boots tastes the most familiar?"

"W— what?"

"Who sent you up here?"

"King," the sniper said. "It was King, but she's… she's acting under Lilith's orders. Please, Ryan. Don't kill us. We weren't supposed to kill you. We weren't *gonna* kill you, either."

He rolled his eyes. "Sure. And I'm emotionally stable."

A flicker of orange appeared in his peripherals. *The fuck...?* He left the sniper and walked over to the side of the deck facing north. The flicker became at once an inferno. Going over the streets in his head, Corman traced the flames to... Outlined in darkness against the Mississippi, Camelot stood engulfed in flames. The bright orange furnace licked the underbelly of the night sky, reaching far into the heavens.

"Oh, God," the sniper whimpered, wiping blood away from their nose. "What has she done?"

"Same shit that she did eight years ago," Corman said. Then, glaring at the sniper, "And *I'm* the idiot?"

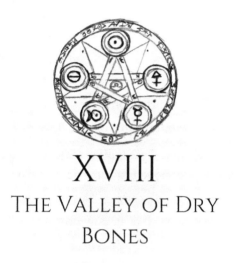

XVIII
THE VALLEY OF DRY BONES

CAMELOT BURNED A BRILLIANT orange. Embers flickered in the wind like lightning bugs, swirling together with snowflakes in a dance to oblivion. The drifts that had once piled up against the building facade and atop the roof melted into rivers; steam arose from sewer grates. But what was the point? Why had it come to this? *How many lives do you have to take?* he wondered. *How much death until you're satisfied?*

Curling his remaining hand into a fist, he marched past the melting doors of the front vestibule into the furnace. Though he'd never tried it first hand, if he had to make an educated guess, his body could withstand ten minutes under one hundred and forty degrees Fahrenheit. It had, up until that point, endured five minutes of one hundred and twenty. *Hope my math adds up,* he thought, right arm across his face. The heat he could stand, but even his lungs weren't immune to carbon monoxide poisoning.

Fire consumed every surface on every side, creating a tunnel of flames, and his vision was obscured by the smoke. *Whatever the hell I'm doing in here, I better make it fast.* Ostensibly, he figured it was a rescue operation. But nobody was outside. He didn't hear sirens. The fire department wasn't coming. Not for a while. If he had to guess, she'd orchestrated all of it, down to the timing of the fire engines pulling up. *She was detail orientated like that.*

Pieces of the ceiling collapsed into miniature tinderboxes at his feet. He might not even make it to that twenty minute threshold if the whole goddamn building came down first. *Think, you idiot, think.* What would any good Knight want to save in the event of a fire?

In the stairwell connected to the sub-basement, he received to his surprise a temporary reprieve from the fiery prison. *It'll come soon enough,* he thought as he approached the door to the R and D department. The door, made of bulletproof steel alloy, was hanging off of its hinges and the keypad was likewise hanging from its wires. Past the door, in the underground parking garage-cum-research lab, he found where all the casualties went. Bodies were strewn across the entire lab, all of them wearing the white lab coats of Knight engineers. They had been blown apart, limbs soaked in blood barely tethered to bodies by a few strands of muscle. Some had been bisected by some brutal instrument.

And the weapons locker had been burglarized. Prototype rifles, grenades, armor pieces, and communication equipment. There were some boxes of ammo spilled out onto the floor, the odd handgun, but everything else had been stolen. *Or signed out*, he thought, picking up a semi-automatic pistol. Its barrel was much longer than a normal handgun's, and upon checking the clip, he found six armor piercing rounds about seven inches in diameter. *There's no way to soak up the recoil*, he thought, tossing it onto a worktable. *Innovation before reason*.

Laying beside it were the components of an artificial limb. It wasn't complete, and likely in the middle of testing, but there it was, waiting to be properly circuited and pieced back together. *If I knew what I was doing...* he thought as he picked up and examined it.

As he did, he heard the death knell of infrastructure above. More pieces of the foundation crumbling into ash. He had to hurry. Across the lab from the weapons locker was the wardrobe. Stands holding gauntlets, cuirasses, and gorgets made of experimental poly fibers lined the walls, their matching helmets hanging from the walls. At the end of the rows of armor, he found a bulletproof display case full of robotic limbs. They were each marked by a prototype number, from a primitive looking bronze hook to a sleek, carbon fiber arm with green accent lighting. Corman grabbed a helmet off the wall and bashed the glass in. He supposed on any other night there'd be an alarm. *Should've broken in now,* he thought as he retrieved the simple, silver arm that fell in the middle of the spectrum. There was a hook for the elbow attached; he figured it was low tech enough for him to make it work.

The first pieces of the lab's ceiling began to crumble; dust and plaster sprinkled onto work stations. He needed just one more thing before he got the hell out of there. *Course I'm stuck with the first drafts.* Nevertheless, without much in the way of alternatives or time, he suited up. He left the armory sporting a flak jacket, helmet, gauntlets, and greaves of dubious effectiveness. Under his right arm, his potential new left. At the busted door, he glanced back at the dead. *They'll be forgotten unless I—* But the ceiling was started to cave in; he felt the rumbling in the doorframe.

Sweat poured forth from his body as he reentered the kiln. Significantly heavier, he calculated he had even less time now. And this goddamn smoke... It was making him see things, shadows that weren't there. At the end of the corridor, he saw something that looked like a person standing amidst all of the destruction, like some sort of fiery wraith. Only, when he got closer to it, he saw that was something far, far worse.

"Ryan," Kyle Woods greeted him from underneath a gas mask, that ridiculous cape still on, even now. "Figured you'd show. You never miss the chance to kill yourself."

"Never took you for a firebug," Corman said, his eyes beginning to water. *Five minutes.*

"Part of our scorched earth campaign," Woods told him. "Between here and highway seventy-seven, there'll be nothing but ashes."

"Never took you for having morals, either," Corman said. "One out of two ain't bad."

"Fortunately for me, I never took you for nothing less than an idiot." From behind his back, Woods swung a gigantic sword around and slid it from its sheath. It was a slab of metal, its blade wider and thicker than the grip.

No practical way to sharpen that thing. Must work on centrifugal force.

"You familiar with Excalibur, Ryan?" Woods asked, brandishing the sword.

"I am, and motherfucker, that ain't it," Corman told him.

"It's not the actual Excalibur. But every Knight chapter gets their own," Woods explained, struggling to make a few practice strokes; Corman squinted through the smoke to see his arm quivering. "And we got this monstrosity. Lucky me, I get to kill you with it."

"That's awfully presumptuous," Corman said, eyeing the cape.

"I'll give you the chance to get on your knees and beg, mooncalf," Woods said, moving into a striking stance.

Corman coughed. "You don't know me as well as you think you do."

"Then you should've stayed dead."

Awkwardly, nearly toppling over, Woods charged him. Despite the smoke, he cut such a large figure that Corman saw him five feet ahead, easily sidestepping his attack. The weight of the sword sent Woods toppling forward, almost into the fire which was growing angrier and closer by the second.

"You wanna live, you cut this shit out," Corman wheezed. "You can't survive."

"Who are you to do tell me anything, you goatfucker?" Woods roared, struggling to keep the sword upright. "You're a goddamn disease! All the fucking billygoats think they can piss and moan and bitch about what we do wrong because of you! You're a fucking poison."

"Listen to me!" Corman coughed. "Your lungs can't take this much carbon—"

"Fuck you!" Woods screamed, heaving the sword at him. It missed by a good foot, and slammed hard into the floor, sending up chunks of tile. "I am so fucking sick and tired of your goddamn—" Swing. "Fucking—" Swing. "Bullshit!"

Corman bashed him across the face with the prosthetic arm and kicked him in the stomach, sending him flailing into the fire. The cape burst into flames, and in a matter of seconds, it grabbed hold of Woods' flesh. He shrieked, dropping the sword. It crashed into the floor as Woods danced wildly, trying to put himself out with his hands. With just his one hand, Corman picked up Excalibur by the grip and heaved it over one shoulder; the prosthetic hung off the blade by its elbow hook.

"Stop, drop, and roll, you idiot," Corman told Woods. Then he turned to leave.

Outside, he could feel the refreshing cold of the night air on his soot-stained cheeks. I need to get to a payphone, he thought as a burning figure flew past him into the street. Doing as instructed, Woods dropped to the ground and rolled. Steam rose from underneath his armor as he flopped onto his back, extinguished. But even as he lay there, what exposed skin Corman could see bleeding and raw, he had nothing but hatred in his eyes.

"You," he croaked, "you did this."

"I did, yeah," Corman said.

"Bastard," Woods muttered. "Get it... over with."

Corman looked at the burning ruins of Camelot, then back at the burned ruin of Woods. "You'll survive. And I'm not in the business of murdering the defenseless."

"You want to, you— you fucking mooncalf," Woods sputtered. "So kill me."

"What I want and what I end up doing are two different things," Corman told him. "Once you get patched up, I'll consider it. Well, if you get patched up, I mean."

"What are you," Woods gasped, "fucking talking about?"

"I'll see that the fire department gets here," Corman said, beginning to walk away. "You'll see if they get here on time."

With Excalibur over one shoulder, Corman strode off into the darkness as pained howls of "bastard" and "mooncalf" echoed through the night, falling upon the indifferent ears of the universe.

So when he heard the shrill, unearthly screeching, Corman was taken aback. Woods didn't have the energy or lung capacity at that point to— He furrowed his brow at what was coming straight for him. Leaping out of windows and and fumbling out of the parking garages were charred corpses, some still very much on fire. They filled into the streets, dozens upon dozens of them. *Behold, O my people, I will open your graves*, Corman thought, *and cause you to come up out of your graves, and bring you to the land of Israel.*

Then a few spotted Woods. Then a few more. Then half of the entire horde. They moved in. Quickly.

And ye shall know I am the Lord., Corman thought, bolting for the mass of the undead.

With one swing of Excalibur, he sliced through a swath of them, cutting the wights in half. Some clawed at him, but he elbowed them off on the backswing, chopping up a dozen of them. Old, dead hands grabbed him by the waist. Wight after wight piled on top of him, dragging him down to the street, fingers digging into his flesh. His cheek scraped against the asphalt, and a cut opened up; he felt the blood ooze out.

He heard Woods scream, accompanied by the squish of organs and the breaking of bones. *Get up. Get the fuck up.* Corman pressed his palm flat against the street and lifted himself to his knees, shaking violently as the hundreds of pounds worth of dead bodies began to fall away. Arching his back and flexing his shoulder muscles, he threw himself up and backward; the wights screeched and danced around him, slobbering. He wound his torso and let the sword fly, smacking into all those around him, cutting them in half and sending dark red blood into the air. More hurled themselves at him, but to avail; Corman sliced through them as he ran for Woods. Arms and legs and organs plopped to the ground as legs buckled and torsos exploded like blood piñatas.

Panting, his shoulders heaving with each sharp intake of breath, Corman surveyed the area. Not another living soul in sight. Just mutilated body parts. *The spirit of the Lord set me down in the midst of the valley which was full of bones.*

At his feet was the corpse of Kyle Woods, his limbs ripped from their sockets. Broken, bent, and tossed aside was his resplendent armor, now soiled with blood and human remains and crushed organs. The cape was no more. Just a piece of cloth charred to ash. So was the legacy of Lancelot and Lancelot's father. Artifacts burned to a crisp over a fire made of their own hubris. *Idiot*, Corman thought sadly. There was no saving him, not from himself. *People who believe they can not err die by their own hand*. He'd learned that for himself well enough.

Sirens blared behind him, but as Corman turned around, he saw they belonged to a single vehicle. The Stingray's tires screeched as it slammed to a stop, and when Sasha burst out from the driver's side, she only got halfway to Woods' body before she stopped dead.

"Corman?" she breathed. "But— you're— you're *dead*. What about to— is *he* dead?'

He approached her slowly while he slid the prosthetic arm off the blade, then presented it to her. "Think Kalebrant can get this hooked up to me?"

Sasha laid her hands on his cheeks. "I saw your body, Ryan. You were *dead*."

"I was, yeah," he said. "But I exploited a loophole in my mortality clause."

She frowned. "W— what?"

He sucked in his breath. Best to just get it over with. "The devil's real, and he brought me back to life to kill Lilith. We can worry about the existential implications of that later. Right now we need to get as far away from here as possible. I'm assuming you got a safehouse set up?"

"Yeah. Yeah," Sasha said, nodding. "At the morgue. Mordred's been hiding us there. How did— Corman, what the hell happened here?"

Corman started to walk over to the cruiser. "I don't know if I'm right, but I think Lilith got as many Knights as she could in there just so she could burn it all down. Trap their souls in a kiln."

"But... King agreed to—"

"Doesn't matter. Lilith doesn't care much for honoring agreements," Corman said, one leg in the car. "She's raising an army of the dead who only answer to her. Now we need to get the hell out of here."

Silently, she got back into the driver's seat and threw it into drive. "But what about Woods? Did you—"

"*They* got to him." Corman sighed. "And they're gonna get everyone else in this city, too. Anyone else still alive?"

"Kalebrant," Sasha replied. "Safir and Yue, too. We were... we were called back to Camelot, just like everyone else, but since none of us thought it'd be a good idea..."

"Wouldn't surprise me if the members of the Round Table are still out there," Corman said. "Especially if Lilith has King hostage. A witch needs her monkeys out on patrol."

"What do we do?"

"We regroup. Try to avoid any of the wights on the way. Kalebrant gives me a new arm, and then we kill Lilith. Easy."

XIX

THE SEVENTH SEAL

T HE COLD STEEL BIT his skin as Kalebrant affixed the prosthetic arm's hinge to his elbow joint. It hung loose, the artificial nervous system yet to be magnetized to Corman's natural
electrons. Safir handed him an instrument that resembled a vise grip
with a meat thermometer sticking out to the side. Adjusting the
arm's position, Kalebrant cinched the flesh and the steel together
with the device and turned a few knobs.

"This is gonna hurt like a motherfucker," Kalebrant warned,
checking the dial. "But you're used to that, aren't you?"

"Oh?" Corman mumbled, staring at anything besides his arm.

"If I had the right equipment, you'd hardly thing anything at all," Kalebrant said. "But I guess our liaison is as underfunded as he claims."

"And I'm gonna be down another eight grand for that hearse," Nathan, standing in the doorframe, muttered.

"What makes you so goddamn certain about that?" Corman barked.

"*You're* driving it."

"What, you don't have insurance on it?" Corman asked. "They really *did* fuck you."

"So he's fucked either way," Yue said, flipping through Corman's notebook. "You actually have really nice handwriting."

"Penmanship is about the only thing you get to work on down there," Corman said.

"You mean writing your name in piss in the snow?"

"How would that translate?" Kalebrant asked, adjusting the elbow hinge again. "Finger dexterity has nothing to do with how you use your dick."

"You think?" Yue said, grinning.

Sasha hung up the landline back onto its wall receiver and sat down across the table from Corman and Kalebrant. "The Kingdom is sending patrols down out to Loring. You have a timeline of when this is all supposed to happen?"

"Within the next twenty-four hours," Corman said. "Lilith has everything she needs to break the Seal. She wouldn't have killed me until she was sure everything else was in place."

"You know how weird it is to hear that said so casually?" Yue asked.

"I have an idea," Corman said.

"All right," Kalebrant said, "I'm about to connect the arm. Get him something to bite down on."

"I got stabbed through the heart," Corman told him. "I can handle it."

"You said you got injected with adrenaline beforehand," Safir pointed out. "You're gonna feel it this time."

"I also got my arm chopped off," Corman continued. "Honestly, I don't think any pain can—"

Kalebrant cinched the prosthetic; it lit the fuse for the nitroglycerine inside of his arm. Corman slammed his fist down onto the plastic table over and over again, barking out any obscenity that came to mind. The phone started ringing, and through tears he saw Sasha get up to answer it. Whatever she said, he swore too loudly to hear.

Then the pressure released, and the last embers of the explosion of pain and nerve damage fizzled out. Corman gasped for breath, clawing where his flesh met metal. It itched and prickled, all the way down to his fingers. He swallowed. The phantom pain had returned, only...

"Congratulations, Ryan, you have two arms again," Kalebrant said.

Corman held up his metal arm and waggled his fingers, closed them into a fist. "There an adjustment period?"

"Should be, but with you, it's hard to say," Kalebrant told him. "I've only done this on humans. Not whatever the fuck you are."

"He's a cambion, Drew" Yue said.

"Nephilim," Corman corrected her, itching his elbow.

"Explains a lot, actually," Safir said.

"Sounds like an STD," Yue murmured.

"What's that mean?" Kalebrant asked, tossing the instrument to Nathan, who fumbled it. As he retrieved it from the floor, he gave him the stink eye.

"Asshole, this thing's like twenty grand."

"Twenty-two," Safir said.

"He'd appreciate it," Sasha said into the phone.

"I'm half-angel," Corman explained, "not half-demon."

"I thought all the nephilim died," Kalebrant said.

Safir asked, "So angels aren't just a different genus of human like demons are?"

"*Homo daemonicus*," Nathan threw out. "Whereas angels don't even have a binomial nomenclature. They aren't thought to actually exist, since they're not material beings."

"How's that work?" Yue asked, flipping through the notebook as if it contained the answer.

"If you see one, it's not what it actually looks like," Nathan said. "It's just your feeble human mind reorganizing the shape its molecules take so you don't lose your mind."

Yue raised an eyebrow at Corman. "And your dad fucked one?"

"Yes, Yue," Corman muttered. "My father impregnated an angel."

"Good news," Sasha announced as she hung the phone up again. "The Zonbi are on their way to a rendezvous point with the Good Earth Tribe. They want to throw their hand in with you."

"You sure that's not a set-up?" Corman asked.

"The Zonbi definitely know by now that the Kingdom has sided with you," Sasha said, sitting down. "If they meant this as a trap, it'd be a declaration of war. There's no possibility they'd align themselves with the Sons, either. And Anansi is too smart to fight a war on two fronts."

"And the Tribe?"

"They're on good terms with the Zonbi. Hawk Sings wouldn't do anything to go against Anansi. Not when they're in the middle of a ceasefire."

Corman frowned. "I don't trust it."

"You really would be an idiot if you did," Sasha agreed. "Way I see it, both Hawk Sings and Anansi see this as a good way to curry favor with the Emperor. If the Sons lose, their territory is going to be for grabs, and no doubt the doling out of that territory is going to fall to him as the *de facto* boss."

"And they think there's a good chance of that happening," Corman said.

"The Sons have been fragmented since Uthor the Elder died," Sasha told him. "Lilith's managed to unite them under her banner, but when she's gone, they'll fall apart."

"Except for the splinter groups that'll pop up later," Yue said.

"The Kingdom's grip will be too strong for any of those to gain any amount of influence," Sasha said. "And King, if she lives through this, is going to have to reckon with the new order. She'll have to figure a way to coexist with them."

"This is all presupposing we win," Kalebrant said.

"Speaking of, how do we do that?" Yue asked Corman. Everyone looked at him. "What are we up against, shortstack?"

Ignore it. "Lilith's made a philosopher's stone using John Kelley's research."

"*That* John Kelley?" Sasha asked.

"The same," Corman said. "She put the half-finished formulas together and figured out how to create one. Based on my understanding of his research notes, the stone itself has a chemical composition identical to a human body, but it's inert without the kinetic energy of the human soul to act as a catalyst. And you need a *lot* of energy to get it going. Lilith set Camelot on fire to get the souls she needed."

"So everyone who went there is...?" Safir asked.

"Now a wight," Corman replied. "Their bodies obey the will of their souls, which are now under Lilith's command."

Sasha frowned. "To what end?"

"In order to open the Sixty-Sixth Seal, you need an amount of energy equivalent to a star going supernova," Corman explained.

"Then what happens?" she asked.

"Our universe is merged with hers. She wants a kingdom, so she's gonna take both and destroy them to get her New Jerusalem."

"So we're talking about the potential heat death of the universe?" Yue asked.

Corman nodded. "Yeah."

"How many philosopher's stones do you need to reach the threshold?" Sasha asked.

"I don't know. But Lilith is going to reach it, somehow."

Nathan approached the table. "And these zombies she's controlling, doesn't she need their souls to open the Seal? Why send them out as soldiers?"

"The soul is still in the stone," Corman answered. "The bodies are only connected to them by a tenuous link. Something like a lower level of the soul chains the two together. The more they kill, the more energy she has. A wight is like a walking philosopher's stone."

"So when she breaks the Seal, I'm guessing they'll consume anything in its wake?"

"We need to evacuate as much of the city as we can," Safir said. "Civilians can't be caught in the middle of this."

"Lilith's already planned for a mass exodus," Corman said. "Blocked off the highways, burned cars. Woods told me that they were going to burn the whole city down between Camelot and seventy-seven. We're closed off until the séance. Only viable option is to kill as many of her wights before the Seal breaks, get people into safe zones. My sister's doing some of the legwork already, but between us and the gangs, we'll have a larger circumference of communication."

"How long until the rendezvous?" Kalebrant asked Sasha.

"An hour," she said. "But we should get this in motion before then. Nathan, you warn any Knights you think will listen."

"Or are still alive," he murmured.

"Yue and me will take the north and west side. Kalebrant, Safir, you get to work on the east. We'll all reconvene with Corman at the rendezvous point in an hour," Sasha instructed, writing out a set of coordinates into his notebook. "Ryan, you do whatever you need to do in the meantime. You're taking point on this. We follow your lead."

He shook his new arm, stared into its empty palm. *How am I supposed to do this without you?*

"When the time comes, I'm facing Lilith alone," he told them. "She'll just kill anyone else. The gangs are gonna need the auxiliary support. Keep the wights inside the perimeter of the Seal, minimize the blast radius if I don't stop her."

"And if you... die again?" Sasha asked.

"Get the gangs together and storm the castle," Corman replied. "But I'm gonna make sure she's the only casualty. And if she isn't, I'll make sure it's just her and me."

He felt Kalebrant lay a hand on his shoulder, his face unreadable. *Maybe I never could do that in the first place,* he thought. *How much did I think I knew? And how much of that do I actually?*

"All right, memorize the coordinates," Sasha ordered. "We're moving out."

As the other end rang, he wondered if she'd even pick up. *Come on...* he thought. *Come on, come on, come on. Answer.*

But no, he was calling her mobile from a pay phone; it went straight to voicemail.

After his brief hope of hearing her voice recording was dashed by the automated message, he sighed and offered what little help he could possibly have to offer her.

"Abigail, it's Corman. Ryan. Look, tonight's—and the foreseeable future—are gonna get... weird. Stay inside. Don't trust any Knights that come looking for you. If anything goes wrong, go to the top floor of the Riverside Plaza. My mom'll take care of you."

He inserted a few more quarters, tried to get ahold of his mother, and again got greeted with an automated message. *I need to get a goddamn phone.*

"Hey, Mom. I'm gonna be fighting Lilith soon, so... I don't know if I'll make it. But, um, thanks. For saving me, and everything else. Love you."

Feels like I should have more apologizing to do, he thought. And he did. But the apologies remaining couldn't be sequestered to a brief message over the phone. It would require more of himself, more of what parts of himself he still had.

In the meantime, he would need to get reacquainted with the world as it stood. He curled his metal fingers, waggled them, felt them with his organic ones. *It's not Ed. But it'll have to do.* It made him wonder, what would she take from him this time? What else was left? *It wouldn't be from you. Not directly. Not—*

Blasting down 101st Street in the hearse, he felt beads of sweat drip down into and sting his eyes. *How didn't I see it? Of course she's pulling this shit. Of fucking course.* How much of his current problems stemmed from his own blindness? But how much of it was deliberate ignorance, and how much was it beyond his control? How much shit did he make everyone in his life wade through on his own behalf? When did it end? When *he* did? *Goddamn it,* he thought, slamming his palms into the steering wheel. *Goddamn it.*

But wasn't this what he always did? Wasn't this what he always ended up doing to the people around him? Mom lost her family because of him. Sasha, Yue, and Kalebrant, Nathan, and Safir too, now, had and were going to get the raw end of whatever deal was offered at the end of all this. *I have to make sure they get out of this.*

And Abigail, how much had he fucked her life up by getting involved in it? *You're goddamn curse,* he told himself. *A fucking harbinger.*

If this was his last fight, then, well. He couldn't exactly shed tears over it. *Maybe life doesn't need me in it. If you live, you're going someplace where no one can find you.* Let the world forget about him, plunge his memory into the cold, unforgiving sea of time. Happened once before, it could happen again. Let it. *World's better off without you*. He'd do what he needed to, but when it was all side and done, he'd be gone. *Let the world breathe.* Hell, maybe Satan would let him stay in Kelzjah. *And if he insists on my passing on...* What that really be the worst thing in the world?

Yet, somewhere inside him, in a place he couldn't identify, a small voice told him not to do any of that. But to stay. *Stay,* he thought, rolling the idea around in his mind. *No.* The rotten part had to be cut out to save the rest of the body. And rotten was all he was, all he'd ever been.

In front of the Hound's Tooth, he didn't see any signs of struggle or even retribution. Unlike in his postmortem visions, the place was still intact. The windows weren't even broken. He slammed on the brakes, the front right tire up on the curb, and burst through the front doors, Excalibur raised. Yet the place was quiet, his steps only accompanied by the squeaking of the floor boards.

All the bottles lay broken on the liquor shelves. Booze soaked into the soles of his boots. The upholstery of all the stools, chairs, and booths were ripped to shreds, stuffing hanging out of holes like intestines. Running a hand across the bar, he felt the scars and bumps laid there by some rough weapon. *Mom would have a shit fit.* A cursory inspection of the bathrooms and the backroom offered nothing else but the same. *What the hell happened...?* He laid Excalibur down on the bar and sat down on the stool that still looked like something to sit on. Where to go from here? Where could she possibly—?

"Corman Ryan!"

He grabbed the sword.

"We have something for you," the voice told him. "Come out and see!"

Whatever that "something" was, he knew it'd send him into a frenzy. Otherwise, why would whoever this asshole was be bragging about it? *Control yourself*, he told himself. *Composure, Ryan. Composure.*

With Excalibur back over his shoulder, he walked outside to see Kay and Bors of all people. But, just as unexpectedly, with them were Sirs Bedivere and Gawain, a couple of other assholes, just of a different, slightly less incompetent sort. *But assholes nonetheless.* Gawain, grinning wickedly, held something in her hand, draped in cloth. Whatever it was, it was leaking.

"We have a present for you," she called out, pulling the cloth away.

No, he thought, his legs shaking. It— he was imagining it. That wasn't actually— No. It was, and he was looking at it. It was real, and it was there.

Inside a plastic evidence bag was Lukkan's severed head. It had been a an ugly decapitation; the cuts were jagged, crude, and entirely too quick. And done within the last couple of hours.

"Guess who found out about the lab explosion?" Gawain asked. "And guess who traced it back to him?"

"Why the hell are you sick fucks showing me this?" Corman roared.

"*You're* the one who got him killed," Bedivere said. "*You* should be the one—"

"Shut your goddamn mouth!" Corman snarled, brandishing Excalibur. "You cocksuckers had something to do with this, didn't you?"

"I see you've given up on being clever," Bors said.

"Again, no, Ryan. The onus is on you," Bedivere said. "Mooncalf."

"Can't just destroy a whole goddamn organ harvesting operation and expect it to just... go away, can you?" Gawain chirped gleefully. "There *had* to be a scapegoat, right? And since you were, well, escaping punishment—"

"I was *dead*," Corman barked.

"Right, and you're back," Bedivere said. "Correct me if I'm wrong, but that counts as escaping the consequences, doesn't it?"

Kay pointed. "You even got your arm back."

This was a typical Knight negotiation tactic. Obfuscate the truth, blend it together with blatant falsehoods, and pretend that, somehow, the facts proved the lies. *And you're falling for it.*

"What do you *want*?" Corman demanded.

"*Your* head," Gawain said. "On the King's orders."

Corman moved into a defensive stance. *King, or Lilith?* "Then come and take it."

Yet none of them so much as drew their weapon. Bors looked to Kay, who did an awkward little dance, as if trying to look intimidating; Bedivere rested his hand on his rapier's pommel but left it in the sheath. Even Gawain, for all her bluster, stayed put.

Furrowing his brow, Corman lowered the sword.

"So that's it, huh?" He heaved Excalibur back over his shoulder. "You show me a man's decapitated head to try and bait me and then you pussy out? Jesus Christ."

"But— You killed Woods!" Kay blurted. "You're a murderer."

"Lilith's wights did that for me," Corman told him. "You gonna keep wasting my time with this bullshit? Or are we done?"

"She's lost her mind," Bedivere blurted out. "She's taken King hostage!"

"And I care?" Corman murmured, already knowing where this was going. *The head was their sick idea of a bluff.* "Tell me who killed Lukkan."

"The Sons," Bedivere said. "But Lilith pointed them in the right direction."

"You want to take control back," Corman told them, "do it yourselves."

"We're outnumbered," Bors said. "Outgunned, and after the fire we—"

"I don't give a shit," Corman said. "That isn't my goddamn problem."

"But if you don't, King'll *die*. You *have* to help her!" Kay pleaded. "*Please*."

Corman gave him a blank look.

"Look, it'll help *you* too, asshole," Gawain barked, arms folded. "You save her, and she might put in a good word with Arthur. You really gonna pass up the opportunity for amnesty? After all this is done, you're gonna be back on our shit list. Cross your name off it while you can."

"That would still mean helping you pricks," Corman said. "I'm not interested."

"Ryan, *come on*," Bors spat. "Don't be a dickhead."

You have leverage here, he told himself. *Use it.*

"Fine," Corman said. "But first you're all gonna do something for me."

"*What?*" Gawain seethed. "Why the fuck would we—?"

"You're gonna do the right thing for once in your miserable, mooncalf-hating lives," Corman went on. "You're gonna give Lukkan's head over to Nathan. Body, too. He gets a decent funeral. And anyone involved in rescuing King this goes dark. No promotions, no commendations, no praise, for any of you."

"You're pushing your luck," Gawain snapped.

"Oh, am I?" Corman grinned. "Good luck."

Bedivere held his arm out in front of Gawain. "Fine. We'll play your little game."

You would think ethics is a game, wouldn't you? "Where's King being held?"

"Blacksite six-hundred and sixteen," Bedivere told him.

"Look at you guys putting all those government subsidies to good use." He walked over to the hearse and popped the door open. *Mom and Rowan are fine. They're fine. It's better you can't find them.* "See you in ten."

Underneath what once was a Vietnamese restaurant, whose windows advertised pho, its lack of public restrooms, and its short window of operating hours, was blacksite 616. Corman pulled into the empty parking lot from Nicollet Avenue, a strip of road once known for its commerce but now whose buildings sat as vacant homes for rat nests. *I'm protecting those rats now,* he thought as he got out of the hearse. Wasn't the first time the pointlessness of all of this crossed his mind, but now he *felt* it. Felt it viscerally. Minneapolis was a dead city, a graveyard haunted by the impoverished and malnourished. Ghosts who hadn't quite finished dying yet.

Two Stingrays pulled up and parked outside of the designated spaces. All four Knights were strapped; shotguns, assault rifles, grenades, and daggers hung from their armor.

"When's the last time anyone used this place?" Corman asked as he retrieved Excalibur from the backseat.

"Whenever the last race riot was," Bors answered.

"I believe they call those protests now," Corman said. "Have, for quite some time."

"Whatever. Six or seven years ago."

"That was before they actually let us put them down," Gawain added, loading her shotgun. "Think those morons would've gotten the message after a dozen of 'em bit it."

"I think they got it just fine," Corman muttered. *Just not the one you wanted.*

"All right Ryan, you're taking point on this," Gawain ordered. "Just kill anything you see in there. "Code's one-five-six-seven-two-four."

"Can I expect reinforcements?" he asked, trying the front door. Locked.

"Only if it gets hairy," Bedivere replied.

"You're the liability here, not us," Kay said.

Corman exhaled, doing his best to not strangle him. Instead, he gritted his teeth and bashed the door's hinges in with Excalibur's pommel. He shoved the busted door in and crossed the threshold.

The place had been used as a squatting site; graffiti, bed rolls, and trash cans full of ash littered the interior. Two-by-fours intersected diagonally in the windows. He walked to the back room, full of empty steel shelves, and came across the bulletproof steel door. *Weren't expecting visitors, I take it*, he thought as he punched in the code.

The door wheezed open, pushing off its rubber hinges to reveal a stone staircase. At the foot of which was a large concrete box. In the center of the room was Barbara Olsen, her ankles tied to a chair, her throat slit, and a bloody combat knife hanging limply in her hand. At her feet, the cut-up bodies of wiemca, their ghoulish faces splayed out against the concrete, coated in blood. *You reap what you sow, I guess*, Corman thought. Despite the mutual hatred they'd developed over the years, he had never wanted to see her like this. Didn't want to see Woods die the way he did, for that matter. *He makes his sun to rise on the evil and the good.*

In the corner of the room was a box covered with a linen cloth. Taking it off, he saw a multitude of instruments coated with dried blood. He could hazard a guess as to what they were used for. Corman laid the cloth over King's body and walked out.

Topside, he saw pitch black clouds gathering above, obscuring the stars. The Knights swarmed around him; still none of them dared to pull their weapons out. They all waited for a moment before Bedivere frowned.

"We were too late, weren't we?"

"He sends rain on the just and on the unjust," Corman replied, moving past them. Before he got very far, he felt someone grab him by the shoulder. It was Bedievere, his eyes not downcast, but afraid.

Corman shrugged his hand away. "What?"

"She warned us," he murmured. "That we had a half hour to save her."

"You wanna tell me what the hell *that* means?"

Thunder boomed; lightning cracked through the clouds. They parted, and in place of the night sky dotted with all those billions of stars, was a crimson moon, whose color bled into the fabric of the heavens. The ground quivered. Then chunks of asphalt and concrete burst forth from underfoot, the city rising up all around him. Across the street, the vacant storefronts were pierced by spikes of the earth reaching hundreds of feet into the air. The storm raged on, growing louder and louder by the second.

Wights burst forth from in between the spires, their gray, decaying faces staring directly at him and the Knights. The horde headed straight for them. The seventh Seal had been broken. The apocalypse was underway.

Corman got into a defensive stance, Excalibur ready to strike.

"God-fucking-*damn* it," he muttered.

XX
THE BLOOD OF THE LAMB

T HE ROTTING, PUTRID FLUIDS flowing inside of the wights spilled out onto the parking lot as Corman swung Excalibur through their chests. As organs squished together and bones rattled, thunder cried and echoed off of the spires. A liver and its liquids splattered on Kay's boots; he whimpered and ducked behind Bors.

"Oh, get a grip," Bors barked, tossing his partner aside.

Corman surveyed Nicollet Avenue as best he could; this was a winter's darkness, exacerbated by the turgid apocalyptic hue. He needed to get to Loring Park *now*. No time to waste on the already dead. *More'll show up soon enough*, he thought as he threw Excalibur into the back of the hearse. The Knights cornered him, their facial expressions running the gamut from enraged to ambivalent to terrified. Corman sighed as he shut the door.

"What?" he asked.

"What the fuck is going on?" Gawain demanded. "You owe us an explanation."

Corman gestured to the restaurant. "The Whore of Babylon is dead, and the Seventh Seal has been broken."

"The hell's *that* mean?" she spat.

"It's the apocalypse," Bedivere said.

"Almost," Corman said, getting into the driver's seat. "The Sixty-Sixth Seal hasn't been opened yet. *Then* it's the apocalypse. Try not to get assimilated into Lilith's army of the undead in the meantime."

Bors grabbed the door before he could lock it. "And what are *you* gonna do about it?"

Calmly, Corman switched on the ignition. "I'm gonna kill Lilith before she gets a chance to kill all of us."

"Yeah, but what about *us*?" Kay asked. "What happens to *us*?"

"If you don't get out of here in the next five minutes, probably getting turned into wights." Corman slammed the door shut, Bors pulling his fingers away just before they got smashed in.

Both sides of the street were raised above the earth, pieces of pavement and asphalt crumbling and smashing together on their way back down. Spires of concrete and metal burst through storefronts and parked cars. The scared, confused masses in the wrong place at the wrong time stumbled out of their homes and businesses, staring agape to the blood red sky or the decimated earth below. Some had already been claimed, their bodies sprawled out at the base of the structures. It was only a matter of time before they all joined the mass of the undead.

They all had lives once, lives lived in complete ignorance. *Not everyone is you*, he told himself. How long had he resented them, the ignorant masses, simply because they hadn't experienced the same things he had? *They know not what they do.* For his own part, he'd lived a privileged life. No, that wasn't quite right. A knowledgeable one. He knew more than most people, had seen more than just about anyone; his elongated lifespan was only partially responsible. How many monsters and foul deeds had he witnessed with his own eyes that so many people couldn't even dream up? And what had he done with all that knowledge, that expertise? Did he bother giving it to other people? *You wasted your own life out of spite.* They would never understand him, nor accept him, or love him, or forgive him. All the things he wanted from them, they had no power to give. And he had hated them for it. *But what stands between them and the monsters? Another monster.*

Maybe that's all he would ever be, all he'd ever been in the first place. A monster with the wherewithal to recognize that. What was the line? *You got to be what you are?* There was nothing else Corman Ryan *could* be, besides a monster hunting his own kind. For he wasn't a cambion, demon, nor human. He was alone in his own genus, his own species, a solitary freak of nature.

While he mulled this all over, he swerved and weaved around the spires all the way down Hennepin on his way east to Loring. The first chimaera he saw came bursting forth from the Electric Fetus, shards of vinyl records mixed in with the mortar and plaster that came spewing out after it. It charged down the street, carrying a dead body in its mouth. Corman cut a hard left to clip it with the back of the hearse. Furiously spinning the steering wheel about, he skidded around to stare it down. The chimaera roared. Corman floored it. Ramming into it, he drove it along toward a spire, then slammed on the brakes. There was a loud crunch and a burst of blood, and the chimaera's body collapsed onto the ground.

"Should've thought of this years ago," he murmured as he backed up.

As he sped down 11th Street, intending to hook a left onto Third Avenue, he ran into a pack of chimaeras parked right in the middle of the intersection, ripping cars and their passengers apart. *Shit*, he thought, hitting the brakes. Too late. The damage dealt to the hearse caused it to clatter; all four of them looked up all at once, then tuned their focus onto the vehicle.

They all charged, beaks and snouts and claws and sharpened tails and extra limbs all poised for attack. No choice left to him; Corman brought the hearse up to ninety miles an hour, and they collided.

Though the seatbelt kept him inside the cab, the windshield burst into a flurry of glass; chimaera body parts split apart and either went flying or went right through the broken window. The hearse tipped over one of their corpses and smashed back down into the street. Face firmly planted in the airbag, Corman could taste blood filling up his mouth. He couldn't tell, however, if that was a stupid idea or not. He leaned back and spat out a wad of blood. *Maybe I got them all in one go*, he thought as claws scraped the side windows. The remaining three chimaera peered inside with their mutilated faces.

Yeah, why not, he thought as he slunk into the back. Just as he did, the chimaera started slamming themselves into both sides of the vehicle, rocking it back and forth in rough waves, all the while making huge dents in the metal; one of them damn near reached him.

"Hope you can cut through steel," he said to Excalibur as he grabbed hold of it. Holding it out, he waited for a break in the rocking. When it came, he unwound himself at the waist and let the sword fly. It broke through the sides of the hearse; he felt it cut right through flesh and muscle.

The final chimaera ripped the back door open and crunched the metal beneath its claws as it approached him.

"You wanna rethink that?" Corman asked. It paid him no mind, so he flung himself forward and rammed the sword through the chimaera's head. Tumbling out into the street, he took asphalt to the shoulder and spilled out into a sloppy somersault. Behind him was the beast, dead. Corman put his boot to its face and slid Excalibur out of its skull.

He took a quick look at the hearse; he'd proved Nathan right. The thing was smashed, its hood was crunched up, the left wheel was missing, and the entire back half of it was split open, plus all the damage the chimaera caused.

Off in the distance, he heard the gurgling and growling of the wights. A few spilled out from behind the spires. *We must have the same destination*, he thought, shouldering Excalibur. Time to go. Corman started off jogging. Wights poured out from alleyways and out of windows, their bodies bisected and torn apart and hanging on by a muscle. *Run, Corman, run.*

It was one of the most excruciating pains he'd ever felt; he sides ached, flames licked his calf muscles, and his chest felt ready to explode. The dry air was hard to breathe in, and only added fuel to the fire in his lungs. Yet he kept running, his joints and muscles crying out for him to stop. But the further he went, the more chimaera and wights appeared. His fingers itched. *I'm supposed to be fighting them*, he thought. But he was out of adrenaline, out of dopamine, out of energy. *What do I do, Ed? How the fuck am I supposed to fix this?*

Only answer he could think of was to keep going. All that mattered now was getting to Loring and stopping Lilith. Nothing else mattered. *Go, go, go.* Soon he scraped his sides bloody and his legs felt ready to give out. All the way down 15th Avenue South he ripped himself apart, past the convention center and the Spanish immersion school, past all the rot that had claimed the city and its people. *Save them*, he told himself. *Save the ones that haven't rotted yet.*

At the intersection of 15th and Willow Street, an explosion rocked him onto his ass. Trees burned, their naked branches all ablaze. Perpendicular spires bordered the entire park, leaving only small gaps to get in through. Corman squeezed himself past, scraping his cheek on the way. There, he saw the battle was already well underway: the Sons, the wiemca, and chimaera and wights clashed against Kingdomers, the Zonbi, and the Tribe; bodies were gored, split apart, and torn to shreds. The snow was coated in a fine sheen of blood. Tentacles reached out from the pond, slamming down into the dirt, ripping up the earth and anyone unfortunate enough to be caught in between. Above them all was a white sun, shining tortuously bright while a jet black sludge oozed over the sides.

Across the park, to the northwest, bolts of lightning burst out from the roof of Saint Mary's Basilica. All he had to do now was somewhere get there amidst the carnage. *If my body doesn't give out first*, he thought wearily. He just needed a breather.

Not that what was transpiring allowed him much respite; every ten feet another skirmish broke out. A chimaera ripped a Kingdomer in half. A Son decapitated a Tribe member. A wiemca stabbed a Zonbi through the chest and ripped their torso off the waist. Bones cracked and limbs were dismembered. Blood gushed forth onto the field of death before him. *They need you*, he thought. *They... need you.* Corman steeled himself, tightened his grip on Excalibur, and took a deep breath. Time to go to work.

Sprinting through the park, he sliced open wiemca, chimaera, and Son alike, ending their lives with a single swing of the sword, the blade so unwieldy and so monumental in its force he never needed to strike another blow. Each kill weighed his arms down, sent another dagger down into his leg muscles.

Yet, somehow, he made it to the north end of the park, to the abandoned community college campus. Out of nowhere, a chimaera charged him, knocked him over. His shoulder struck a planter right at the edge, and the corner went through his muscle. As the beast pivoted for another go, Corman pulled himself off and up, bleeding, and with one hand rose Excalibur into the air. The chimaera came running; Corman threw the sword down into its head, slicing it in half. Then he collapsed onto the pavement; his fingers felt locked into place around the sword grip. *Can't let go, even if I wanted*, he thought.

The shuffling of robes caught his attention; standing in between him and Maple Street were five Witches, each one holding a bone-hilt spear and accompanied by a chimaera. One stepped forward, lifted their spear, and screeched out a command. They fanned out, joined in on the screeching.

Too far apart, he thought as he stood. His right arm was violently shaking; any more exertion and he was fit to vomit. Corman shook his head out and swallowed what little saliva he still had. He hoisted Excalibur up.

Then a bullet cracked through the air and one of the Witches went sailing toward the ground. Another shot rang out, and a chimaera got hit right between the eyes. Then another, and another, until a full volley rained down on them.

"On your left," came Yue's voice from the rear. With her were Safir and Kalebrant, all staring down the scopes of assault rifles. "Open fire!"

They all dropped to one knee and riddled the Witches with bullets, their thick blood and roting organs bursting from their emaciated chests. Bodies toppled over each other as the chimaera ran around in an attempt to disperse. Before any of them could get very far, Corman swung Excalibur around; all four of their heads fell off their bodies, their decapitated necks jetting out blood.

Panting, Corman fell onto the same planter that stabbed him and threw up. Coughing out the last bit of it, he looked over to his saviors.

"This is easier—" He spit. "With other people."

"Who could've guessed," Yue said. She helped him to his feet. "What the hell's going on? Did the rendezvous happen?"

Corman shook his head. "I need to get to Saint Mary's."

Yue held two fingers to her ear. "Sasha, you got eyes on anything between here and the church? No shit. Real ugly-looking bastard out in front."

"Par for the course," Kalebrant said.

"Do you have a strategy in mind?" Safir asked Corman.

Charge in headfirst and kill anything that moves doesn't seem appropriate. "Stay behind me, attack at a distance. If it gets too hairy, you retreat."

"And if it gets too hairy for you?" Yue asked.

"It never does," he said.

Although this might qualify.

Skulking about in the front of the basilica was a giant, centipede creature whose neck extended into a thin appendage ending in a bleeding skull. Inside its open chest cavity were rows of horizontal teeth, an unyielding fleshy darkness below. Its legs were all human, though its body was a meaty pulp of other body parts rammed together. As its feet stamped on the ground, its neck swung to and fro, a loud gurgling erupting from its narrow throat.

"What in the actual fuck is *that* thing?" Yue blurted.

"Don't think about it," Corman told her, walking toward it. "Just kill it."

The creature twisted around to face him as he approached, its chest opening wide to

screech a protest at the intrusion.

"And I thought *I* was ugly," Corman said, throwing Excalibur off his shoulder. He took a swing at it, slicing across its gaping mouth, only to get kicked in the small of the back. The force was so great it sent him crashing into the front steps. Two grotesque parodies of arms, twisted and gnarled, bubbled up from its corpus, and it made to grab him; Corman bashed the sword against its arms. It tried again, its head lowering to meet his eyes. He swung Excalibur into the air, ready to decapitate the thing when...

"You..." it whispered. "Killed... us."

Corman blinked. "What?"

It dug its many fingers into his side and lifted him off the ground, and just as he was becoming aware of what was happening, he felt the pavement. He shuddered, coughed out a little blood, scrambled to his knees; the thing pressed a milieu of feet onto his back, forcing him back down. The head returned to his side and through impossibly sharp teeth, whispered, "You... left... us..."

His hand was still wrapped around the sword grip. But his shoulder was pinned down. No way to strike.

Guns fired, and bullets struck the creature all over its body, even the neck, as small a target as it was. Spinning to face this new threat, its chest bent backward to roar. It was forced to swallow bullets, and Corman saw them leave exit wounds in its back. Its blood was thick and green, oozed out like pus. The creature charged away, screeching. With a shaking hand, Corman propped the sword up, got to his feet. *What do I do, Ed? What do I fucking do?*

But what else was there? He had to fight. As he always did.

The creature barrelled toward the Knights, splitting them up as they retreated. Flailing its skinny neck around in a pathetic show of force, it swiped at the empty air with its arms. One stroke, and he could slice it in half. He lowered Excalibur, held it sideways, and wound up at the waist. *One stroke of the sword.* He ran, panting and sweating and bleeding. *Please God let me fucking kill this fucking thing*, he thought as he swung.

With a mighty crunch of bones and a splattering of meat, Excalibur tore through the creature's waist. It shrieked as its head smashed into asphalt, blasting open to reveal brain matter and bits of skull. The legs abruptly stopped moving; its torso went rigid and collapsed over from its own weight. A shower of its pus-like blood came pouring down over its corpse. Excalibur landed gently on Corman's shoulder. Then he fell to a hand and knee, breath coming in hard and fast. The Knights approached silently.

"Guess you really didn't need us, huh?" Safir asked.

Corman shrugged. "More than you... than you think."

No time to rest on his laurels. More bolts of crimson lightning flashed overhead; a clap of thunder boomed so loud Corman worried it might crack the atmosphere open. The ground rumbled and burst forth into more spires, dirt clods smashing into the street, which was now being torn asunder.

"Did she expect it to kill you?" Yue asked.

"No," he said, "she meant it as a warning."

He jogged up the basilica steps, another quake sending him careening into a cracked pillar. Pushing himself off his shoulder, he shouted for the others to stay outside. Inside the chapel, the plaster of the ceiling crumbled dusting the pews. Another quake. As he flew into one, a spire bursting up from underneath the altar. Stained glass windows burst, shattering onto the marble floor. *Come on, come on. You gotta go.* Corman climbed over the busted pew, stumbling once more as a spire shot up mere inches from him. *Son of a bitch,.*

His ascent to the roof was marred by his flying backwards every other step. It was a narrow staircase, and without much to hold onto. Yet somehow, he manged to make it to the next floor, the circular glass window visible from the basilica's front entrance now visible once again. Some of the spires had even burst through up to here. And, as he was infuriated to discover, *another goddamn creature.* In the dark red of the room, he could barely make out some deformed monstrosity, bulky and dripping with *something*. Eyes opened up all over its body, from head to chest to arms, all the way down to its amorphous lower body.

"You killed them," it croaked. "Killed us."

"Not yet," Corman muttered, raising Excalibur. "And if you're gonna try killing *me*, hurry it up. I have places to be."

It charged him, the slimy sound of tentacles squishing across the floor. All four of arms went for this throat; Corman strafed and slammed the edge of the blade into its back. It turned on him, and he got a close look at its gigantic, bulbous head for the first time. Tentacles hung limply from a beaked mouth, its eyes placed haphazardly and seemingly without purpose. All what looked like two hundred of them glared at him.

"You killed them!" it squawked, throwing itself at the sword. Corman blocked its attack, and countered with a diagonal slice. It tried hopping backward, only for the sword to cut its chest open. Corman raised the Excalibur to finish the job when one of its back tentacles blasted forward and punched him directly in the ribs, sending him flying onto his back. More tentacles slithered over and wrapped themselves around his body, squeezed his bones to near collapse. He got lifted into the air and brought close to the creature's face once more.

"You killed *us*," it gurgled. "*Failed* us."

He could feel his bones beginning to break; he couldn't ask who this used to be or why it thought that. Corman could only try in vain to gulp down what little air he could. Then he heard the blast of an assault rifle; phosphorescent blue blood blossomed from its bullet wounds and the creature dropped him. In the stairwell appeared Yue, Safir, and Kalebrant.

"Open fire!" Yue screamed.

"No!" Corman wheezed.

All three assault rifles lit up the room, bullets making their way into the pulpy flesh of the creature. It shot its tentacles out at them, grabbing all three at once.

"And now *we* kill *them*," the creature cackled.

"Mother... fucker!" Corman roared, charging into a full sprint.

As the creature laughed manically, as Corman heard the unmistakable sound of bones crunching, he stabbed Excalibur through the thing's giant head. All three tentacles loosened and the creature flopped to the side, blood bursting forth from its wound. Lying on the floor beside its corpse were three more. Corman fell against Excalibur, barely able to stand. Vomit bubbled up in his throat.

"Ryan?" Yue rasped. He hurried over to her, dropped to his knees. Her chest was practically caved in, her left arm was bent in wrong direction, and he could see her femur sticking out of her skin. "Oh, good. You're... you're alive."

"I told you to stay outside," he said, tears welling up and burning his cuts.

"Hypocritical, coming from... from you," she whispered. "Since when did *you* ever listen..."

"Don't... don't fucking die on me," Corman whispered. "It's not that bad. You'll live."

"Ha." Her head lolled to the side and her eyes closed. "Ha."

Corman rested his head against Excalibur's blade. He let a primal roar exit him, screamed until his throat was bloody and raw. Then he began to weep, his vision blurred by the tears.

XXI

WOMAN CLOTHES IN
SUN

I T WAS SNOWING AGAIN when Corman reached the roof of
Saint Mary's; two inches had already accumulated. Crunching
through it on his way to the belltowers, the wicked sharp wind bit
into his wounds, clawed at his flesh. In ragged overcoat, torn jacket,
and soiled shirt, he approached the source of the hell that had befall-
en this city. Her raven black hair fluttered over her malformed shoulders, her matching robes flapped underneath them. Lilith turned.
Her face now resembled what it once had, but something still struck

him as off. It wasn't right. *She's not the same person,* he thought, touching his horns, *and neither are you.*

"So you finally decide to show up. About time."

"My family," Corman said hoarsely. "My mother, my sister. Where—"

"Do you really think I would stoop to so low a level?" Lilith barked. "Did you really believe I would take them to lure you here?" She raised both of her hands; her nails were dangerously sharp. "No, no. I knew, one way or another, you'd come. It doesn't matter how far you would have to go, or how long it would took, you'd come just the same. For love, or revenge, I don't know. But you'd cross the world twice over if it meant seeing me."

"I'm not here for either," Corman said.

"But you're here to kill me," Lilith told him. "Not that you'll be able to, not in the state you're in. Look at yourself, Corman. What sort of hell have you put yourself through to get here?"

He lifted Excalibur, pointed it at her. "Enough talk."

"Not quite," she said, stepping to the side.

Corman nearly dropped the sword. Kneeling in the center of the Seal was Abigail, bound at the ankles and wrists, tears in her bruised eyes. Rings of blood encircled her nose. her face was covered in cuts.

"I just need one more soul," Lilith said. "Just one more, to complete the final stone. And I thought to myself, whose would be more appropriate than hers? You foiled my last attempt, but I refuse to allow you to repeat that insult."

"Use mine," Corman said. "It's my own again."

"You think me an idiot," Lilith growled. "I'm no fool, Corman. I know the only way you could've come back is if you made a deal with my father. A bastard knight serving a bastard king. So no, your soul is not your own. Not until you, what, bring me to 'justice?' Whose justice would that be, Corman? Yours? My father's? And for the crime of... what exactly? Refusing to bow to that arrogant son of a bitch? Demanding I be treated as an equal? As his *heir*? Insisting upon my rightful place as his successor? What justice would there be in refusing me my birthright? I'm taking what is owed me, nothing less, nothing more. *That* is justice. Not whatever horseshit you two decided on without my input. Not that you could possibly—"

"I just want you dead," Corman told her wearily. "That's it."

"You've grown callous in death," Lilith said. "Unfortunately for you and my father, you will fail. You *lost*, Corman. Have you managed to understand simple concepts as winning and losing yet? Perhaps allow me to put it another way. No matter how many chimaeras you put down, or how many wiemca you kill, or how many people you rescue from them, you can't win. Not against me. *You. Lost.*"

He glanced at Abigail, her eyes pleading with him. *Save her. Save the one person who hasn't rotted yet.*

"I know," Corman said, gently laying Excalibur on the ground. *Doesn't matter what happens to you now.* "I just thought I'd give it one more shot."

Lilith rolled her eyes. "Quaint."

"Do what you were gonna do," he said. "I won't stop you."

"As if I needed *you* to tell me that," she scoffed. She hobbled over to the sword and picked it up in one hand. "Fine blade. Shame it was wasted on the likes of you."

Excalibur soared through the snowfall; it clattered on the ground below. *Goodbye, old friend.*

Back at the Seal, Lilith rose her arms and began to chant the Liturgy of the Witch's Sabbath; soon, Abigail's soul would be ripped from her body and infused with a philosopher's stone as the Seal broke open. *Do what you were gonna do*, Corman told himself as he grabbed hold of his right horn. It was still just a stump, but even a stump would be sharp enough.

As he curled his fingers tight around the bone, Lilith's voice grew louder and angrier; the ground shifted and quivered beneath them. Roof tiles went flying and the bells began to clang. He grit his teeth and pulled. She screamed; he howled. Like a hundred knives stabbed through his brain all at once. Like losing Edgar. Like all those nights spent in a frozen wasteland, waiting to die. Kalebrant had been right. He'd known far worse pains than this. With the beginning of the final verse, Corman's ripped the bone from his head. Blood burst from his torn flesh and dripped over his face.

A bright red light burst forth from the Seal under Abigail in the form of dozens of tendrils; their long, gangly fingers wrapped around her body. She began to convulse, her cries of pain coming from nowhere and everywhere. And then, abruptly, Lilith stopped chanting.

Stuck into the side of her neck was Corman's horn, forced down to the jugular. The tendrils shrieked and retracted into the Seal. His hand still on the horn, he twisted it, and then plunged it even further inside. Then she opened him up with her fingernails, four long, jagged lacerations across his chest. As he stumbled back, trembling hands failing to dam the flow of blood, she stabbed him through both shoulders. When she had him raised in the air, she shook him about wildly.

"You bastard!" she wailed. "You fucking *hellspawn*! You goddamn *filth*! How dare you! You insolent son of a bitch, I'll *murder* you, damn my father! You *dare* presume to touch me with your unclean hands? You foul, repulsive *thing*! I'll—"

And then his back slammed into ground, blood pouring forth from his wounds onto the snow. As far as he could manage to crane his neck up, he saw standing behind Lilith Abigail, grasping his horn in both bound hands. The crimson lights of the Seal enveloped her, this woman in the dread sun of the end.

"You little *bitch*!" Lilith shrieked. As she made to wrap her hands around Abigail's throat, her own was pierced with the horn. Blood spurted out, and as Lilith tried to remove it, she lacerated herself with her own claws. "No! No!" Snow crunched under her as she fell to her knee, screaming in an increasingly incomprehensible shrill.

One last time, Corman told himself as he lifted himself off the ground. Those knives in his forehead had fallen down to his chest, and as he crawled to his former lover's writhing form, he felt life beginning to leave again. *It's no great thing to die. Easiest thing in the world, really.*

He wrapped his prosthetic arm around her throat and jerked it toward himself; as he crushed her esophagus, he could feel life leaving her, too. Though he could no longer understand her, not that he ever did, he knew her last words were curses. Even now she refused to relent, to compromise. To love anyone besides herself. In the end, the only one who ever mattered to Lilith was Lilith.

With a sharp twist of his arm, he snapped her neck. Her lifeless body slumped against his as his head hit the snow. In the dimming of the light, he saw Abigail kneeling above him, cradling his head in her hands. They were still bound; he felt the roughness of the rope.

"Corman?" he heard her cry out. "Corman? Don't go, don't go, don't..."

For maybe as long as a second, he did. Then something punched him in the back of the skull and he shot up, the breath back inside his lungs. The sharpness of the cold air made him cough; the gust of hot wind at his back made him shiver.

"Corman?" Abigail asked, pointing to something behind him.

He turned to see the devil approaching them. Satan offered a hand, which Corman accepted. The amalgamation of corpses that once housed Lilith's soul tumbled off of his lap. Without a word, Satan walked to the Seal and knelt before it. Pressing a single finger into the center, the crimson world faded away; it was replaced with the old, frozen, white one.

"C'ymaerlothyan," Satan said softly as he turned to face him. "Thank you."

Their contract appeared in his right hand, all two hundred and sixty pages of it. It ignited, and ash flakes twirled in the frigid winds, joining their snowy cousins on their way down to earth. "You have fulfilled your end of the bargain. Your soul belongs to no one but you."

"What do I do with it?" Corman asked.

"That's not for me to say," Satan said. He bent down and picked up his daughter, cradled her in both arms.

"What'll happen to her?"

"She will face a trial for her treason," Satan said, his misty eyes frozen over. "And then I will lose her, for good. Oh, my sweet girl, what have I done to you? How did I fail you so miserably?" He pressed her deformed body against his own. "Oh, little one."

He carried her to the circle of ash that marked his arrival and faced Corman one last time. "You're a better man than your father, C'ymaerlothyan. A good man."

Another burst of hot wind encircled them, and in a vortex of smoke and fire, the devil disappeared. Snow fell where he had once been, but melted just as quickly.

Corman turned to Abigail and took hold of her restraints. With a single tug, he unwrapped the ropes around her wrists; she removed the rag inside of her mouth. Then she fell into him.

"Please tell me it's over," Abigail said, cheek against his chest.

"It's done," Corman told her. "It's done."

Although it's never really over, is it? he thought as Abigail helped him down the steps. The bodies of the creature, Yue, Kalebrant, and Safir all laid lifeless in the dark. *Only for the dead.*

In the main chapel, a lone figure rushed from the doors, her arms outstretched. Sasha caught him as he was about to stumble, and together with Abigail, propped him up against a pew.

"What happened? Is she dead?" Sasha asked. "All of the wiemca just retreated out of nowhere. The chimaera, too. Did you kill her?"

"Sasha," he said, "you have to turn me in."

She frowned. "What?"

"You can't look like you had anything to do with this," he told her. "They'll eviscerate you. Find something worse than last time. Hand me over to the Knights."

"You just stopped the apocalypse," she said. "You don't think that'll grant you a pardon?"

"It's not that," Corman murmured, barely shaking his head. "It's for everything else. I'm still a fugitive. Arthur won't forgive that. All the Knights who died, all the shit that's happened, that's gonna be on me."

"You don't know that," Sasha said.

"Turn me in," Corman told her again. "Do me one last favor."

"Are you sure?" Abigail asked. "What if you never get out of prison or—?"

"Only way this ends well," Corman said, "is if I get the shaft."

Outside, the clean up was already underway; the victorious were counting and identifying their dead, corpses of slain enemies were being carted away in the back of moving trucks to God-only-knew where. Prisoners were being taken away in the same trucks. On either side of him, he had Sasha and Abigail prop him up from under his arms as they made their way out of the basilica.

Waiting for him was an armored prisoner transport, about thirty Knights, and to his surprise, the deputy secretary of the entire bureau. A severe, grim, and altogether unpleasant woman, as far as the stories went.

"Lieutenant General Guinevere," Sasha greeted her as they reached the bottom of the steps; she offered a halfheartedly salute.

Guinevere returned it. "This him?"

"He's..." Sasha glanced sideways; he nodded. "He's in my custody."

"Who's this, then?"

"A civilian who helped apprehend him," Sasha said.

"If only the rest of the Knights in this godforsaken city were as competent," Guinevere muttered. "Is Barbara still MIA?"

"KIA," Sasha said. "By Lilith."

"And Lilith?"

Sasha nodded to Corman. "KIA. By him."

The lieutenant general glowered down at him. "I suppose you think that means you'll receive amnesty for your crimes?"

"No," he said.

"Good. I'm glad you understand how things work now. As disturbingly late as it was. Hector, Lohot, seize him."

"I invoke the path of the exile," Corman announced as the Knights came for him, raising his head as much as he could.

"Excuse me?" Guinevere snapped. "As if you have the authority to invoke *any*—"

"'Any anointed Knight," he said weakly, "whose behavior has reflected poorly on the brotherhood of the Bureau, and whose titles and honors have been stripped from their name, may request in lieu of death or other such punishment, permanent exile from their home on the basis of some appropriately chivalric action. Even if they regain their former merit, they shall never set foot in the place of exile again, on pain of death.'" Corman cleared his throat. "I demand exile for my chivalric act of slaying Lilith, thereby preventing the apocalypse."

"And just where in the handbook does it say—"

"Article nine, section eighteen, subsection five, paragraph two," Corman recited. "Punishment for the abnormal wicked."

"Hector?" Guinevere spat. "Find it."

The short, pudgy Hector appeared at her side, flimsy, laminated handbook already open. "He's right, Sir. He recited the rule verbatim."

"Your killing of Lilith does *not* qualify you for that," Guinevere told him. "It was merely you undoing the damage your previous exploits wrought."

"It also says that should three or more people testify for the validity of the chivalric act, that he shall then be—"

"I do," Abigail said. "I mean, I testify for its... um, validity."

"I second that," Sasha said.

"Doesn't matter," Guinevere scoffed. "There's only two of you, and your sentiments are outside a court of law. The decision won't stand until you are formally tried."

"Then perhaps we could sway the court's opinion." Emperor Wukong, dressed in combat regalia, rode up to the basilica steps on horseback, whose own armor was equally as ornate. "I am afraid, lieutenant general, that this Corman Ryan is a friend to the Sun Kingdom. He shall be exiled."

"Likewise," came another voice of authority. Anansi and his Zonbi arrived, dressed in their bright, vibrant armor. "Henceforth, Corman Ryan shall be exiled."

"As if I'm going to be intimated by thugs," Guinevere spat. "You two gentlemen are making a mockery of our bylaws. He will tried and convicted as any other criminal. I will not abide by this ridiculous idea of justice. Lohort, *Priamus, Seize him.*"

Corman could feel Sasha and Abigail's grips tighten around his arms. With as much strength as he could muster, he removed himself from their protection and walked forward.

"You don't have to do this, Ryan," Sasha said.

"Corman, don't—" Abigail began.

He turned to the two of them. "It's okay. Enough people have suffered for me. Tell my mom and my sister what happened to me. That I'm alive."

The two Knights grabbed him roughly by the arms and threw him to the ground. One of them stomped on his prosthetic, screwed his face up when no sounds of pain arose from Corman's throat. So the other one kicked him in the ribs.

"Get up, mooncalf," he demanded. When Corman got to his hands and knees, a boot slammed him back down to the street. By then there were cries of protest all around, and the gangs moved forward; the Knights, however, readied their assault rifles. As demands for his freedom and commands to ignore those demands were doled out at the same frequency, Corman let the Knights shove him into the transport vehicle. With one last slam of the butt of a rifle into the small of his back, Corman was locked inside, alone.

He breathed, heavy and deep, and sat down on one of the metal benches. If this all led back to HADES, and he realized it very well might, then he would live out the rest of his days there without qualm, and he would find peace in the fact that he had done, for once in his life, the right thing. His debts were erased. His conscience was cleared. Corman Ryan, despite himself, had won. *And if I die,* he thought as the vehicle shivered to life, *then I die knowing that.*

As the transport pulled away, he could hear pleas to let him go, to stop the truck. Hands slapped the side, and guns fired. *They better not try anything if they don't want a martyr on their hands.* But the

Knights were short sighted enough. They might do it. Hell, he might even *tell* them that's what would happen, and they'd hit him, tell him to shut the fuck up, and do it anyway. The gangs would no doubt see this as a slap to the face, and then they'd rage war. But it would be Mom and Rowan, Corman knew, that would be the most dangerous enemy to make. They'd join the gangs, fight for his freedom. He smiled. *Now that would be worth breaking out for*.

XXII
PENTECOST

H ANDLING THE AXE FOR the majority of the day had rendered his hand bloody and raw. Through this effort, he had
also rendered himself a good number of logs. The pile would last
him for at least two weeks, maybe three. It had taken some time, a
good few days or so, but what did Corman Ryan have to do with his
time now? *Too much of it, and still too little*, he thought as he stacked
the logs together on a wooden sledge, itself made of logs he had also
chopped. This was just laborious a process as cutting them, since
he didn't have a second hand to help balance it out. Yet, as opposed

to when they dropped him off here seventeen years ago, he'd gotten used to doing things with just the one.

Knots remained an issue, albeit downsized to a minor inconvenience. To remedy his, he frequently used bobby pins to keep things tied, such as the left sleeve on all of his clothing. Most of the time, he'd fallen back on just bunching it all up and hoping it stuck. It never did. Not as long as he wanted it to, anyway.

After he'd gotten the logs arranged, he wrapped the leather reins of the sledge around his chest and under his arms, then fed it through a buckle. The legs of the sledge glided smoothly over the snow, fresh from that morning. This chore, like everything else, had taken some getting used to, but as dealing with his disability, it became routine. Alaska wasn't so different from the other frozen wastelands he'd been stuck in. It was, in practice, just more of the same. That familiar weight around his throat, however, had left him years ago.

In the end, the jury had acquitted him of most of his plethora of crimes; the charges of trespassing, contempt of court, and fleeing police custody were forgiven. His impersonation of a federal officer, theft of government property, and exaggerated third degree murder of Kyle Woods were left on his record and resulted in his permanent expulsion from Minneapolis. Though the prosecution attorney representing the city demanded he be imprisoned in HADES again, he was granted one small reprieve. Mom, Rowan, Sasha, Abigail, Anansi, the Emperor, and even Nathan testified on his behalf in support of his demand for exile. And so, as was befitting a disgraced

Knight, he was freed from the jaws of death by the small mercies of humankind. The judge added the stipulation that despite this, he must also serve a minimum sentence of twenty years in isolation. Otherwise, he argued, it wouldn't have constituted an actual punishment. His court-appointed attorney cried foul, but no appeal was granted. His associates were furious. This led him to having to, in a strange reversal of roles, be the one to assuage *their* rage.

"They're letting me live," Corman said. "That's more than most people like me ever get." Ultimately, he knew that the punishment, especially in regards to the murder charge, was nothing more than damage control. The Knights, the city bureaucracy, and local law enforcement needed a scapegoat to cover up their blatant incompetence, and hey, blaming him for everything worked once. So why not try it again?

It was an economic hail-Mary; the Knight Bureau was lavished with donations from private citizens, which they used to lobby against one councilmember or another to keep them operating despite their flagrant disregard for civil rights. Although Corman figured they could withstand a scandal on this scale, Guinevere didn't appear to be taking any chances.

After three days of being out on bail, he was shepherded into a Knight helicopter and flown out into the middle of the Alaskan wilderness. As they flew over what was once northern Ontario and the Yukon, both made barren wastelands outfitted for oil pipelines, Corman was surprised to see across the American border, the natural world remained. They set him down a mile from what was to be his home for the rest of his five-hundred year long life, and gave him one final warning: should he be seen by any government official outside of his designated area, whether American or Canadian, he would be shot.

"Yeah, sure, why not," he said, no longer enraged enough to argue. Somehow, the universe conspired to let him live; the last thing he was gonna do was push his luck.

Fighting against the injustices of the world, over the course of the succeeding seventeen years, ceased to be a priority. Keeping his family out of his turmoil was all that mattered to him. What Mom and Rowan and Sasha and Abigail failed to realize was that he, too, understood how this was profoundly unfair. He just didn't care. Unfair or not, no one else was punished. No one else lost their freedom, or home, or livelihood. And they let him spend the rest of his days in the open air, surrounded by the birds and the trees and the rivers. They could've let him rot in a blacksite for half a century. But the mere fact they didn't meant that life was still a viable option. Corman could live without making a mess of things. *They'll never know how big a favor they did me.*

Almost two decades of solitude had passed since then. For most, it would become unbearable, a cruel and unusual torture. But to a nephilim, seventeen years was barely any time at all. Maybe one day he'd lose composure and claw at tree trunks and slam his head into the frozen dirt, desperate for any sort of escape, even if it meant horrendous pain. But nothing like that had come to pass. Corman had been dead to the world, and in this case, death really did mean peace.

He unloaded his sledge inside the shed connected to the main cabin. It was here, in this makeshift workshop, that he'd built a good many things with just one hand. The sledge, some tables, a few chairs, even had a statue of a bear going. Working with his hands was nothing new, just the medium.

With a few of the logs tucked under his arm, he went inside to lay them in the fireplace. As the flames consumed the kindling and torched the wood, he inhaled the delicious scent. No longer full of resentment, he could enjoy small things like this. Impossible to imagine all that time ago, in his arrogant self-denial. *I'm lucky, always have been.* Had he been anyone else, he might've been unceremoniously shot dead in the street. How long had he hidden from the world, while in plain sight of it? Here, though, his horns grew as long as his beard did. He could be seen, for what he was, always had been. No one would curse him here. It was, despite the punishment's intentions, freeing.

As the flames danced, he watched with something like reverence, lost in his thoughts again. He'd been doing that a lot as of late.

Your life's no longer about solving everybody else's problems, he told himself. *Just managing your own.* He knew that a part of him would always yearn to fix the world's bullshit, but had he ever done so out of any sense of actual altruism, or had his solutions always come at a price? He hadn't tried to protect those women because he loved them, felt for them. He did it so everybody would forget what he'd done. *I no longer want your forgiveness*, he thought. *It's not mine to beg for.*

The Corman Ryan he'd become was not altogether a different person, but one that was no longer marred by self-loathing and vitriol. So what did that leave him as? Who was he? Who was Corman Ryan, if not hatred and resentment and anger incarnate?

He was a fool, he thought, lying in bed that night. *A fool who looked back while he fled the underworld. Who lost everything to gain nothing. Who took what good was given him and threw it away. A fool who demanded godhood. A fool whose wax wings melted. A fool who fell. And now? Now he is a man. Nothing more, nothing less.*

Early the next morning, as the sun rose and caressed the frozen cheeks of the slopes and hills, Corman tied his snowshoes to his boots. He wanted to get some fishing in before they stopped biting, get himself decent for dinner. Though he was running short on bait, he figured he could catch some of the small fry to use instead of dead crickets and mealworms.

As he started out for the lake, some two miles north of his cabin, he heard the unmistakable cacophony of helicopter blades. Patterned in camouflage, there were large letters stenciled on the side.

No missile ports or mounted machine guns or turrets, however. That vague fear of being gunned down that haunted his dreams had long since left him, but suddenly he found himself searching for cover. The helicopter landed some ways away; not as far as a mile, but too close for comfort. Corman dropped his fishing pole and tackle box and jogged into the shed. He didn't have much in the way of weaponry, never had much of a need for self-defense up here. All that was available to him was his wood axe and a paring knife. Brandishing both, he waited outside for his attackers to show their faces.

Been long enough, he thought. *Might as well get this shit over with.*

Instead of a squadron of soldiers, just one person drove up on a snowmobile. Bizarrely, he looked to be the clerical type; it didn't even look like he had a pistol on him. The man killed the engine and took off his helmet; he was Native American or Aboriginal, long strands of thick black hair hanging from his knit cap.

"Hey, I come in peace," he said. "I'm not packing."

Corman lowered his weapon, but kept his glare up.

"You're Corman Ryan, right?" the man asked. "Hate to think I wasted five hours to meet the wrong guy."

He raised the axe again.

"All this time alone has made you kind of paranoid, I'm guessing," the man said. He held up one hand while the other went fishing inside his coat. It retrieved a leather badge. "I'm Agent Noah Pendergrass, here on behalf of the Canadian People's Defense Agency.

We're an NGO that deals with chimaeras, the wiemca, all the same sort of stuff you did."

Corman stuck the axe into the snow. "I still got a few years left on my sentence. Compulsory solitude. Talking to me is technically a felony."

"That's no longer the case," Pendergrass said. "You've been issued a full pardon by the U.N."

Corman reached for the axe.

"Hey, hold on, hold on, I have proof." Pendergrass picked up a briefcase from the back of the snowmobile. He took out a leather portfolio and handed it over. "Figured you'd want to see it for yourself."

"If this is a summons for jury duty, I'd rather you just shoot me," Corman murmured. Inside the portfolio, printed on cream-colored paper, was an official declaration of amnesty for one Corman Ryan, as endorsed by the secretary general of the U.N.

"Took a lot of pressure from the international community and about a million and a half in lobbying, but you're no longer on the United States' shit list. Officially, anyway. I'm sure plenty of people still bear resentment toward you. We tried getting your entire criminal record expunged, but with the statute of limitations on some things, we—"

Corman glanced up. "We?"

"A whole committee was formed to protest for your freedom," Pendergrass said. "The man who prevented the apocalypse twice ought to be treated better than this."

"You're really not bullshitting me, huh?" Corman muttered as he scanned the document a dozen more times.

"You're a free man, Mister Ryan," the agent told him. "Albeit one who can't vote, which I'd argue puts the whole notion into question, but—"

"What's the catch?"

This caught the agent off-guard. "What?"

"What do you people want from me?" Corman closed the portfolio, shoved it back into Pendergrass's hands. "You wouldn't spend a million and a half dollars on a two decade old charity case. So, out with it. What're the terms and conditions?"

"Your release was already approved, before we got involved," Pendergrass told him. "Your mother was the one who orchestrated most of this, headed the committee."

My self-appointed parole officer, Corman thought; he smiled. "So what were you hoping to gain out of this seventeen-year long shit show, Mister Pendergrass?"

"That you'd come work for us," the agent answered simply. "The chimaera threat has been on the rise all this time you've been locked away. I could read you the statistics, but I don't think you're one for figures."

"Never interested me, no."

"You'd be a field operative, doing what you're best at," Pendergrass continued. "Hunting monsters, keeping people safe. And with a salary, this time."

"I had a salary with the Knights," Corman said.

Pendergrass seemed to understand what he meant. "I don't suppose there's anything I could say that would convince you we're not like them?"

"I'd have to see for myself," Corman said.

"Your mother and sister would be delighted if you did," Pendergrass told him. "They're back at headquarters in Montreal. I can come back some other time if you want to weigh your options. I'm sure if they waited seventeen years, they can wait a little longer."

Corman felt a prickle where his left hand had been. "Nah, I'm ready."

"Are you sure?"

"You tell me," he said, "if you'd been stuck here for this long, would you wait?"

"I don't think I would."

Corman nodded. "Yeah, so I'm sure."

Pendergrass started up the snowmobile; Corman sat behind him.

"I think you'll like working for us, Mister Ryan," Pendergrass said, putting on his helmet. "We don't function on such strict hierarchies as you're used to."

"We'll see," Corman said as they rode for the helicopter, which sat in a large clearing in a nearby thicket. He helped the agent load the snowmobile up into the cargo hold, then took his place in one of the passenger seats.

A minute later, the rotors spun furiously overhead, and he felt the ground fall away beneath his boots. As the chopper soared over the vast, uninhabited wilderness, Corman had to admit he felt a little ambivalent about the whole thing. Reintegrating himself after only eight years had been tricky; what kind of return would it be after seventeen years? *But then again*, he thought, *does it even matter?* He'd see his family again. That'd be enough. The world had no doubt grown colder and angrier in his absence, but he was more than familiar living with outside hostility.

Over the decimated, empty wasteland of northern Canada, his vision for his future began to solidify. He didn't believe anyone was put on Earth for any reason, but if he was ever proved wrong about that, he figured his was fighting for people. People who loved him, who hated him, it didn't matter. He didn't need to strive for atonement in their eyes. Forgiveness for God's territory; his was cleaving a chimaera's skull in half. He was there to protect the weak and defenseless, the ones who couldn't fight for themselves. For the Abigails. The Edgars. All those forgotten women.

So let the masses curse his name and spit on the ground he walked, rage against his very existence. Cambion, human, everything in between. He'd fight for them anyway; for amongst the throngs of the ravenous wolves, there were sheep that needed a shepherd. If he had to protect the former to save the latter, so be it. He'd been torn down, ripped apart, chewed out, and spat back out a hundred times, just like the lands beneath him now. And he, like the earth, kept coming back. *Can't get rid of either of us*, he thought.

This was his pentecost, his return. His revival. The helicopter flew toward Montreal, toward the world, toward Hell. And Corman

Ryan would meet it with a dagger in his teeth, righteous fury in his blood, and love for the damned in his bones.

Printed in the USA
CPSIA information can be obtained
at www.ICGtesting.com
JSHW062149151023
49994JS00010B/66

9 781957 893297